"I haven't been as understanding as I should've been. I know you didn't intend to hurt me or anyone else. You did what you had to do, and I can't fault you for that."

Stepping close, his pant legs brushing her skirts, he very carefully cupped her cheek. A rogue sigh slipped through her lips. The rasp of his work-roughened palm against her skin wrought an intensely heady feeling inside. If only this wasn't a platonic caress.

"My sweet Janie-girl," he murmured. "The memories of your laughter, your sweet smile, the way things were always easy and fun between us, kept me going this past year. You represented peace and calm at a time when my life was falling apart. I need your friendship."

Friendship. Not love. Not devotion.

If he guessed how badly she yearned for more, he'd be revolted.

"Friendship," she croaked. "Always. You have it."

Karen Kirst was born and raised in East Tennessee near the Great Smoky Mountains. A lifelong lover of books, it wasn't until after college that she had the grand idea to write one herself. Now she divides her time between being a wife, homeschooling mom and romance writer. Her favorite pastimes are reading, visiting tearooms and watching romantic comedies.

Books by Karen Kirst

Love Inspired Historical

Smoky Mountain Matches

KAREN KIRST

The Bachelor's Homecoming

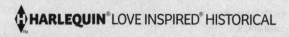

HHARLEQUIN® LOVE INSPIRED® HISTORICAL

Recycling programs for this product may not exist in your area.

TM LOVE INSPIRED BOOKS

ISBN-13: 978-0-373-28336-1

The Bachelor's Homecoming

Copyright © 2015 by Karen Vyskocil

www.Harlequin.com

Printed in U.S.A.

Delight yourself also in the Lord,
and He shall give you the desires of your heart.
—*Psalms* 37:4

To the ladies of Southside Baptist Church
who are fans of the O'Malleys—
thank you for your encouragement and support.

Mary Blakley, I'm blessed to know you
and to count you as a friend.

Retha Smith, your smile brightens my day.

Gina King, I love when we chat about the
characters. Thanks for the cards.

Carole Gresham, Wilma Hayes,
Greta Griffin and more,
thanks for liking my books.

Chapter One

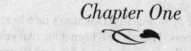

Gatlinburg, Tennessee
May 1884

"Do you, Jane O'Malley, take this man to be your lawfully wedded husband?"

Jane opened her mouth. *Say no. Say you've made a mistake.*

"I—"

Family and friends had crowded into the quaint mountain church and were looking on with hushed expectation. Roy's fingers tightened around hers, gentle brown eyes offering silent support. He'd been nothing but kind throughout their courtship. A perfect gentleman, save for the one time he'd attempted to kiss her—a proper kiss, not simply a buss on the cheek—and she'd shied away. How patient he'd been. How understanding.

What was the matter with her? Here was a hard-working, responsible man who desired to marry her... the too-quiet, too-shy, unexceptional O'Malley sister. She couldn't throw away this one chance at a normal life for a man who didn't want her, whose whereabouts and well-being were a mystery.

Moistening her lips, blood rushing in her ears, she struggled to push out those two simple words. Words that would change her life forever, bind her to a man she liked and admired but didn't love.

The lace at her throat scratched. The blooms in her hair enveloped her in their cloying scent, nearly gagging her. Surely her sisters had tied her corset too tightly. Her lungs clamored for air.

She closed her eyes, and Tom Leighton's face loomed in her consciousness. Though he'd been gone two years, his image was still crisp and clear. Like a photograph inscribed on her mind.

Dear Lord, give me the strength to follow through with this. Marrying Roy is the only way to purge Tom from my heart and soul.

"Jane?" Roy leaned in, his whisper threaded with anxiety. "You're not gonna swoon, are you?"

The church doors crashed open. Jane jumped. Everyone twisted in the pews, craning to see who dared interrupt the ceremony. Roy dropped her hands as a petite brunette hurtled down the aisle, thunderclouds scrunching her features.

"I object!" The unfamiliar young woman jabbed a finger in Roy's direction.

The groom audibly gasped as the color drained from his face. "Laura?"

Seated on the first pew, Jane's identical twin sister, Jessica, mouthed something she couldn't make out. Their mother fanned herself furiously. Her overprotective cousins exchanged looks of foreboding.

The reverend leveled a stern stare at the intruder. "What is the nature of your objection, Miss…"

"It's missus." Smirking at Jane, she planted her hands on her hips. "I'm Mrs. Laura Crowley. Roy's *wife.*"

Chaos erupted. Several of Jane's family members, including her cousins Caleb and Nathan, shot to their feet, forbidding features radiating anger. Her newest brother-in-law, Quinn, restrained them both and appeared to be urging them to stay calm. Her sisters shared matching expressions of dismay.

The reverend attempted to restore order. "Is this true, young man?"

"Y-yes. We were married at one time, but she deserted the marriage." He threw up his hands. "I thought you had it annulled, Laura."

"I didn't draw up any such papers."

"Why not?" he growled. A vein bulged in his neck. The telltale sign of rage in the otherwise even-tempered Roy gave Jane yet another shock. "You abandoned me. The least you could've done was set me free."

"You drove me to leave."

"That's a lie."

The reverend cleared his throat. "Ah, perhaps we should take this discussion to a more private setting."

"What's there to discuss?" Laura said. "Roy and I are husband and wife, which means there will be no wedding today."

Jane must've made a noise, because Roy turned to her, entreaty and a slight edge of panic in his eyes. "Hear me out, Jane. Please—"

"No."

By now, the truth was sinking in that she'd nearly taken part in a crime. Unknowingly, of course, but the damage would've been done regardless. If she'd gone through with it, she would've been living with him without the protection of a valid marriage license. And if she'd had children with him...

The room tilted dizzily. Perspiration dotted her brow.

Looking out over the rows, she realized every single person in attendance was staring straight at her. Some with pity. Some with suspicion. And some with anticipation, as if taking pleasure in this spectacle.

"I can't do this," she said, more to herself than anyone else.

Scooping up her voluminous skirts, she fled.

Through the narrow door of Reverend Monroe's office she ducked, slamming it behind her. Raised voices reverberated through the barrier. She banged her hip against the desk corner in a desperate bid for escape. Rubbing the sore spot, she tumbled through the door that opened into the graveyard. The heat and humidity of a cloudless spring day closed in on her, suffocating and relentless.

She couldn't face anyone just yet, not even her twin. She needed solitude. Privacy. A moment's peace to process the destruction of her hopes. Not the hopes one would expect a prospective bride to have, nor the ones the attendees likely thought the arrival of Laura Crowley had crushed.

The loss of Roy wasn't the cause of her devastation.

It was the loss of what marriage to Roy might've finally accomplished...rooting Tom out of her heart once and for all.

Tom Leighton was almost home. After nothing but rolling plains and endless wheat fields these past years, the verdant, forested mountains were a feast for the eyes. Patches of brilliant purple phlox peeked out between soaring sugar maples, yellow buckeyes, white ash and basswood trees. Like an open-air cathedral, the thick canopy high above was a bird-filled roof, allowing only slivers of sunlight in. Cool air scented with moist earth and magnolia blossoms evoked lifelong memories and an overwhelming sense of relief.

They'd made it.

Glancing over his shoulder at the slumbering child curled up between crates in the tightly packed wagon bed, he offered up a prayer of thanksgiving. Traveling alone with a five-year-old girl across four states had presented a myriad of dilemmas. By the grace of God, he'd dealt with each challenge and was now a couple of miles from the Leighton farm and the cabin he'd grown up in.

Coming home to Gatlinburg hadn't been the easiest decision. Folks would not have forgotten the reason he'd impulsively sold his barbershop and skipped town. Still, moving back here among friends that were like family had made the most sense now that he was officially Clara's guardian.

The familiar disappointment and anger knotting in his chest, thoughts of the difficult past year crowding in, he almost didn't see the woman weaving through the dense trees to his right. A vision in pure white, waist-length hair flowing free, she walked with her head bent, oblivious to her surroundings.

Guiding his team to a halt on the edge of the lane, Tom set the brake and simply watched her. Who was she? Why was she alone? Unwilling to leave without offering his assistance, he disembarked. He checked to make sure Clara hadn't stirred before rounding the wagon and, not wanting to spook the stranger, took halting steps into the forest.

The sun's rays slanted through the leaves, and her hair came alive, a deep, glistening red. The air left his lungs. He knew of only two women in this town with hair that color. He'd been particularly fond of one of them.

Intrigued and a little hopeful, Tom moved to intercept her. "Hello there."

Startled, she pulled up short, one hand flying up to clutch her throat. Her sweet countenance was the same and yet different. More mature. Womanly. Her cheekbones were more pronounced, her rosy mouth fuller. Her moss-green eyes reflected wisdom that hadn't been present when he'd left.

"Jane O'Malley."

Grinning, he closed the distance between them. She'd grown several inches, the top of her head coming even with his nose, and her gangly form had blossomed into that of a young woman—tall and graceful in her elegant, beaded white dress.

Hold on...was that a *wedding* dress?

"T-Tom?"

Her cheeks, he noticed belatedly, were wet with tears, and her already pale countenance went whiter still. She swayed on her feet.

He caught her against his chest, hands instinctively curving about her waist. Too late to worry about his gloves soiling the pristine material.

The faint scent of lilac hit him. "Jane? What's wrong? Are you ill?"

Clutching his biceps, she blinked up at him. "I must be dreaming."

The smooth voice like rich, warm cream belonged to Tom. And those vivid green eyes shining like stars against tanned skin? Tom's.

But it couldn't be him. There was nothing left for him here. He'd sold his barbershop. His mother was dead. And the woman he'd adored—her older sister, Megan—was happily married to another man.

"What's happened?" He brought his face closer, a frown pulling his brows together.

She studied that face, muscles locking up as she struggled to absorb the truth of what she was seeing—Tom Leighton...not a figment of her imagination...real flesh and bone.

His pleasant, boyish features had thinned out, grown leaner, tougher, the angles of his face more pronounced and cheeks hollowed. His wavy, rich brown hair spilled onto his forehead and curled over his shirt collar. Longer and messier than before.

Reaching up, she explored the scruff on his jaw with her fingertips. "You're really here. I'd thought..."

His Adam's apple bobbed. "What are you doing out here all by yourself? Does your family know where you are?"

Disappointment set in, followed by outrage. This was how he greeted her after all this time? No *I'm sorry for worrying you, Jane.* No *you're all grown-up and I can't believe I ever left without saying goodbye.*

She pushed out of his arms.

"I'm not a little girl anymore. I don't need a keeper."

He frowned. "That's not what I meant."

"You've been gone two years, Tom. Two years without a word. No letters. No telegrams. Would it have killed you to tell me you were leaving?"

A sigh gusted out of him. "I'm sorry about that."

"Didn't they have paper and pencils where you were?"

"I should've written. I see that now—"

"You have no idea how many unfortunate scenarios I've entertained. Not knowing whether you were alive or dead..."

An active imagination was both a blessing and a curse. Oftentimes the endless scenarios playing out in her head didn't have happy endings. Countless nights she'd tossed in her bed, unable to sleep for worrying about him.

Turning away, she swiped at the moisture on her cheeks and fought a fresh onslaught of emotion. She pulled at the dress's itchy collar. Had her sister Nicole not known how uncomfortable this confection would be when she'd designed it? One last remaining purple blossom fell from her hair. She crushed the fragile petals beneath her heel. His inadequate words did nothing to ease her deep-seated hurt.

For so long, she'd struggled to accept that she'd likely never see him again, never hear his warm laughter or gaze into those shining eyes. Tom represented all the heroes she'd ever read about. And while she knew he hadn't viewed her as anything more than a little sister, she'd missed his friendship in the most dreadful way.

His casual apology was more of an insult than anything.

Tom touched the spot between her shoulder blades. Gentle. Imploring. "I truly regret causing you worry, Jane. I was in a bad place when I left."

He didn't have to remind her. Her older sister Megan had rejected his proposal and chosen to marry Lucian Beaumont, a wealthy aristocrat from New Orleans who'd come to town for a brief visit and wound up falling for her. Megan's choice had effectively ended her and Tom's long-standing friendship.

In their small mountain town, there'd been no escaping the gossip. His dreams had been crushed, his pride wounded. Crazily enough, Jane had hurt for him. She'd hurt because she knew how it felt to care and have no hope of those feelings being returned.

"I suppose the main reason I didn't contact anyone

was because it was easier to sever all ties. I realize now how selfish that was."

When she didn't comment, he audibly exhaled. "Have you come from a party?"

"A wedding, actually."

Silence. Then a stunned, "You're married?"

"Ah, no," she murmured. "Turns out my intended groom already has a wife."

"What?" Tom encircled her wrist and turned her to face him, manner unyielding. "You'd better start at the beginning."

Amid the birds' intermittent chirping came a soft cry. She tensed. "What was that?"

Releasing her, Tom strode in the direction of the lane. Jane picked up her skirts and tripped after him, dense carpet of ferns catching on the delicate lace. "Sounded like a child. Do you think someone's lost?"

Intensely focused on the wagon that came into view, he went directly to the rear and held out his arms. Jane's steps slowed when she caught sight of a blur of pink calico and bouncing brown curls rushing into his hug.

"It's okay, Clara. I'm right here."

Planting a quick kiss on the little girl's head, he eased away and jerked his chin in Jane's direction. "There's someone I'd like you to meet."

Her frock wrinkled and creases from her blanket lining one cheek, the girl lifted a shy gaze to Jane. Her green eyes matched Tom's exactly.

Jane pressed a trembling hand to her middle. He had a child? Mind racing, she tried to calculate the girl's age. Four, maybe five years old? It didn't add up. Unless, like Roy, he'd been harboring a terrible secret before he left.

No, she couldn't let Roy's perfidy influence her outlook. Tom had been desperately in love with her sister.

Besides, he was an honorable man who patterned his life after the Bible's teachings.

"Who is she, Tom?"

Countenance solemn, he said, "In the eyes of the law, you might say she's my daughter."

Chapter Two

This second, mountain-size shock robbed her limbs of strength. Jane sank onto the ground, skirts puffing around her like a giant, satiny cloud.

His face a mask of concern, Tom swung Clara down and quickly approached, crouching to her level. Open at the collar, showing the column of his throat, the gray-and-white-striped shirt hugged his broad, sturdy shoulders and defined chest. She recalled the leashed strength in his arms as he'd propped her up.

There was one question answered. Wherever he'd gone, he hadn't been working in a barbershop. That kind of indoor profession didn't add bulk to a man's frame.

"I've never known you to swoon, Janie girl, but you look seconds away from it right about now. I've got a canteen in the wagon. Water's not cold, but it might help. Want me to get it?"

"No, thank you."

Behind him, Clara edged closer, eyes wide with wonder. Such a pretty, delicate child, with a round, inquisitive face and a pert nose.

"Clara, this is my friend Jane O'Malley."

Friend. An innocent word that sounded hateful when

he spoke it. Had he had the same reaction when Megan insisted on being nothing more than friends?

"Hello, Clara." She dredged up a smile. "It's nice to meet you."

Clara continued to stare first at Jane's hair—no doubt a wild mess since she'd plucked all the pins out to rid herself of the flowers—and then at her apparel.

"You have the same eyes," Jane told him quietly. "And hair."

Shadows gathered in the green depths. "She's my niece. I'm her legal guardian."

Tom's only sibling, a brother named Charles, was ten years older than him. He'd left town years ago and hadn't returned.

"You were with Charles and his family all this time?"

He gave a short nod, lips tightening. "On his ranch in Kansas."

She'd imagined him in all sorts of places and situations, none of them as ordinary as Kansas. Piloting a riverboat in Louisiana. Cutting hair in New York City. Sailing to Europe on a huge ship. Those pursuits would've kept him so busy he couldn't be blamed for not thinking of her. But working on a ranch in the middle of nowhere?

The reality stung. He'd had ample opportunity to contact her—he'd simply chosen not to. She bit back the urge to ask about Clara's parents, to ask anything more of him. Pride prevented her, as did consideration for the girl's feelings.

Clara dared touch one of the seed pearls on Jane's sleeve. "Are you a princess?"

"No, sweetheart."

Tom's perfectly formed, expressive mouth softened

into a slight smile that held affection for the little girl. "She sure does look like one, though, doesn't she?"

Then he turned that smile on Jane, and her foolish heart hummed a happy tune.

She flinched.

No. She couldn't do this. Not again.

"Jane?" Confusion colored his tone.

Struggling to her feet, she shook out her skirts and tugged the tight bodice down, backing away as she did so. "I have to go."

He stood to his full, impressive height, one hand outstretched. "Let me take you home."

"No." Her harsh tone elicited a frown from Clara. Tempering it, she continued her retreat. "I mean, no, thank you."

"Jane—"

"I don't need your help, Tom. I'm perfectly capable of finding my own way home."

She hadn't finished expelling him from her storybook dreams. If she allowed him to reclaim what progress she'd made, she'd never know true peace or contentment.

And for the second time that day, she fled.

Frustration pushed Tom to call after her. "I don't remember you being this hardheaded."

She paused long enough to glance over her shoulder. Her luminous eyes challenged him. "People change."

Framed by the forest's varying shades of green, her startling white wedding garb and flowing red mane carved an image on his brain he wouldn't soon forget.

He, more than anyone, was acquainted with the truth of that statement. His brother had transformed into someone unrecognizable after Jenny's death, and there'd been nothing Tom could do to stop it. As for

Jane, the sweet, adoring girl who'd followed him around like a lamb after its mother had been replaced by a self-assured, stunning young woman.

With a dismissive shake of her head, Jane ventured deeper into the forest, hem flaring with each stride of her long legs.

He didn't like the thought of her on her own out here, especially considering her current mental state, but he couldn't very well tie her up and toss her in the wagon.

"I'm hungry, Uncle."

Clara tucked her hand in his, the utter trust she'd placed in him a humbling thing. He was all she had now. That she depended on him for everything weighed heavily at times. Not because she was a burden, but because he'd come into this upside down. He'd never been married. Didn't know what it was to be responsible for another human being, although he'd had plenty of practice these past months.

"Come on, then, my little bird. I've got a can of tinned peaches with your name on it."

Her rosebud mouth parted. "Really? Clara Jean Leighton is right there on the label?"

Chuckling, he lightly tapped her nose. "Not exactly."

When he had her settled with her snack in her spot between the crates, he climbed onto the hard seat and put the team in motion. Impatience kept his bone-deep exhaustion at bay. These final miles felt like the longest of the entire journey.

Pulling into the shaded, overgrown lane leading to his place, memories bombarded him, and he wished his ma were here to welcome him. To meet her only grandchild. She would've relished the role of grandmother.

"We're here, Clara." His throat grew thick, and he had to blink away the gathering moisture.

Gripping the side, she observed her surroundings with solemn curiosity.

Tom hadn't expected his family farm to be in good condition—his ma had been gone a long time—but the disintegration of his former home gutted him. Set against the magnificent backdrop of the Smoky Mountains, his land used to be lush and vibrant, the yard around the one-story cabin kept neat and his ma's roses flanking the narrow porch. Now vegetation consumed the buildings. The cabin's shingled roof was barely visible beneath bands of ivy, the porch running the length of the building completely obscured. To the left and slightly behind it were the barn and toolshed, the smokehouse and corncrib looking like stacks of weathered wood amid a profusion of man-size weeds. The handful of apple and peach trees were in desperate need of pruning. The snake-rail fence separating the yard and fields beyond had completely fallen apart in some spots.

He was in for a massive job. Chest tight, he wondered how he'd manage to set things to rights before the first frost in six months' time. Unearthing the vegetable garden and readying the ground for seed alone was going to take days of hard labor.

And what to do about his niece? She couldn't very well accompany him to the fields every day.

Leaving her in the wagon, Tom used a hatchet to carve a path through the waist-high weeds and hack out an opening in the ivy. Stepping through onto the porch, he passed the single window with its dusty, cracked glass and had to shoulder the door open.

He stopped short on the threshold. If not for the layer of grime coating the cast-iron stove and the cobwebs in the corners, he'd have thought his ma had gone to the mercantile for the day's necessities. His gaze landed on the gray knitted shawl she'd favored, draped over the rocking chair beside the fireplace, and he picked it up, catching a whiff of her floral scent beneath the overwhelming odor of dank air and dust.

The unreality of her death coalesced into a truth he could grasp. She wasn't at the mercantile. She wasn't in the henhouse gathering eggs with her gnarled, age-spotted hands. She wouldn't be welcoming him home.

She wouldn't learn that her firstborn had descended into debauchery to the point Tom hardly recognized him. And that her youngest was now charged with the care and raising of a vulnerable five-year-old child.

Oh, Charles. What have you done?

"You should try to eat something."

Gripping the pot, Jane scrubbed harder at the stuck-on bits. "I'm not hungry."

Jessica shared a worried look with their mother, Alice, who was bustling about the kitchen packing for her extended trip to Cades Cove, a day and a half's ride from Gatlinburg. Their eldest sister, Juliana, lived there with her husband and two boys, and Mama had been counting down the days until she could see them again.

Abandoning a loaf of sourdough bread on the worktop, Alice came and put her arm around Jane. "I'll postpone this trip if you need me to, honey. I can send a telegram to Juliana. She'll understand."

"That's not necessary. I'll be fine."

"You're sure?"

Her ma's troubled look mirrored the one from yesterday when Jane had finally stumbled home, the same one from this morning when Jane had announced she wasn't attending church services.

"I'm positive."

Jessica carried her dinner plate over. "With the amount of desserts the café requires, we'll be so busy she won't have time to spare a single thought for that snake Roy."

The café owner, Mrs. Greene, had been stricken with a lingering illness this past January. Unable to continue running the café without assistance, she'd approached the twins with a job offer. Getting paid for doing something they enjoyed and excelled at made sense. Their afternoon hours were used to bake and decorate pies, cakes and cookies, which they delivered before the supper rush. The additional income helped with all sorts of things, from extra fabric and hair ribbons to replenishing their chicken flock and luxuries such as store-bought chocolates.

Alice's lined face pinched. "I wish you could've been spared all this."

"You couldn't have known," Jane rushed in. "Roy's a relative newcomer to the area. No one was aware of his history."

"He could've mentioned having a wife before he proposed." Her twin rolled her eyes. "While I hate that you had to suffer public humiliation, I'm glad you didn't wind up with him."

Jane fell silent. Her sister had made her feelings plain from the moment of their engagement. While Jessica had been all for her getting over Tom, she hadn't approved of Jane's choice. That her instincts had been right didn't help Jane's flagging self-confidence and made her question herself. What was it about her that had prompted Roy to keep his past hidden? Was she not the type to inspire confidences? Trust?

"Speaking of being busy, I have a favor to ask." Alice retrieved a second basket from the shelf. "As you are both aware, the Leighton farm is in a terrible state. Tom will have his hands full the coming weeks trying to clean it up and won't have time to see to meals. I've baked some bread and gathered jars of apple butter, jam and vegetables. There's a wheel of cheese, as well. Would you mind delivering it for me?"

Jane lent extra attention to drying the pot, tummy doing a somersault at the prospect of seeing Tom again. She'd made up her mind to steer clear. Resuming their friendship wasn't sensible or safe.

"I'm meeting Lee for an afternoon ride in an hour. I'd be happy to accompany Jane over, though."

Missing the glare Jane shot her twin, Alice patted her shoulder. "Thank you, dear. If I'm going to leave at dawn, I must finish this packing."

When Jane had gathered her satchel and the journal she kept on hand—one never knew when inspiration might strike—she met Jessica at the wagon. Several crates lined the bed.

She plopped onto the high seat. "This is a bad idea."

Jessica snapped the reins, and they rumbled out of the yard. "Look, it's just a simple errand. We'll drop off the supplies, stay long enough to be polite and then you can return home with the team. I'm meeting Lee in town, and it's a nice day. I'll walk home."

"I guess."

"I still can't believe he came back. And with Charles's daughter, no less. Where are her parents, do you think?"

"I didn't ask." Though she'd fretted over it since their run-in yesterday.

She'd mentally reviewed their encounter more than once, the distance of time and ebbing of her initial shock allowing her to recall his slightly haggard expression, the weariness that had clung to him. Whether it was due to their long journey or the events that had prompted him to leave Kansas, she couldn't be sure.

When they rode onto Tom's property fifteen minutes later, Jane experienced a surge of dismay. This was far worse than she'd imagined, too much for one man to tackle.

Jess let loose a low whistle. "Ma wasn't exaggerating."

On the porch, Tom hacked away at the profusion of vines.

Jess chose a shady spot in which to leave the horses. "Are you ready?"

Her younger sister—by four whole minutes—might not be a sensitive soul, but she understood how difficult seeing him again would be.

"We say hello. Drop off the food. And go." Sounded straightforward. "I'm ready."

They each grabbed a crate and waded through the path of trampled weeds to reach him. Grasshoppers jumped out of their way. A fat beetle crunched under Jane's shoe.

Grimacing, she eyed the chimney and wondered what creatures had lodged inside.

Engrossed in his task, Tom hadn't noticed their approach until they were almost upon him. His eyes widened. "Jane. Jessica."

Brushing his shirtsleeve across his damp forehead, he rushed to take Jane's crate and, setting it down, relieved Jessica of hers. He was out of breath and his blue-gray shirt clung to him in places. Caramel-hued trousers hung low on his lean hips, encasing solid, muscular legs that seemed to extend for miles.

He was healthy and virile and too handsome for her peace of mind.

"Welcome home, Tom." As his hands were full, Jessica gave him a quick side hug. "I could hardly believe it when Jane told me she'd run into you. How have you been?"

"Not bad." His answering smile slipped a bit when his gaze connected with Jane's. Concern flickered.

"Ma thought you could use some supplies." Jessica seemed oblivious to the undercurrent of tension as yesterday's encounter hung between them.

"That was thoughtful of her. Thanks for bringing it by."

"How's Clara?" Jane said.

"Not impressed with her new home. Can't say as I blame her." Shifting his burden, he cocked his head. "Come on in and say hello, if you'd like. She's supposed to be resting, but I'm certain she's playing with her doll instead."

He was right. Wearing the same pink dress that she'd had on yesterday, she danced a worn corn husk doll across the kitchen table's grimy surface. She stopped what she was doing to stare openmouthed at the women. The reaction wasn't an unusual one. Children—and sometimes even adults—rarely encountered identical twins, much less redheaded ones.

"Clara, say hello to Miss Jane and Miss Jessica." Sidestepping the bedrolls laid out on the floor, where they'd obviously slept instead of on the musty beds, he deposited the foodstuffs on the table. Red slashed his cheekbones. "Sorry about the mess."

Jane couldn't halt the sympathy welling up on his behalf. He'd always been a tidy person, had kept his barbershop and tools of the trade as clean as a whistle. Of course the cabin would cause him embarrassment. Cobwebs hung from the rafters. The mantel sported an inch-thick coating of dust. And while the floor had recently seen a broom, it would benefit from a good scrubbing.

In its current condition, his family home wasn't fit for a child. Tom, either.

How would he manage with his niece underfoot?

Not my problem. She tried to harden her heart. *I can't afford to care. Can't fall into that dark, desperate place again.*

Clara came up to Jane and touched her wrist. "Princess."

She shot Tom an incredulous look. "How can she tell us apart?"

"I don't know." He scraped a hand along his unshaven jaw.

"We do tend to wear our hair differently," Jessica mused, finger combing her long ponytail. While Jess didn't give much thought to her hairstyle, Jane tended to wear hers up in twists or tidy buns.

"Jane's hair was loose yesterday," he said.

She must be mistaking the admiring light in his eyes. He'd made a habit of teasing her about the color. And of course, he preferred blondes, like Megan.

Bending down, she indicated the doll. "What's your baby's name?"

"Jenny."

"That's a pretty name."

"That was my mama's name."

"Oh." Unaware of the child's situation and the whereabouts of her parents, Jane refrained from further comment. She straightened and risked a glance at Tom. Deep grooves appeared on either side of his mouth. In him, she glimpsed a curious mix of regret and anger.

The news was likely not good. Why else would he have guardianship?

"I hate to ask, but would you mind keeping Clara company long enough for me to take a quick inventory of the property? I need to determine the most pressing tasks."

Jessica turned to her, unwritten apology in eyes that matched her own. "I'd stay if I could, but Lee will be waiting for me."

So much for making this a brief visit. Refusing Tom this simple request wasn't something she could find it in her heart to do. "It's all right. I don't mind staying."

Slapping his battered black Stetson on his head, he cupped her upper arm and ran his hand down the length of it, setting her nerve endings on fire. "Thank you, Jane."

To his niece, he said, "Mind your manners, birdie."

"Yes, sir."

Jessica waited until he'd gone. "I'm sorry, sis."

"I'll be fine." She'd continue to say the words until they rang true.

"I know. It's just that you don't need this on top of everything else."

Clutching her doll against her, Clara watched them with too-serious scrutiny. What troubles had befallen this precious child?

Jane ushered her twin toward the open door. "I'll see you at home later."

Turning back, she lifted her satchel off her shoulder and, hanging it on a peg near the door, pasted on a bright smile. "How would you like to help me clean up this kitchen for your uncle Tom?"

Chapter Three

"What do you think you're doing?"

Hot, overwhelmed and running on an empty stomach—the tin of beans and handful of jerky they'd had for lunch long gone—Tom's question came out more sharply than he'd intended. He'd come upon Jane and Clara at the creek with what looked to be the entire inventory of his kitchen laid out across the grass.

Bent over the water, Jane sat back, the cup in her hand dripping a trail of dark splotches on her navy skirt. "Clara and I are helping you." With a significant glance at his niece, who was carefully drying a saucer, her tone carried a hint of reproof.

Slipping off his gloves and shoving them in his pocket, he removed his hat and fluffed his sweat-dampened locks. He motioned her farther down the line of shade trees. "Can I speak with you for a minute?"

She came hesitantly. He smoothed his expression. No matter his current mood, the near despair that had set in as he'd inventoried the seemingly endless list of repairs, he wouldn't take it out on her. She'd endured the worst kind of humiliation yesterday, and he wasn't about to add to her distress.

"I didn't expect you to work while you're here," he said. "This is my problem. My responsibility."

"You can't do it all yourself." Standing in a patch of light, she squinted, doing a slow inspection of the undulating fields and blue-toned mountain peaks rising to the sky. "How are you going to manage with Clara?"

Focusing on his niece, the familiar drive to provide for her settled in his chest. "I've no idea." Life had delivered more than her fair share of harsh blows. She deserved a bit of happiness, deserved better than trailing him around the farm day and night while he worked. "Suppose I'll have to find someone to watch her during the day."

Jane stared at the ground, teeth worrying her lower lip. Sunlight glinted in her glossy locks pinned into a simple twist with short strands about her ears. Dainty pearl earbobs matched the line of pearl buttons on her bodice. A pleasing mint green, her blouse was crafted of the softest cotton, the hue a perfect foil for her flame-colored tresses, expressive eyes and sun-kissed skin.

This close, he could make out the faint smattering of freckles across the bridge of her nose and the crest of her cheeks. In the past, he'd taken great pleasure in teasing her about those freckles. Now he experienced the strange urge to trace them with his fingers.

Tom shook off the unsettling thought. This was Jane, after all, the baby sister he'd never had.

"Thanks for befriending Clara."

"She's a delightful child." Her smile was there and gone too quickly. "I'm still wondering how she was able to recognize me."

"I don't have any trouble." Their eyes and mannerisms set them apart. Jane's were soft, dreamy. Innocent.

Jess's contained a boldness, a yearning for adventure. And Jane's voice was huskier than Jessica's.

"That's because you've known us your entire life." One cinnamon brow inched up. "And we haven't attempted to trick you."

He kicked up a shoulder, fully confident. "You could try, but you'd fail. I'd know you anywhere, Janie girl."

Something akin to anguish passed over her face, and he wondered what he'd said to cause it. Then it dawned on him. Here he was teasing her as if she wasn't suffering from a broken heart, as if the man she was supposed to marry hadn't deceived her in the most horrific way.

Taking her fine-boned hand in his larger one, he skimmed a thumb across her knuckles. "How are you holding up?"

Head bent, she seemed engrossed by their linked hands. "I'm fine."

"You never did tell me who you were supposed to marry."

"No one you know. He moved here last summer."

She sounded lost. Dejected. Anger sparked and simmered in Tom's gut. How could anyone willingly wound her like that?

Jane gestured toward the pile of dishes. "I should return to Clara before her interest wanes and she wanders away."

His niece had indeed abandoned her task and was tossing pebbles into the water.

"You two have already made friends." Jane was sensible and sweet natured. She'd treat Clara with kindness. The more he considered this potential solution to his dilemma, the more he warmed to it. "Would you be willing to be her caretaker?"

Her jaw sagged. "Me?"

"Yes, you." He smiled at her astonishment. "You're wonderful with her. And besides, I trust you whole-heartedly. I wouldn't worry about her if she was with you."

Her expression shuttered. "I can't."

Surprised by her vehement refusal and the lack of forthcoming reasons, he said, "It's a paid position."

"I wish that I could help you, but Jessica and I bake in the afternoons. The café owner, Mrs. Greene, has been ill and has cut back her hours. She hired us to provide the desserts."

Something wasn't right. Her words of regret didn't ring true. The fact he couldn't interpret her true state of mind drove home the fact she'd grown up. Changed.

"Are you still angry with me?" In the old days, he would've slung his arm about her shoulders and cajoled her out of the doldrums. He didn't feel comfortable doing that now. He hated that his insensitivity had created this distance between them. Couldn't have guessed his departure, and the cowardly way he'd gone about it, would trouble her to this extent. Oh, he'd surmised she'd be miffed at him for a month or so. But two years?

"I truly am sorry, Jane."

Tom was holding her hand.

The soft-as-a-feather scrape of his thumb across her skin mesmerized her. Hot tingles arrowed up her arm and into her midsection. He was standing so near, wide shoulders filling her vision, his brilliant green eyes earnest.

"I...I'm not angry anymore."

"But you're disappointed."

She couldn't lie. "Yes."

"And hurt."

"That, too."

This close, his lips looked firm yet yielding. If Tom tried to kiss her, she wouldn't shy away. She'd welcome his embrace. It hit her then that marrying Roy wouldn't have accomplished anything. Laura's arrival had saved her from a catastrophic mistake.

Pulling free, she adopted a casual air that was difficult to pull off. "Not sure why I expected you to write to me. I was just a silly kid with a bad case of hero worship."

His forehead creased. "That's not how I remember it. We were friends. I—"

"Uncle Tom?" Clara twisted her hem in both hands. "I'm hungry."

Tom continued to stare at Jane, obviously conflicted. After a moment, he slowly nodded. "I am, too. Guess it's time for a bite to eat."

Glad for the interruption, Jane held out her hand to her. "My ma packed lots of goodies. Why don't we go and see what all there is to choose from? We can finish the dishes when we're done."

Clara's hand in hers was small and warm, her expression trusting but with a hint of sadness and uncertainty. Jane found herself pondering how to elicit a smile from Tom's charge.

Her hope that he would busy himself with another chore fell flat when he stacked the already washed plates in his arms and followed them to the cabin. He even joined them in riffling through the foodstuffs, his excitement matching Clara's over the jars of apple butter and assorted jams. They decided to appease their hunger with thick slices of bread smeared with butter and blackberry preserves. Jane insisted on scrubbing the tabletop beforehand, so while she tended that task, Tom readied the food.

A giggle caught her attention. Twisting, she saw them standing together at the long counter beside the cookstove. His hair was a shade darker than hers, but the family resemblance was strong. He dipped his finger in the jar and swiped a tiny bit of sweet jam on the tip of Clara's nose. He grinned. "Try and lick it off."

Clara stuck out her tongue. No matter how hard she tried, she couldn't reach. "My tongue isn't long enough."

"Let me try," he said, swiping some on his own nose.

Clara giggled again at his antics, and Jane couldn't suppress her mirth. She'd forgotten how good he was at that. Making others laugh. Making them forget their problems, even if just for a little while.

He looked across the room at her and winked. She quickly resumed her task before she could act on the impulse to join them. She wasn't part of their family.

And she couldn't allow herself to be a part of their lives, no matter how much the idea appealed. When the surface was at last clean, Tom carried three plates over.

"You're joining us, right?" He pulled out a chair for her.

Jane hadn't planned to. She could use the time to wipe off the wall-mounted shelves above the counter or clean out the stove's firebox. But she didn't want to disappoint Clara, who was waiting expectantly.

"Sure." Taking her seat beside him, she scooted the plate closer.

"I haven't had a chance to purchase a milk cow. We'll have to make do with water." He angled his thumb toward the saddlebags in the corner. "Unless you'd prefer coffee. I could wash out the kettle and brew us some."

"Water's fine."

"Do you even drink coffee? You didn't use to like it."

"Sometimes. I require lots of milk and sugar when I do."

He nodded, the bread balanced in his large, work-roughened hand. "I'll be sure to have those items on hand next time you visit. And this place spick-and-span."

Jane didn't mention she wasn't planning on doing much of that. Quietly taking in the interaction between uncle and niece, her questions mounted. Tom was completely at ease with the child, his manner natural. He loved her. How had such a rapport between them built? How long had he been her sole caretaker?

By the time he'd gotten her settled on her pallet for a nap, Jane couldn't resist questioning him. Pride be hanged.

They'd gone out onto the porch, the cloying heat hinting at an impending rain shower, and he'd tugged on his buckskin gloves and begun removing the remainder of the vines. Bit by bit, the sagging railing became visible.

She hung back, out of his way. "What happened to Clara's mother?"

The muscles in his broad back rippling with effort, he ripped away a handful of vines and tossed them in a growing pile near the porch. Pushing his hat farther up his forehead, he met her gaze squarely, rioting emotions near the surface.

"Jenny died a year after I went to live with her and Charles. Pneumonia."

"I'm so sorry." Sympathy squeezed her heart. Poor Clara.

"Me, too. She was a fine woman."

"How old was Clara?"

"Four."

Lips pressed in a tight line, he attacked the last section.

So he and his brother had been left to comfort the small girl. Cook for her. Do the wash. Mend clothes. Hard to fathom how they'd managed it in addition to ranch work.

"Where is Charles?"

Was it her imagination, or did he yank on the stubborn vegetation with greater force? He discarded another bunch before answering.

"I have no clue where my brother is," he bit out.

Shock carried her forward. "I don't understand."

"Me, either." He snorted. "It's not a topic I like to dwell on."

His rigid spine and closed-off expression warned her to abandon the topic. There was a mystery here, one she would've liked to unravel. Short of tying him up and forcing it out of him—something her bolder, braver twin wouldn't have hesitated to try—she'd have to accept his silence on the subject.

Besides, the less she knew about his life, the less involved she'd be. Keeping her distance—emotionally and physically—was the only way to survive his homecoming.

Chapter Four

❧

Jane's heart and mind were at war. Her heart insisted she stay and attempt to draw him out. Learn what had happened in Kansas. Her oh-so-practical mind, on the other hand, was insisting she leave.

"I'll go and finish those dishes."

By now, he'd uncovered the entire porch railing. "Don't worry about it. I'll get to them later."

"I like to finish what I start." That was the only reason she wasn't climbing in her wagon right this minute. "I have extra time on my hands since the café is closed on Sundays."

"That's kind of you, Jane." He dropped the last bunch onto the pile. "Least I can do is pitch in."

Not giving her a chance to decline his offer, he took her elbow and assisted her through the thick vegetation. She was very conscious of the strength of his fingers through the gloves, his gentle hold. He didn't release her until they'd reached the stream.

Jane remained close to the tree trunk, letting it support her weight. Removing his gloves, he crouched at the water's edge, dipped his hat's crown below the surface and tipped the entirety over his head. He laughed when he caught her staring. "Feels amazing." Finger combing the excess water from the wet strands, he extended the hat with a grin. "Want a turn?"

"No, thank you."

Trailing his right hand through the water, he approached and flung tiny droplets on her exposed neck. "You sure? Won't hurt to unwind every now and then."

Jane shook her head, even though the cool moisture did feel wonderful. Somehow, she'd forgotten Tom's playful side. All this time she'd remembered him as he'd been after Megan's refusal. Somber. Disappointed. A man whose life plans had been thwarted.

"Why haven't you asked about Megan?" she blurted, cheeks burning when his eyebrows hit his hairline.

"No particular reason. I've had a lot on my mind, what with Clara and the farm. Yesterday, my mind was too full of your predicament to give anything else much thought."

Right. Her spectacular *non*wedding.

"So?" he prompted. "How is she?"

"Happy. Not only are she and Lucian the guardians of two adolescent siblings, but they recently adopted a three-year-old girl from New Orleans."

"She always talked about having a large family. I'm happy for her."

Jane studied him closely. He struck her as genuine, his interest in her sister casual. There was nothing to indicate he yet nursed a broken heart.

Propping a hand on the branch above her head, he leaned in, bringing a whiff of his distinctive woodsy scent. "Why are you looking at me like that?"

"Like what?"

"Not sure exactly. Do you suspect I came home with the intention of making things difficult for your sister?"

Jane gasped. "Of course not."

"I respected Megan's decision. I didn't like it, but I learned to accept it."

Mouth dry, heart beating frantically at his proximity, Jane desperately wanted to ask if he still loved her. Her lips refused to form the words.

His brow creased, and he pushed off the branch to pace. "If you think me capable of such behavior, other people might, too. Maybe even Megan herself." He slapped his hat against his thigh. "I have to see her. Make sure she understands I harbor no ill will. No grand illusions about us."

Jane stepped into his path, forcing him to stop. "I don't think that. I know you'd never do such a thing. Megan knows it, too."

He closed his hands over hers. "Even so, it would be best if she and I had our first encounter in private. Will you go with me? Having you there would put her at ease."

Tom had no idea what he was asking. No idea how difficult it would be for her to witness their reunion. What excuse, then, could she possibly give?

Caught in his imploring gaze, his touch both wonderful and torturous, she pulled free. Sidestepping him, she sank onto the bank, blindly seizing the nearest dish and soap sliver. She should've stayed away. Although it wasn't in her nature to refuse her ma anything, she should've invented a chore that needed immediate attention.

He followed and, taking up the spot beside her, began to wash without a word. She sensed his quiet perusal.

"When would you like to visit her?" she said at last.

"In a few days, once I've had a chance to clean out the cabin and round up a milk cow and several hens.

But, Jane, I get the feeling you'd rather not go. Has something happened? Have you two had a falling-out?"

"Nothing like that."

She recalled the day all those years ago when she'd confessed her feelings to Megan. Her sensitive sister had been heartbroken. Megan had known there was no hope Tom would ever love Jane. Not that she would ever voice such a hurtful truth, of course. She hadn't had to. The evidence was in the way she'd gently tried to reason with Jane, reminding her of their age difference. Back then, seven years had seemed an impossible chasm.

All these years later, he in his late twenties and she of marriageable age, she didn't register the gap any longer. But while the age factor wasn't an issue, something Megan never would've admitted made a future between them impossible—Jane didn't possess the qualities Tom desired in a wife. She couldn't measure up to Megan.

"You and Lucian get along, right? If he isn't treating you well, I'll—"

"No." Surprised by the promise of retribution in his voice, Jane jerked her head up. "Lucian is a wonderful man. He's good to my sister. To all of us."

The tension in his shoulders eased somewhat, and he returned his attention to his task.

Studying his profile, she placed the clean dish on the quilt behind her. "We can visit her any day this week. I'm free in the mornings."

"That's right. You bake in the afternoons." Reaching across her, he snagged an extra washcloth for drying. "The townspeople must love that. I often dreamed about your ribbon fruitcake."

Their desserts were indeed popular with the locals. She used to take such joy from making Tom his favorite treat. That particular item had been off the menu for quite some time. Too many memories.

"Any chance I might get to purchase a slice soon?"

"Right now, we're taking advantage of the fresh berries for pies and strudels. Perhaps in the fall."

"I'll have to be patient, then." He moved into her space. "Hold still. You have a stray eyelash."

His fingertips lightly stroked the tender skin beneath her eye. He was close enough that she could feel the cool fan of his breath across her nose. Her pulse rate tripled, and her head felt too light. What Jane wanted was to erase the scant inches separating them, wanted his arms around her, his chest beneath her cheek.

It wasn't fair that she should possess these feelings for him, suffer these reactions when he wasn't the least bit affected. She was nothing but a friend to him. Worse, actually. She was the little sister of the woman he'd wanted for his *wife*.

"There," he murmured huskily. "I think I got it."

Tom pulled away slightly, confusion tugging his brows together as his gaze roamed her face as if seeing her for the very first time. As if she were a stranger to him. His eyes flared with surprise just before he turned away and resumed washing without a word.

The creak of wagon wheels had them both twisting to see the new arrival.

"Josh." Jane wasn't surprised to see her cousin. He and Tom had been close friends since childhood.

A second wagon pulled onto the lane behind it, driven by Josh's younger brother, Nathan. The blond hair glinting in the light belonged to his pretty spitfire of a wife, Sophie.

"Looks like an official O'Malley family welcome."

He flashed her a quick smile that struck her as a bit strained. Helping her up, he quickly stepped away.

"Nathan's brought you a milk cow."

"Yes, I see."

Jane wondered at his distant manner. Was he worried her family would hold a grudge because of his lack of correspondence? Was it her? Hanging back while he strode ahead, she surreptitiously sniffed at her blouse, relieved when the lilac-infused washing soap was the only scent she detected. It was a rather humid day, after all, and he'd been very close.

If it wasn't an offending odor, was it something she'd said?

Oh, no. She stopped in her tracks. Had he glimpsed the truth in her eyes? The secret she worked so hard to keep hidden?

Tom hoped the astonishment ricocheting through his system wasn't written across his face for all to see. He couldn't have known a simple eyelash would incite this peculiar reaction to Jane. *Jane*, of all people. His best friend's younger cousin. Megan's baby sister.

But, oh, her skin had been incredibly soft. Her eyes luminous, the deep, true green of mysterious forests, drawing him in, making him forget who and what they were.

He'd always fancied himself as a stand-in big brother. Someone to tease her out of her introverted shell. Protect her from guys with questionable intentions. He'd always seen her as young and innocent. Vulnerable. The little sister he'd never had.

Seeing her as an alluring, intriguing young woman wasn't natural.

"Tom Leighton." His old friend pulled him into a

back-slapping hug. Josh hadn't aged in the years he'd been gone; he still wore his wheat-colored hair short and had a neat goatee. "Hard to believe you're here. I've missed you, brother."

"I should've written." Beyond Josh's wagon, the middle O'Malley son was swinging his wife to the ground. He'd been surprised to hear Nathan had married the O'Malleys' neighbor, tomboy Sophie Tanner. She certainly didn't look like a tomboy anymore. "Only now that I'm here do I realize what a mistake not writing was."

Josh's hand remained on his shoulder. "If I hadn't known where you were going or why, I would've been tempted to come searching for you."

Jane gasped. Pivoting, Tom saw the tremor in her hand as she lifted it to her throat. Anguish pinched her features.

"You knew where he was all this time and didn't tell me?" Her gaze hit upon Tom's and skittered away. "N-not just me. The entire family has been worried."

Josh shifted his stance. "I'm sorry, Jane."

"It's not his fault," Tom said. "I discussed my decision to go to Charles's ranch with Josh. I asked him to keep it quiet." Not thinking straight after Megan's refusal— he'd been one big mass of hurt and disappointment—he hadn't stopped to evaluate the rightness or wrongness of his actions. "I'm the one to blame."

He resisted the urge to touch her, something that up until a few minutes ago had been as instinctive as breathing.

Nathan and Sophie approached. Tom had no choice but to greet them both, noting Jane's swift departure out of the corner of his eye. Josh trailed her to the cabin, delaying her at the steps. She was upset and, as in the past, all Tom wanted was to hold her until she wasn't anymore.

It struck him again that things had changed. She had changed. And maybe so had he.

Nathan lifted the Jersey cow's lead rope. "We heard your niece is with you. Thought a milk cow might come in handy. This here's one of our best producers." He rubbed between her ears. "Her name's Belle."

"Let me get my wallet and settle up with you."

"No need. Consider her a welcome-home present."

He hadn't forgotten the O'Malleys' generosity or their stubborn natures. Arguing the point was useless. "I appreciate it, Nate. Thank you."

"I'll get her settled in the barn."

Tom sighed. He hadn't cleared out any of the outbuildings yet. Making Clara feel comfortable in her new home had been his top priority, and he hadn't made much progress on that front. "You won't reach it without a machete."

"So lend me one." He shrugged.

"Wouldn't you rather pass a pleasant Sunday afternoon with your wife?"

Arm linked with Nathan's, Sophie smiled. "He's promised to take me fishing later. For now, I'm going to help Jane. Good to have you home, Tom." She bussed her husband on the cheek before slipping away.

Silver eyes sparkling with good humor, the other man drawled, "Don't be stubborn, Leighton. We're family, got it? And family helps each other out. Now, point me to the tools."

Tom complied. He expected Jane to leave right away. Instead, she and Sophie carted buckets of water to the porch and began scrubbing the windowpanes, conversing in low voices so as not to disturb the still-sleeping

Clara. She did avoid looking at him, however. Having kindhearted Jane upset with him was not a pleasant experience.

With company around, he'd have to wait to try and smooth things over.

While he, Josh and Nathan attacked the overgrown vegetation around the barn entrance, more O'Malleys arrived—the men's parents, Sam and Mary, who were like a beloved aunt and uncle to Tom, and the youngest son, Caleb, who brought his wife, young sister-in-law and adorable eighteen-month-old son, Noah. Everyone pitched in. And there, in the midst of the sweaty, back-breaking work, surrounded by these people he considered family, he acknowledged how much he'd missed them all. Missed this town.

Despite the grief and turmoil that had spurred him home, he was glad to be back.

Leaning his scythe against the barn wall's weathered boards, Josh motioned for Tom to follow him to the stream. Resting a knee on the grassy bank, Josh submerged his handkerchief and mopped his face and neck.

"How did Jane seem to you yesterday?" Josh said.

Scooping up water with his hat as he'd done earlier, Tom reveled in the cold shock of it as it slid down his head and beneath his shirt collar.

"Distressed."

He wouldn't soon forget that encounter. Her breathtaking beauty. The fact she'd come close to fainting in his arms.

Josh tunneled his fingers through his hair, a disgusted noise gusting out. "The ceremony was a disaster of epic proportions. I'm not surprised she took off."

"Who's the lout she was supposed to marry?" Anger at an unknown stranger bloomed inside. Not many men were worthy of Jane. She deserved someone truly special, someone who'd recognize her true worth and cherish her gentle spirit. Not someone who lied to her, humiliated her in front of the entire town.

"Newcomer named Roy Crowley." He stood.

"You allowed her to get engaged to a man like that?"

"She didn't ask my permission. Besides, he struck me as a solid, responsible man. Treated her well. Everyone approved of the union."

Her misery fresh in his mind, Tom clenched his fists. "She must be devastated."

"Jane's not one to confide in me, but I got the sense she wasn't as invested as she ought to be."

"What do you mean?"

"I mean, she didn't have the look of a young woman in love."

Turning so that he had a clear view of the cabin, Tom crossed his arms and sagged against the tree base. She wasn't hard to spot, what with that shining red hair and cool mint-green blouse. At the moment, she and Sophie were emptying the bed mattresses of the old and no doubt moldy corn husks.

Was Josh's assumption true? Tom hoped so. If she didn't love the guy, she wasn't suffering more than bruised pride. Marrying for convenience's sake was a practical solution if one was facing financial difficulties or needed a spouse to help with farm chores. But Jane and her family weren't struggling with either. Why would she agree to such a union?

Chapter Five

"Time for bed, birdie." Tom folded back the freshly washed quilt and patted the mattress. "Hop in."

Taking a final sip of her water, Clara plunked the cup on the table and climbed onto the bed pushed up against the main room's wall. The same one he and his brother had shared when they were young. Here on this farm, the memories were everywhere. Inescapable. At least at the ranch, there hadn't been anything to remind him of the good times. Nothing to resurrect futile yearning for what used to be.

Making herself comfortable, his niece clasped her dainty hands together over her chest, big eyes blinking up at him. "I don't wanna sleep in this bed."

Sitting on the mattress's edge, he flicked a stray piece of hay from his pant leg. "Miss Jane and Miss Sophie cleaned it out today just for you. There's fresh straw inside to make it comfy."

"I want my old bed." She surveyed the cabin's interior. "Our other house was bigger. I wanna go home."

The plea in her tone punched him square in the chest. "I know this place doesn't feel like home yet. It's been empty a long time. No one's been around to take care of it." His attention wandered to the empty rocking chair, the basket of knitting needles and yarn near the hearth, and a fresh wave of grief crashed over him. He could use a bit of his ma's insight right about now. "Did you know that your pa and I were born in this very cabin?"

Her face reflected astonishment, and she looked so much like Charles that he could hardly catch his breath. "Really?"

He made do with a nod. Sometimes he despised his brother for not being strong enough to cope with Jenny's death. For abandoning Clara. *He abandoned you, too. Don't forget that.*

Giving up wasn't in Tom's nature. He hadn't thought it of Charles, either.

Granted, he didn't understand what it felt like to lose the love of his life, the mother of his child. But Charles had a daughter who needed him. Going off on a reckless self-pity binge was just plain selfish.

"Uncle Tom?"

"Hmm?"

"When will Pa meet us here?"

Snapped out of his reverie, Tom worked to conceal his emotion. He covered her folded hands with his own. "I'm not sure, Clara."

He hadn't told her that he had no idea where her pa was. Whether or not he was safe.

This is how Jane must've felt when I bolted, he thought dumbly. *All those months of wondering where I'd gone, how I was faring...* Knowing her proclivity to imagine the worst, it would've been torture for her.

No wonder she'd been so devastated. She had a right to be angry.

Like Charles, he'd selfishly disregarded her feelings. And the one person who'd known, who could've eased her worry, had been sworn to secrecy, thanks to him. *Stupid move, Leighton.*

Clara yawned widely and snuggled deeper into the mattress. "Will you tell me a bedtime story?"

Exhaustion had seeped into his marrow, and he longed for his own bed, but he couldn't deny her. Tucking the quilt under her chin, he wove a tale of adventure.

Her lids heavy by the time he'd finished, she mumbled, "Is Miss Jane coming to see us tomorrow?"

"Jane has her own farm to take care of."

She wouldn't be visiting again soon, he was certain. After overhearing Josh, she'd made sure not to be alone with Tom the remainder of the day, giving him no chance to apologize. Would she change her mind about accompanying him to Megan's?

"You like her, don't you?" he said.

"She's nice."

"Yeah, she is."

Nice wasn't the only adjective he'd use to describe Jane. Insightful was one. Sensitive. Beautiful. That moment by the water resurfaced, the mental image of her upturned face, eyes closed, pale lashes resting against her cheeks as he brushed away the stray one filling his mind.

"Amy is, too." Clara's voice jarred him. "She played dolls with me."

With much effort, Tom refocused on the present. He'd seen Caleb's young sister-in-law playing with Clara beneath the big maple tree in the yard. In Kansas, Clara had been somewhat isolated from feminine company, surrounded by rowdy, manners-challenged ranch hands. Having the O'Malley women around would benefit her.

Despite the difficulties, coming home to Gatlinburg would be good for her. He'd make sure of it.

* * *

"I can't believe you agreed to this."

Jane didn't look up from her journal. Tom and Clara would be arriving any minute to pick her up, and she wanted to finish her entry. Expressing her thoughts and feelings on paper helped her make sense of her world.

"What excuse could I possibly have given him, Jess?"

Her twin popped up from the top step and paced the length of the porch, blue paisley skirts swishing with each step. "I don't know. Chores? Errands? Visiting the sick?"

With a sigh, Jane shut the clothbound book and slipped it and her pencil into the leather satchel at her feet. She started the rocker moving with the tip of her boot. "He's concerned how Megan will react if he shows up there alone. As her sister and his friend, I'm the obvious choice to accompany him."

"He's concerned about Megan." Jessica snorted. "Of course he is."

Anguish arrowed through her. "He loved her, Jess. Once you love someone, that never goes away."

At least, it hadn't in her experience. How many times had she yearned for the empty hole in her heart to mend? Or be filled with someone else? She'd thought that, with time, Roy would've come to mean more to her. "Besides, Tom hasn't the slightest idea how I feel. In his mind, this is simply an opportunity for me to visit with my sister."

Jessica knelt before her, halting the rocking motion with her hands on the armrests. Looking into her face was like peering into a mirror.

"I'm worried about you, sis. Not only are you dealing with Roy's deception, but the return of your infatuation. The hero of your daydreams. The man you haven't been able to forget."

"Don't worry. I have a plan."

Interest kindled in Jessica's rounded eyes. "You're going to confess everything?"

The mere idea had her heart doing palpitations. "Can you honestly picture me doing that?"

"Yes, as a matter of fact. If you were to work up your nerve. It's not a horrible idea." She snapped her fingers. "I know, I can pretend to be you and do it for you."

Jane glowered at her twin. The handful of times they'd switched identities as children had been spectacular failures. And they'd gotten punished for their efforts. "Forget it, Jess."

"Okay. How about flirting with him? Giving him subtle hints that you're open to a relationship?"

Gently nudging Jessica aside, she pushed to standing and went to the railing. "My plan is to live my life apart from his. After today, I'm going to see to it that our paths rarely cross outside church. I won't even sit with him during the service." Not like old times, side by side with Tom and Megan on the wooden pew.

Jessica joined her, retying the shiny blue ribbon that had come loose about her thick mane. "He'll be included in all the O'Malley events."

"I can handle it."

"Has he told you what he's been up to all this time?"

"Not exactly."

"You do realize he might be married. Or engaged. Not all men wear wedding bands. Anything could've happened in two years."

Married. The possibility hadn't occurred to her. Surely he'd been too distraught over Megan to notice other women! Dread and something too much like desperation cut into her. She couldn't bear the thought, and that frightened her. Because it meant she wasn't over him. It meant she was right back in the same impossible spot she'd been in when he'd been dreaming of forever with her sister.

Sucking in a shaky breath, Jane stiffened her spine. "Falling back into the same detrimental cycle is not an option. I refuse to waste any more time mooning after a man who doesn't want me."

"Good for you." A wide smile blossomed on Jessica's face. "Because now that I'm with Lee, I have no intention of letting you become a spinster."

The longing for a husband and children of her own would have to go unfulfilled until she could successfully slay her hopes concerning Tom Leighton.

"I can't dwell on the future. I have to focus on one day at a time." The thudding of horses' hooves against the hard earth alerted her. "He's here."

Retrieving her satchel, she looped it over her shoulder and entered the yard.

Jess followed. "Be strong, sister of mine. I'll say a prayer for you."

Tom guided the team to a stop. His motions fluid despite his impressive height, he jumped down and, after advising Clara to remain in the wagon bed, strode across the yard. Neat charcoal-gray trousers encased his long, muscular legs. A button-down shirt the color of spruce trees hugged his fit upper body, the rolled-up sleeves revealing corded forearms lightly dusted with fine hairs. His eyes glowed even brighter than usual. His dark hair hadn't yet seen a pair of scissors, nor his chiseled jaw a razor. Strange. She'd thought he would've cleaned up for this first meeting with Megan. Personally, she preferred the rugged look. She linked her hands behind her back, away from the temptation of that beard, lest she succumb again to the need to touch him.

As he neared, his intense gaze lit on her, and he flashed an endearing smile she felt all the way to her toes.

She pitched her voice low. "Better pray hard, Jess. I'm going to need it."

"I wasn't sure you'd come."

Beside him on the high seat, prim and proper and delicately beautiful in her high-collared russet-hued dress, she sat rigid with tension. Her knuckles were white where she gripped the wood.

"I wasn't sure myself," she said softly.

"I messed up, Jane. I was so absorbed in my own problems, I didn't stop to consider your feelings." If his brother was here, would he be saying the same things? How difficult would it be to come to a place of forgiveness? "I don't blame you for being angry. Never should've asked Josh to keep my whereabouts quiet."

"No more apologies, okay? What's done is done."

Frustrated at his inability to gauge her true state of mind, he dared take her hand. He wished he wasn't wearing gloves so he could enjoy, however briefly, the soft texture of her skin. "You probably won't believe me, but you were never far from my thoughts."

Her gaze lifted from their joined hands to his face, searching, probing for answers. Opening up about what happened wasn't easy. He'd do it for her sake, though.

"In those first months of trying to get my head on straight, I often asked myself what you'd think about this or that…if you'd appreciate the stark wildness of the land, the unending flatness of it all, a sky so blue it hurt to look at." He smiled a little. "The ranch hands liked to sit out by the fire at night. There was one guy, Cookie, who played the guitar and sang the worst ditties you've ever heard in your life. Made me wish you were there to show them what a talented singer was supposed to sound like."

Alone on his cot in the bunkhouse, he'd think back to those times he'd drifted off to the sound of her lyrical voice. Picnics with the O'Malley sisters, joined sometimes by Josh and his brothers, had been one of his favorite pastimes. Good food. Great company. When he could eat no more and the sun had lulled him into a sleepy state, he'd lain on a quilt, hat over his face, and listened to Jane's soft singing as she poured her thoughts into her journal.

Jane didn't comment. Face angled away, her attention was on the roaring river tumbling over moss-covered boulders and under the wooden bridge they were crossing. The air had a moist twang to it, a pleasant earthiness typical to this area. In the near distance, people bustled up and down Main Street conducting their daily business.

He was both surprised and pleased that she hadn't removed her hand.

"The situation in Kansas..." His fingers subconsciously tensed on hers. "It deteriorated quickly after Jenny's death. I found myself in charge of a very sad, confused little girl. Whenever I neared the end of my rope, tempted to give up, I'd think of you."

Head tipping toward his, her fine brows crashed together. "Why?"

"You said it yourself. You finish what you start. You're so strong, Jane. You handle difficulties with a grace I could only hope to mimic."

"I would've given anything for one letter from you."

She looked incredibly sad, and a little surprised she'd admitted it.

"That's how I feel about Charles. He's doing to me what I did to you. I'm not sure I'd forgive me if I were you."

The wagon dipped to the side as the right front wheel hit a shallow depression. She didn't flinch, didn't remove her tumultuous gaze from his. "Our situations are vastly different. You didn't owe me anything. Not really."

"Our friendship mattered to me. *You* mattered. And I made you feel like you didn't."

He regretted that more than he could express.

Emotion slid behind her eyes. Mercy? Understanding?

Her mouth softened. "You're home now. Let's put the past to rest."

She took her hand back then, and he stifled a protest.

Reins firmly in his grip, he glanced into the wagon bed to check on Clara, who'd been quiet the entire ride. Propped against the far side, she observed the passing scenery. Her springy curls were freshly washed—he winced at the memory of her protests as he'd tried to untangle them with a comb—but her yellow dress was too short, the puff sleeves a little too snug about her small arms. He was going to have to hire someone to fashion her a couple of new dresses. Maybe nightgowns, too. Even if he knew how to sew, there simply weren't enough hours in the day.

Returning his attention to the rutted road, he said, "Something smells delicious. What's in the basket?"

"Rhubarb pie."

Tom groaned, his mouth watering at the prospect of

sampling Jane's cooking after so long a drought. "I sure hope your sister is in a sharing mood."

At that, she stiffened. He wondered at the cause.

She twisted around to address his niece. "Do you like rhubarb, Clara?"

"I don't know."

He felt Jane's speculative regard. "Did your sister-in-law not like to bake?"

"She did." He lowered his voice. "Clara was only four when she passed and probably doesn't remember a whole lot. And neither Charles nor I are that handy in the kitchen. We managed to get simple meals on the table. Nothing fancy."

Lots of beans and corn bread. Slabs of pork fried in hog fat. Fried chicken. Sometimes vegetables made an appearance on their plates. Greens from the yard. Potatoes or carrots he'd purchased from a neighbor. After Charles lost himself in the bottle, preparing breakfast, lunch and dinner fell to Tom. The entire situation had exhausted him, mentally and physically. That wasn't the kind of life he wished for Clara.

Not for the first time since he'd received guardianship, he considered the prospect of a wife. Clara would benefit from a woman's presence. There were things he simply couldn't teach her. With all the upheaval in their lives, however, he lacked the time and inclination to search for a suitable bride.

Admit it, marriage for convenience's sake doesn't appeal. You want the real deal. Like what Charles and Jenny had shared. Love. Mutual respect and affection. A true partnership.

As if she'd read his mind, Jane said haltingly, "Perhaps she could spend some afternoons with me and Jessica. I'd be happy to teach her the basics. She's not too young to learn how to make dough for biscuits and bread. You'd have to tend the stove, of course."

"I think that's a fine idea."

"Have you found a caretaker for her yet?"

Spying the turnoff to the Beaumont home, he shook his head as he urged the team onto the shaded lane. "Getting the farm into working order has dominated my time. You haven't changed your mind, have you?"

"I wish I could help you." She bit her lip. "I can't."

He didn't speak as the trees thinned out and there atop a gentle incline sat the grand yellow Victorian. A ribbon of colorful blooms hugged the front of the house. More formal flower gardens were laid out behind the two-story home, with winding walkways and hidden benches and fountains. This place had once belonged to Lucian Beaumont's grandfather. Lucian had come to Gatlinburg with the intention of selling it. Meeting Megan had changed his mind.

They stopped beside the barn. Setting the brake, he rested the reins in his lap and angled toward Jane. The light freckles stood out in sharp contrast to her skin. Even her lips had gone pale.

"Are you all right? You're not ill, are you?"

"Ill?" She plucked at her stiff collar. "No."

"Then what's the matter?"

"I had a restless night, that's all."

Her smile had a brittleness to it that troubled him. This was more than merely being upset with him. Was she hurting because of her deceitful fiancé? Was it the humiliation of the public revelation keeping her up at night?

"Is it Roy? Did he come to see you?"

"He has no reason to."

Curving a rogue strand behind her ear, she adjusted

one of the pins supporting her elegant hair arrangement, swoops and twists and miniature braids that made her appear older than her years.

She gathered up her skirts and made to descend on her side. He thought he heard her mumble, "Let's get this over with."

"Wait." He left his gloves under the seat. "I'll assist you."

His boots met the ground and, after swinging Clara free of the bed and making her giggle with how high he swung her, he reached up to grip Jane's waist. She balanced herself against his shoulders. Once she was on the ground, Tom discovered he was reluctant to release her. She was warm and supple beneath his hands, the raised design on her bodice rubbing against his palms. A tiny gold cross suspended from a thin gold chain nestled in the hollow of her collarbone. It was the only piece of jewelry she wore, and he recognized it as a gift from her deceased father.

Quickly moving out of his reach, she held out a hand to his niece. "My sister has a little girl about the same age as you. Her name is Rose, and she has a beautiful, handcrafted doll house and a number of dolls that I'm sure she'd let you play with. Would you like that?"

Clara's eyes grew large. Slipping her hand in Jane's, she nodded, contemplative as they headed through the short grass to the sweeping front porch. Having retrieved the basket containing the pie, Tom walked behind the pair, thoughts in turmoil. He had to get a grip. If Jane guessed these strange notions bombarding him, she'd be deeply disturbed. Josh would throttle him.

Tom rationalized with generic facts. It was natural for him to notice the physical changes in her. Any man would be thrilled to be near her.

His mind was on Jane as they ascended the wide steps, crossed the porch boards painted white and rang the bell on the fancy, carved wooden door. As a result, he wasn't prepared for the sight of his former love standing in the open doorway. All social graces abandoned him, and he stood gaping at Megan like a nervous young buck.

"Tom." She blinked. "Jane."

She hadn't changed at all. Petite, shorter than him by several inches, Megan possessed an ethereal beauty that ought to be preserved in a painting. Ringlets the color of moonlight framed a face unblemished by the sun, her peaches-and-cream complexion in contrast to large sea-blue eyes.

"Hello, Megan. You're looking as lovely as ever," he blurted, regretting it when color surged in her cheeks and next to him, Jane's harsh inhale punctuated the silence.

Great. No doubt they both assumed he was still madly in love.

Pulling open the door, she gestured for them to enter the small alcove, the sleeves of her pink-and-white-striped blouse fluttering. An ornate wedding band adorned her left hand. At his insistence, she'd worn his ring for a short time while considering his proposal. The day she'd returned it was high on his list of painful memories. Only after spending time with his brother and sister-in-law and witnessing their devotion to one another had he recognized she'd been right to refuse him.

Megan hadn't loved him. A truth that didn't inflict pain like it had before.

"Lucian mentioned that you'd returned. Is this your niece?"

Pulling himself together, he introduced the two and asked after her husband. While he and the New Orleans native weren't friends, he respected the man.

"He's out hunting with Patrick, our son."

Josh had told him that the couple had experienced difficulties having children. Years ago, when the wounds from her rejection were still fresh and his jealousy toward Lucian Beaumont had raged in him, he might've experienced a twinge of satisfaction. But no more. He couldn't rejoice at their troubles. He was glad they'd found a way to have a family.

Megan enfolded Jane in a brief hug. "How are you, sweetie?"

"Perfectly well."

Jane stood slightly apart from him and Megan, as if she didn't want to intrude. The siblings exchanged a look he couldn't interpret. What was going on? And why did Jane look so miserable?

Chapter Six

Jane had lied. She was ill. Very ill, indeed.

Her whole body felt as if it wasn't quite tethered to the ground. Her limbs trembled. And a vise was squeezing her insides until she could hardly breathe.

In that initial moment when Tom saw Megan, his reaction had confirmed her suspicions...he still loved her. There could be no arguing the fact.

As they followed her sister down the long papered hallway to the back porch, Jane was once again confronted with a heartbreaking truth—she was not what he desired in a wife. The epitome of delicate beauty, Megan's personality was such that people craved her company. She was comfortable reading storybooks to scores of children while their parents looked on. She even dressed like the characters! There wasn't enough money in the world to induce Jane to do such a thing. No, she preferred solitude to crowds. Peace and quiet to outright attention.

It made sense that Tom would prefer a woman with well-honed social skills. He was open and friendly, able to strike up a conversation with anyone he came in contact with. That was part of why he'd been such a successful barber. He'd treated his customers like dear family members.

There were any number of such single women in Gatlinburg who'd welcome his interest. Best that she start preparing herself for that event. Once he got the farm situated, he'd be on the lookout for a wife. A daytime caretaker was merely a short-term solution for Clara's needs.

As they exited the house, she stumbled over the doorjamb, and his hand came to rest against her lower back, guiding her over to the grouping of painted metal chairs with cushioned seats. The familiarity of his touch reminded her of old times, the weight and heat registering through her cotton dress and igniting a roaring inferno of longing within her chest. Such an innocuous gesture and yet devastating.

Urging them to sit, Megan waved to her daughters, who were inspecting a butterfly hovering above the patch of bleeding heart flowers. Seventeen-year-old Lillian said something to the small child at her side and, taking her hand, walked her over to the steps. Tom remained standing, his focus on the girls.

She knew what he was thinking. Lillian, with her waist-length blond curls and pale skin, could pass for Megan's sister. Rose, on the other hand, had dark brown hair and olive skin like Lucian.

As the girls neared, Clara tucked closer into Tom's side. He gently stroked her curls and murmured encouraging words. Jane winced. *This* was the reason she couldn't be Clara's caretaker. She couldn't be in their presence every day, couldn't witness his patience and affection without yearning to be included. To share in the care and nurturing of this sweet, vulnerable child.

And, impossibly, to give him more children. Build a family with him.

Please, God, let this visit be brief.

Motherly pride on her face, Megan brought them over. "Girls, I'd like you to meet a dear friend of our family, Mr. Tom Leighton. And this is his niece, Clara."

Lillian blushed and smiled. "How do you do?"

"It's a pleasure to meet you," Tom said warmly.

Rose observed Clara with keen interest.

"Girls, how about you show Clara the gardens?" Megan said.

"Certainly. Rose has some dolls on the table there." Lillian pointed to the white wrought-iron setting on the garden's perimeter. "Would you like to come and play?"

Clara looked up at her uncle, silently questioning. He bestowed her with a bright smile. "Go ahead, little bird. I'll be right here."

Megan lifted the basket Jane had given her. "I'll have our treat dished out in a few minutes. I'll prepare tea for you, sis. Tom, would you care for coffee?"

"I'd love some." Striding to her side, he relieved her of her burden. "I'll help you get everything ready."

Jealousy flushed her skin hot, then cold. Jane hated that she was jealous of her own sister. *Forgive me, Lord.*

"I'll stay with Clara," she scraped out, throat burning. He'd invited her here to smooth things between them. Apparently he didn't require her presence, as he'd initially thought.

Megan flashed her a look of apology. Tom thanked Jane, already leading the way to the door, holding it open like a proper gentleman.

Clara tugged on her sleeve. "Let's go, Miss Jane."

Gazing down into wide, solemn green eyes so much like Tom's, she realized how immature she was being.

This child had endured the loss of her mother. Her father had willingly abandoned her. She was in a new, unfamiliar town far from Kansas, surrounded by people she didn't know. Jane's shallow problems were inconsequential compared to Clara's.

Summoning a smile, she squeezed her hand. "What shall we do first? Play dolls or explore the gardens?"

Two days later, Tom couldn't get the image of Jane and Clara out of his head. He and Megan had emerged carrying trays brimming with pie and hot drinks and there, in the midst of the stone path flanked by a profusion of pastel blooms, sat Jane, his niece on her lap, heads bent as they studied a caterpillar in her cupped hands.

A rare smile had graced Clara's rosebud mouth. She'd been relaxed in Jane's arms. Content. And when they'd lifted their heads, he'd been struck by the compassion on Jane's face.

He shouldn't be surprised at the evidence of his friend's maternal instinct. Jane was one of the most kindhearted, loving people he'd ever met. That's why he was here on her doorstep unannounced, ready to get down on his knees and beg if need be.

At his knock, the door swung open and there she stood, an apron over her nut-brown skirt and buttercup-yellow blouse. Shiny strands had slipped from her simple twist to form a halo about her appealing features, the hair at her temples damp from the afternoon heat. One hand clutched a small towel. He'd interrupted her baking.

"Tom." Varying emotions surged and waned in her shadowed eyes. She dusted flour from her apron. "I wasn't expecting you today." She looked beyond his shoulder to where Clara was crouched in the grass, picking dandelions. "Is everything okay?"

Of course it wasn't. He was overwhelmed with the massive task of setting the farm to rights while trying to keep an eye on Clara, not to mention taking time out to prepare meals. He hadn't even addressed the issue of Clara's new wardrobe yet.

"Do you have a minute?"

Draping the towel over her shoulder, she opened the door wider. "Sure. Come on in."

Inside the main living area of her family's two-story cabin, the tempting aroma of apples and cinnamon curled around him. The low-ceilinged rectangular room looked pretty much the same as he remembered it—a stacked-stone fireplace dominated one wall. Oval-backed chairs surrounded one long chocolate-brown settee and a yellow-gold fainting couch. Sewing baskets, fabrics and supplies occupied a low table in the far corner. A cramped dining space led to the kitchen.

"Smells amazing in here."

"I'm working on a stack cake for Hattie Williams's wedding tomorrow. Do you mind if I give Clara a treat?"

"She'd enjoy that."

He followed her to the kitchen, attention on her hair and her exposed nape. She'd nearly caught up with him in the height department, the crown of her head about even with his nose. The twins were tall and slender like their eldest sister, Juliana, and shared the same flame-colored hair.

Being in her kitchen was like being in the bowels of a bakery. The pie safe's doors were open, the shelves crowded with baked goods. A five-pound sack of flour, containers of sugar and fresh butter occupied one end of her work surface, while bowls and spoons of various sizes fanned out around the stack cake in the middle. Even the table had been put to use. Spice bags and a crate of eggs lined the nearest edge.

"Where's Jessica?" Tom propped a hip against the counter, wishing he could have a taste of the towering confection.

"At the mercantile. I ran out of vanilla extract." Removing the covering on a large plate, she counted out four ginger cookies the size of his palm.

"Are all of those for Clara?"

Humor played about her generous mouth, and she started to replace the top two. "I thought you might like to indulge your sweet tooth, but if you'd rather not..."

For a moment, he was struck dumb by her almost smile, the first true glimpse of the lighthearted girl he used to know. One long stride had him at her side. Chuckling, he swiped them from her hand and took a huge bite. "Mmm. You, Janie girl, are the best baker in the state. Maybe even in the east."

Her green gaze clung to his, something akin to fascination in the mysterious depths, as if she was loath to look away from his enjoyment of her creation. Clearing her throat, she moved away to pour milk into a pair of mason jars.

"I'll be right back."

His mouth full of cookie, he watched as she carried the jar and a small plate out to the front porch. Clara came running. Jane bent to her level, a full-fledged smile transforming her face into something so pure and lovely he nearly choked as he fought to catch his breath.

She had to agree to his request. Her affection for Clara had surely grown greater than her reasons for refusing him the first time.

Taking up her spot behind the waist-high work space,

she resumed her work, carefully slathering apple butter across the top layer. "What did you wish to see me about?"

"You've seen my kitchen."

"Yes."

"It's not as large as yours, but it has everything you'd need to do your baking there. Jessica, too."

Slowly lowering the spoon, she stared at him. "What are you suggesting, Tom?"

"I'm asking you to reconsider watching Clara for me. I understand it would be a bit of an inconvenience for Jessica to have to come to my home every afternoon, but I'm willing to pay her what I can."

"I don't know—"

He lifted a hand. "Please, hear me out. Clara's had a rough year. After Jenny died, Charles and I couldn't make her understand why her ma wasn't coming back. We struggled to console her during those first weeks."

"I'm sorry." Her voice dropped to an almost whisper. "I can't imagine how hard that must've been for you."

He recalled the many sleepless nights. In the beginning, they'd taken turns comforting her after yet another bad dream. "Months passed, and she started improving. Charles, on the other hand, got worse. He and Jenny, they shared a love few people get to experience. He was furious with God for taking her. Couldn't handle the loss, so he started drinking. I tried to stop him."

And had gotten a handful of black eyes in the process. Knowing the depth of his brother's despair, Tom hadn't had the heart to put up much of a fight. He'd merely wanted Charles to snap out of it.

"Charles disappeared. I waited for him to return. Had the sheriff contact nearby towns looking for him. I have no idea if he's alive or dead."

"Oh, Tom." Coming around to his side, she clutched his forearm. Sympathy rendered her eyes the color of the dusk-darkened forest.

"I didn't tell you this to guilt you into agreeing. The fact is, I don't want just anyone to be her caretaker. I want you." Ignoring her quiet gasp, he continued. "I trust you. And she does, too. You're the first woman she's taken a shine to since her ma passed. You'd be good for her, Jane. Please say yes."

She stepped away, shoulders slumping a little. "I can't."

Disappointment swirled in his chest. Jane might not be as outspoken as her sisters, but she had the O'Malley stubborn streak. There'd be no changing her mind. If only she'd tell him why. She'd given him the impression she'd forgiven him for demanding Josh's silence. Holding a grudge wasn't in her nature, but it was the only valid reason he could come up with.

"I can't say that I understand, but I respect your decision. I won't ask again." Heading for the exit, he forced his voice to remain upbeat. "Thanks for the cookie. Good luck with the cake. Hattie will no doubt love it."

"Wait."

Foolishly, hope surged as he pivoted in the doorway.

"There's an elderly widow in town. You may remember her. Lorraine Drummond?"

Swallowing hard, he nodded. This wasn't going the way he'd envisioned.

"She's been saying recently how lonely she gets now that her husband is gone and her children have moved away. She'd be the perfect caretaker for Clara."

"Thanks, Jane. I'll look into it." He hooked a thumb at the door. "I'll let myself out."

Outside, he discovered his niece wasn't alone. A stranger stood with his hat in his hands, fingers worrying the brim as he turned it in a never-ending circle. Shorter than Tom, dressed much like the locals in pants, a band-collared shirt and suspenders, his black hair was rumpled and beads of sweat dotted his brow. From the looks of his mount, he'd been in a hurry to get here.

"Can I help you?" Crossing his arms, Tom deliberately blocked the steps. The man wasn't sporting a holster or gun belt, but there could be a knife hidden somewhere on his person.

The man scowled. "I'm looking for Jane."

"Who should I say is calling?"

"Roy Crowley."

Jane hadn't felt this low in a long time.

Seeing the hurt and confusion in Tom's eyes, knowing there were things about his time in Kansas he wasn't telling her, she'd come close to giving in to his plea. Whatever he'd endured was bad. So bad he wouldn't voice it.

Tom was adept at masking his troubles with his carefree, upbeat manner, something she hadn't recognized as a young girl. Interpreting his words and gestures through the eyes of a mature woman gave her fresh insight into the man she'd assumed she knew everything about. Just now, he'd attempted to hide his disappointment from her. To protect himself? Or was he doing what he'd always done—protecting her?

He wouldn't want her to feel guilty for not helping him. But she did. Jane genuinely liked Clara. Ached for what she'd endured. She had it in her power to help her, make her life a little brighter, and she was choosing not to. That went against everything her ma had taught her.

Desperate times call for desperate measures.

Her future was at stake. Her peace of mind. She'd

concocted a sensible plan to get over him, and she must stick to it at all costs. Even if it meant putting her own needs above a little girl's.

The sick sensation in her middle belied such thoughts.

Mrs. Drummond will be wonderful for Clara, she reassured herself, *like a substitute grandmother*.

"Jane."

Startled out of her reverie, she jerked her head up. "What is it?"

Anger blazed in Tom's eyes, which glowed like the most brilliant peridot gems. Hands fisted at his sides, his jaw worked. "You have a visitor."

"Roy?" Who else would evoke Tom's murderous expression? The sick sensation intensified. This day was getting better and better.

"I'll get rid of him if that's what you want."

His hard, lean body filling the doorway, tension coming off him in waves, he looked like a stranger. A lethal one.

Always her protector. If only... *Stop. Wishing for the impossible has gotten you nothing but heartache.*

Untying her apron, she hung it on a hook beside the back door. "I can't avoid him forever."

"You don't have to see him today."

She stopped in front of him. The temptation to seek refuge in his arms was strong. "Better here than on a street corner, with the townsfolk for an audience."

"Fine," he clipped out. "But I'm not leaving you alone with him."

This was where she should point out she didn't need him watching over her, that she could handle Roy on her own. Instead, she nodded her acceptance. His fierce determination to protect her, despite that it was motivated by friendship alone, made her feel cherished.

Tom had directed Clara to remain in the main room. She sat on the couch, big eyes taking in the paintings on the chinked-log walls, the photographs on the mantel. "We won't be long," he told her on their way outside.

The sight of her former fiancé in her yard evoked fresh waves of humiliation. Her cheeks burned. Maybe agreeing to Tom's presence hadn't been the wisest idea. Surely this fiasco called into question her sound judgment. Her ability to discern people's true natures.

"Why are you here, Roy?" At least she sounded calm. Unfazed.

He came to the porch's bottom step, brown eyes pleading. "I came to apologize. You ran out of the church so fast, you didn't give me a chance to explain."

Behind her, Tom made a sound of disgust.

Roy's lips thinned. "Can we speak in private?"

"It's too late for explanations. If you'd been honest with me from the beginning, we would've been spared a public spectacle. Go home to your wife, Roy."

"Laura." He shook his head. "She's been trouble since the day I met her. That's why you were so refreshing, Jane. You're sweet and biddable."

Biddable? He might as well have likened her to a sheep!

Tom moved to stand beside her, large hand curving against her spine. "Hit the road, Crowley."

"I'm not finished here."

"If you don't leave of your own volition, I'll be happy to *escort* you off the property." Undeniable threat laced his words.

Jane shivered. She hadn't known this side of Tom existed.

"We need to talk, Jane. Alone. Think about it." With that, Roy smashed his hat on his head and stomped to where he'd left his horse grazing.

Tom turned to her the moment he was gone. "He's a first-class idiot." Running his hands lightly down the length of her arms, he studied her closely. "You okay?"

"I'm fine. I just wish he'd been honest with me."

"Do you love him?"

They were moving into dangerous territory. He couldn't know her reasons for accepting Roy's suit. Besides, what right had he to ask?

"That's not something I'm willing to discuss with you."

A muscle ticked in his jaw. "I'm asking as your friend."

Pulling away, she hugged her middle. "You've been gone a long time, Tom."

"I wish you wouldn't shut me out. You told me once I was a good listener."

Jane closed her eyes, recalling all too vividly how he'd sat and simply let her vent. Sometimes about some petty argument with one of her sisters or a problem at school. More rarely, he'd held her as she'd cried for her father, a man she barely remembered but whose absence she felt every day. Tom hadn't ever made her feel as if her problems were insignificant, although to him they probably had been.

"Considering everything that's happened, we can't go back to the way things used to be."

"Is that why you won't watch Clara?" He passed a weary hand over his face. Bewilderment colored his tone. "Because of how I handled things?"

"No. I understand why you did what you did."

"Then why?"

At a loss, she paced to the far end of the porch, not really registering the neat rows of vegetable plants and the line where the forest took over the land. "I think you should leave. I—I have a lot of work to do."

Stilted silence met her words. "I won't keep you from it, then."

She flinched at the defeat in his rich-as-cream voice. When he'd beckoned his niece to join him, Jane managed a quiet farewell to Clara, all the while avoiding his scrutiny.

This is for the best, she told herself. Reclaiming their former friendship wasn't a possibility. Creating distance was the wise, practical course.

She simply hadn't anticipated the depth of pain such a course would inflict.

Chapter Seven

Jane entered the mercantile, wincing when the overhead bell trilled and customers in the aisles and at the long sales counter stopped what they were doing to gape at her. Seventeen days had passed since her almost wedding, and today marked her first foray into public. Jessica had tried to convince her to attend services again this past Sunday, but she hadn't been able to summon the courage.

She was here this morning only because Jess had refused to come in her stead. Why be ashamed about something that was out of her control, she'd argued. Roy was the one who'd behaved badly, not Jane.

Her twin had a point. And so, she'd dressed in her most sensible frock, sturdy green calico trimmed in black ribbon, with a stiff high collar and three-quarter sleeves. Her scalp hurt from a brisk brushing, the thick mass pulled into a severe knot at the base of her skull. Not one hair was out of place.

Gripping her reticule in nerveless fingers, she took a bracing breath. *I can do this.*

Her favorite brother-in-law, Quinn Darling, was behind the counter tallying up his customer's bill. He caught her eye and winked, a roguish grin brightening his handsome face. Sidestepping to the doorway that led to the storeroom and office, he called, "Nic. I need you out here."

Nicole appeared, hands on her hips. "You bellowed, my dear?" Jet-black eyebrows arching above her stunning violet eyes, a sparkle of affection belied her dry tone.

Quinn tipped his head in Jane's direction. "Your sister's here."

Jane approached the counter, gaze trained on Nicole, whose gently rounded tummy was barely visible beneath the ice-blue ruffles of her dress. They were expecting their first child, and Jane could hardly contain her excitement. Quinn would be a natural, of course. Nicole, on the other hand, hadn't had much experience with children. It would be fascinating to observe her with a newborn.

"Jane, sweetie." Coming around the counter, Nicole draped an arm about her shoulders and guided her right back through the entrance and onto the boardwalk, choosing an empty bench tucked up against the building. "We'll have more privacy out here, believe it or not."

They sat and fluffed out their skirts. "I'm glad to see you out and about," she said, brushing an errant curl behind her ear.

"I'm done with hiding."

An older couple passed, whispering together when they noticed Jane. The woman even glanced back over her shoulder and would've stumbled if her husband hadn't caught her. Across the dusty street, a gaggle of young girls pointed their direction. What was she, a circus act? She fought the impulse to bolt.

Nicole covered her hand, an unusual display of affection. Marriage to Quinn had wrought many positive changes in her previously standoffish sister. "This will pass. A month from now, they'll have forgotten. Moved on to the next bit of news."

"I hope you're right."

"There's no question," she quipped with a smile.

"How are you?" Jane tried not to stare at her expanding waistline. "Still exhausted?"

"Not as bad as before. Quinn's insisting I get off my feet every couple of hours. He's being very careful with me."

"And you love every minute of it," Jane teased softly, truly happy for her sister.

For all her sisters. Juliana, Megan and Nicole had married honorable, loving, God-fearing men. Even Jess had found someone special and believed her beau would soon propose.

Her thoughts turned to Tom, and her smile faded. She hadn't seen him in nearly a week. True to his word, he hadn't visited again. His absence left her aching. Not seeing him, all the while knowing he was but a couple of miles away, was torture. Her nights had been dominated with dreams of him…repentant and sad, pleading for her help. She'd woken each morning with a heavy heart.

Have I done the right thing, Lord? Protecting myself at Clara's expense?

She'd heard from Jessica that Tom had taken her advice and enlisted Mrs. Drummond.

Nicole squinted in the overly bright sunshine. "Who's that little girl in front of the barbershop? I don't recognize her."

Easing forward, Jane searched the length of the boardwalk, seeking out the last business on this side

of Main Street. She recognized the pink dress immediately.

"Clara," she breathed.

"Tom's niece?"

What was she doing alone, peering into the shop's
window?

"You haven't met her?"

"They haven't been to church. I thought at least
they'd come into the mercantile."

"You didn't see the state of his farm." Jane stood,
reticule swinging from her wrist. "Come with me. I'll
introduce you."

Ignoring the curious passersby, she walked briskly
to Clara's side, Nicole following in her wake.

"Good morning, Clara." Crouching to her level, Jane
smiled to hide her concern.

She turned from the window. "Miss Jane."

Spotting Nicole, her petite mouth formed an O. Jane
hid a grin. With her raven hair, porcelain skin and unusual eye color, her sister was very beautiful. Her talents
as a seamstress meant she was always dressed stylishly.

Once introductions had been taken care of, she said,
"Where is your uncle?"

"In there." The child pointed to the boards beneath
her feet. "I'm to wait here and not move."

"I see." She straightened. Through the warped glass,
she spotted Tom's unmistakable profile. His back was
to the window as he conversed with the barbershop's
new owner. Had he given Mrs. Drummond the morning off while he completed his errands?

"Want to see my hurt knee?"

Clara was pulling up the fabric of her too-small
dress. Nicole's soft, "Oh, my," was followed by Jane's

sharp exhale. Her entire knee was swollen and an ugly purple color.

"Oh, sweetie—" she squeezed her shoulder "—what happened?"

"I fell outta the tree."

Dismay skittered through her. A glance at Nicole revealed similar emotions. "Mrs. Drummond allowed you to climb trees?"

"She was sleeping." Clara's nose scrunched. "She likes to take lots of naps."

Jane's eyes squeezed shut. Guilt flushed through her system.

Nicole poked her ribs. "He's coming."

Opening her eyes, she saw the door swinging open.

"Nic, would you do me a favor? Watch her while I speak to him?"

"Sure." Holding out her hand, Nicole aimed a dazzling smile at her. "Miss Clara, how would you like to come to the store with me and pick out a piece of candy?"

She hesitated, weighing the allure of sweets against the prospect of going with someone unfamiliar.

"It's okay," Jane told her. "Your uncle and I will be there in a few minutes to get you."

Gingerly placing her hand in Nicole's, she allowed herself to be guided away. Nicole kept up a steady stream of chatter all the way to the mercantile entrance.

"Where are they going?" Tom's low voice addressed her from behind.

Spinning, she grabbed his hand and tugged him around the corner. "Walk with me."

"Jane, what—"

"I wish to speak to you. Away from prying eyes." Fingers interlocking with his, she pointed to the river rumbling behind the businesses. Massive willows, maples and oaks dotted this side of the bank. On the opposite side, the forested mountain rose up sharply.

Tom allowed her to pull him along, his long strides matched to hers. They reached the lone bench and, releasing him, she swept out an arm to indicate he should sit. He didn't. Instead, he propped his hands on his lean hips and stared her down.

"What's this about?"

Mirroring his stance, she tried not to notice the way his rich brown hair slid over his forehead and curled about his collar. Tried not to stare at the play of his chest muscles beneath his cream-hued shirt. "When did Clara's accident happen?"

Understanding dawned, and his arms fell to his sides. "Saturday afternoon."

"You dismissed Mrs. Drummond, I hope."

"The whole thing really shook her up. She quit before I had a chance to."

Jane massaged her temples in an attempt to slow the blossoming headache. "I can't believe this. I thought... She's such a dear lady. Adores children. I had no idea she'd neglect Clara."

This was *her* fault. Tom had hired Mrs. Drummond on Jane's recommendation.

What if Clara had broken an arm or leg? Or worse? Her imagination kicked in, and she pictured the little girl balancing on a high limb—

"Hey." Tom tipped her chin up with his thumb and forefinger. The tenderness in his gaze was almost too much to bear. "I don't blame you."

"But—"

"You weren't there. You couldn't have known something like this would happen."

His thumb was grazing her chin, the tip sweeping the outer edge of her bottom lip, making it very difficult to think.

"I should've been there. And I will be. I'll be her caretaker for as long you need to find the right person."

The motion stopped. He released her chin. "I don't want you agreeing because of a guilty conscience. Neither you nor Clara would benefit."

"I want what's best for her. I want her to be safe and properly cared for." At his obvious indecision, she voiced the thoughts that had been plaguing her this past week. "I'm sorry for what I said before."

He stilled, intently examining her face. "What are you referring to, exactly?"

"I know how devastated you were following Megan's decision to marry Lucian. I understand how impossible it would've seemed for you to remain here and stand by while she pledged her life to someone else." An image of Tom standing in the church with a faceless bride flashed in her mind, and she cringed. No wonder he'd left. "I haven't been as understanding as I should've been. I know you didn't intend to hurt me or anyone else. You did what you had to do, and I—I can't fault you for that."

Stepping close, his pant legs brushing her skirts, he very carefully cupped her cheek. A rogue sigh slipped through her lips. The rasp of his callused palm against her skin wrought a heady feeling inside. If only this didn't feel like a platonic caress.

"My sweet Janie girl," he murmured. "The memories of your laughter, your sweet smile, the way things were always easy and fun between us, kept me going this past year. You represented peace and calm at a time when my life was falling apart. I need your friendship."

Friendship. Not love. Not devotion.

If he guessed how badly she yearned for more, he'd be revolted.

"Friendship," she croaked. "Always. You have it."

Encircling his thick wrist with her fingers, she allowed herself scant precious seconds to revel in the contact before tugging his arm down.

When she began spending days at his farm, she'd have to deter these types of gestures. Maintain a reasonable distance. Natural affection had existed between them from the start. He was comfortable expressing that with her, unaware of the devastating effects.

Scooting back, she smoothed her hair and wished for a fan or light breeze to cool her skin. "I'll be at your cabin first thing tomorrow morning. I'll have to speak to Jessica. She may wish to divide our work whenever possible."

His gaze had followed the slide of her fingers over her hair and was now brighter than usual. Indefinable emotion crossed his features before he twisted away to observe the glide of brown-feathered ducks across a smooth section of water.

"I'm fine with whatever you decide." Clearing his throat, he turned back. "You're welcome to use my supplies. I've come today to stock my kitchen."

"Thanks, Tom. I'll bring my own, but there may be instances when I forget something and have to borrow something of yours. And don't worry, I'll clean up after myself."

A slow grin tilted his lips. "As long as you let me sample your creations, I don't mind a mess."

Orange streaks of dawn were stretching across the lightening sky when Jane arrived on his doorstep the next morning. The sight of her filled him with confidence that everything would work out. Clara would be safe and happy. He could tend his responsibilities without worrying about her.

Still in the process of dressing, he opened the door in his stocking feet.

She stared at his snug undershirt and flushed to the roots of her hair. "I brought breakfast." She indicated the basket looped over her arm. "I have more things in my wagon."

Flicking a glance behind her at the now-cleared yard, his fingers went to the buttons on his outer shirt and nimbly started fastening from the bottom up. "I'll bring everything in and then see to your horses." He waved her in. "I don't expect you to provide breakfast for us, you know."

"I came early today because I forgot to ask what time Clara usually wakes." She placed her burden on the table, looking at everything except him. "Is she still sleeping?"

Choosing the nearest chair, he sat and tugged on his boots. "She's in the bedroom. The plan was for her to sleep in here." He jerked a thumb at the bed tucked against the opposite wall and separated from the room by a quilt divider. "I couldn't convince her she'd be safe by herself, so I fixed her a pallet on the floor in my room."

"She's still adjusting to the change. Give her time." She tucked a pin deeper in her upswept tresses. "Jessica decided to work from home. We'll be splitting the orders. It's easier for her."

"Like I said, I'm fine with whatever the pair of you work out."

Fiddling needlessly with the handle, slender body

drawn tight as a bow, she reminded him of a skittish deer, ready to bound away if he made a sudden move. Considering their history, it struck him as strange that she'd be uncomfortable in his home. Wasn't as if they hadn't spent time alone together.

He frowned. Had she perceived his thoughts yesterday down by the river? He was quickly learning there was no such thing as a casual touch where Jane was concerned. Not anymore. Being that close to her, exploring her petal-soft skin, had him entertaining wild ideas about her and him. Ideas that had absolutely nothing to do with friendship.

He had to get a handle on this. Especially now that she would be spending her days here.

"Did you forget your razor in Kansas?"

Dropping his booted foot to the floor with a thud, he laughed outright. Scraped a hand over his unshaven cheeks. "What? You don't like the scruffy look?"

"It suits you." She shrugged, cheeks pinking again. "I was just wondering… Never mind."

Spinning away, she went to the wall-mounted shelves above the dry sink and chose three plates.

Tom stood. "Wondering what?"

She set the plates on the tabletop and started to peel away the cloth covering on her basket. He covered her hand to stop the movement, quickly removing it when she stiffened.

"You can't start something and not finish it," he cajoled with a smile. "Tell me."

He could see that she wished she'd kept quiet, and his curiosity was piqued.

"You were gone a long time. Jessica mentioned you might have someone special there. I wondered if you did and if she's the reason for your new look."

Surprised by the question, he hastened to lay down the facts. "The truth of the matter is, there wasn't much socializing going on. The ranch isn't close to town. We attended church, of course, and a handful of socials, but that's about it. I wasn't in the right frame of mind in the beginning. And then Jenny took sick…"

He shook his head to dislodge the memories. He'd never felt so helpless. He could do nothing to stop his sister-in-law's worsening health. Nothing to prevent his brother's slow unraveling. "The answer to your question is no. There's no one special in my life."

Busy doling out boiled eggs, sausage slices and biscuits, she spoke without looking at him. "I told Jessica that Megan was the love of your life and that you were ruined for anyone else."

He jerked his head back.

The love of his life? He'd thought so at the time, hadn't he? "I wouldn't go that far."

Slowly, she lifted her face, dark eyes full of questions. "You wouldn't?"

"Seeing Charles and Jenny together made me realize something. If Megan had chosen me, she would've been settling for something less than real, abiding love. Sure, she loved me as a friend, but that's not what I want. I want someone who's as crazy about me as I am about her."

"Oh. I—I see."

She bent her head. Once again, she'd scraped her hair into a schoolmarm bun. He was starting to think of their first encounter as a dream. With her lustrous red mane flowing free, she'd been gloriously unreserved. He found himself thinking of possible ways to shake that reserve.

"Am I making any sense?" he said.

It wasn't often he spoke of such private matters, but he could tell Jane anything and not worry she'd laugh or criticize. She used to feel the same about him. His absence had driven a wedge between them. A chasm he didn't know how to cross.

"Yes." She took her time arranging the settings. "Perfect sense."

A sleepy, tousled Clara entered the room then, putting an end to the conversation. Just as well. He sensed Jane's discomfort and figured she'd appreciate a break from him.

As he prepared to head to the barn and milk Belle, he remembered she once hadn't found his presence upsetting. These unexpected, and unwelcome, developments troubled him. He'd known his return wouldn't be without challenges…he just hadn't counted on Jane O'Malley being one of them.

Chapter Eight

Jane breathed easier once Tom left for the barn. His disheveled state when he'd first answered the door— his hair falling in his eyes, the stubble on his cheeks and chin making the contours of his mouth more noticeable, undershirt outlining the lean musculature of his torso— had jolted her with the energy of a lightning bolt.

Being in his home, in the early morning stillness and without Clara as a buffer, had imbued their interaction with a false sense of intimacy. Far too easy for her to envision living here. Sharing breakfast with him every morning.

Stay strong. Stay practical. He's just a companion. A pal. One who needs my help.

"Let's get you dressed, sweetheart. Then we can eat."

Blearily rubbing her eyes, Clara padded into the cabin's only bedroom. Jane hesitated to enter. This was Tom's private domain. It couldn't be helped, however.

Inside the generous-size room, she discovered he hadn't had the opportunity to put his stamp on the space. His mother's trinkets, photographs and jewelry box cluttered the plain wooden dresser. The tall wardrobe still held his mother's dresses and shawls. Certainly the feminine bed quilt, dominated by whimsical rose, green and cream flowers, was Edith Leighton's creation. Three massive trunks lining the interior wall contained his and Clara's clothing and other sundries.

"Which one of these holds your things?" Her fingers skimmed the metal bands on the nearest trunk.

Clara pointed to the last one. Jane hefted the heavy lid open, the distinct scent of cedar wafting upward, and took stock of the contents. There wasn't much to choose from, as most of the dresses were faded and clearly too small for the child. Thankfully Tom had enlisted Nicole's services. After their chat yesterday, he'd returned to the mercantile and chosen enough fabric for five everyday dresses, a pair of nice ones for church and several nightgowns.

"How about this one?"

They agreed on a solid navy blue. Jane assisted her into it, careful of her bruised knee, then directed her to sit on the bed while she brushed her curls. Clara bit her lip when the brush caught on a snarl.

"I'm sorry. I'll be more gentle, all right?"

Carefully untangling the soft strands, she wondered how long Tom had had the sole care of his niece, seeing to every need, soothing hurts, both emotional and physical. Her admiration for him increased tenfold. Never one to shirk responsibility, he'd cared for her as if she were his own daughter.

She'd just finished tying the matching ribbon in Clara's hair when the main door opened and closed and his heavy tread crossed to the kitchen. "Your uncle's brought in the milk. Are you hungry?"

"What are we having?" She slid off the bed, cautious green eyes fixed on Jane.

"Biscuits, sausage and eggs."

"I'm *very* hungry."

Unable to hide her amusement, Jane was still smiling as they emerged. Tom lifted the milk pail onto the counter and, with a quick glance at his niece, answered her smile with a wide one of his own. Gratitude shone in his bright gaze.

Breakfast was a relaxed affair. There was one tense moment when he blessed the meal and expected them all to join hands. His grip had been gentle, palm dry and warm against hers, and Jane hadn't heard a single word of his prayer.

Before he returned to his chores, he showed her the pinto beans he'd left to soak overnight. "We can have these for lunch, if you don't mind fixing them. There are onions and enough meal for a skillet of corn bread. I believe your aunt supplied several jars of sauerkraut, as well."

"Of course I don't mind. Feeding us all is part of my job."

His mouth kicked up in a lopsided smile, and he ran his hand down the length of her arm. "What would I do without you?"

He said that now, his appreciation for her assistance fueling his fervor. But one day, he'd find a woman he wished to pursue, and Jane didn't plan on sticking around for a first-row seat.

"I'm only here until you find a suitable replacement," she felt compelled to remind him. And herself.

He grew serious, disappointment flitting over his features. "I don't want to rush it. I have to make sure your replacement is the right fit. Clara's experienced enough upheaval."

"I understand."

Striding to the door, he swiped his Stetson from the

row of hooks. "Come and find me if you need anything. I'll be in the barn." He winked at Clara, whose mouth and chin bore witness to the meal. "Mind Miss Jane, you hear?"

"Yes, sir."

"Tom, wait." Jane rushed over. "If you don't have any objections, I'd be happy to pack up your mother's clothing so that yours and Clara's can be put away."

"That's kind of you to offer, but it's not part of the job description. Your being here and seeing to her needs is enough."

"I'm here to help you both. Besides, you know I don't like being idle."

"I do know that. I also know I don't deserve you as a friend." He stunned her by leaning over and kissing her cheek. His lips were firm yet feather soft. "My world would be a worse place without you in it, Janie girl."

Tom forced himself to stay in the barn until noon, sorting through the equipment. A few tools were rusted through and couldn't be fixed. Most were able to be salvaged. Setting aside those he intended to take to the blacksmith, he tried not to dwell on that spontaneous kiss.

Not the best way to make her feel comfortable, Leighton.

She'd stood frozen immediately afterward, fingers pressed to the spot where his lips had brushed, a maelstrom of emotion in her green, green eyes.

"She's just coming off an engagement, you fool," he muttered, checking his pocket watch again and deciding she probably had lunch on the table by now.

Logically, he understood Jane was emotionally vulnerable right now. Whether or not she'd had feelings for Crowley—a question she'd stubbornly refused to answer—she'd still suffered a public humiliation. She'd be smarting from that sting for weeks, maybe months. The townsfolk's ongoing scrutiny would serve to complicate matters. His private, reserved friend would not welcome such attention.

But why an innocent display of affection should evoke such a reaction was beyond him. Unless…was she as aware of him as he was of her? Had she also noted the change in the dynamic between them?

Whatever the case, he must strive to be more circumspect. Restrain his inherent demonstrative behavior. Otherwise, he could find himself without a caregiver once again.

Fat, gray clouds had rolled in while he'd been inside the barn. Rain would delay his plans to fix the fences that afternoon. Striding through the grass, he eyed the unturned earth where the vegetable garden used to be. He'd have to get seed in the ground this week if he planned to harvest vegetables this season.

When he entered the cabin, neither female was in sight. A pot of beans bubbled on the cast-iron stove, infusing the room with a hearty aroma, and a golden corn bread round occupied the space beside it. Three jars of milk waited beside clean plates. A silly grin curved his lips. Amazing how a simple act could make him feel like a king. Not counting eating establishments, he couldn't recall the last time someone had prepared a meal for him.

Still standing on the dingy hooked rug his ma had crafted years earlier, he tugged off his boots and left them there. He was halfway to the bowl and pitcher to wash up when he heard Clara crying.

Changing course, he halted in the bedroom's open doorway, arrested by the sight of his niece curled up in

Jane's arms, tiny face awash in misery. Seated on the side of the bed nearest him, they hadn't noticed him yet.

"Where's my pa?" she sniffled. "Why hasn't he come for me?"

Tom's throat closed up. Aching for Clara and at the same time furious with his brother, he clenched both edges of the door frame until the wood bit into his skin. Charles had every right to grieve his wife. But there came a time when a man had to deal with the unpleasantness of life and see to his responsibilities.

Jane didn't speak at first, methodically smoothing Clara's curls with one hand, the other tenderly wiping her tears. "I don't know, sweetheart. But you know who does?"

Eyes big and shiny, she slowly shook her head. "God."

Her wispy brows hit her hairline. Such a notion hadn't occurred to her young mind.

"God knows where your pa is right this moment. He knows exactly what he's doing. What he's thinking and feeling. And I think it would be a good idea to pray and ask the Lord to watch over him. What do you think?"

Shame washed through him. He'd been lax in his prayer life lately, had allowed the business of this move to edge out his Scripture study and quiet time with his Creator. Charles needed help. Divine help. And Tom hadn't spared more than a few desperate pleas for him. Mostly selfish ones, he conceded, more focused on what Charles's return would mean for him.

"Can we pray now?" Clara asked.

"Absolutely."

Tom watched as Jane pulled her closer, bent her head and began to offer up a humble petition. He soaked in the sight of them together, comfortable, natural, like mother and daughter. Jane's features reflected an earnestness that touched the deepest hidden parts of him. She was incredibly wise. Some people would've blurted meaningless platitudes with the sole aim of calming Clara. Or promises they had no power to keep.

She'd make a wonderful mother someday.

At the end of her prayer, she finally registered his presence, and there was a hint of despondency in her look.

"Your uncle is here," she said quietly.

Clara clambered down and rushed over, arms coming round his legs and holding tight. He picked her up so that she could hug his neck instead. Warm, wondrous emotions expanded in his chest.

He might not have come into this parenting role the normal way, but he felt like a father. The drive to protect her was there, as was the need to make things right for her.

Turning, he carried her to the table and lowered them both into her chair. When she lifted her head and sniffled, he ran his knuckles along her cheek. "I love you, birdie."

"Love you more."

"Uh-uh. I love you most." His words were bittersweet, having heard this same conversation between Clara and Charles.

You're missing out, brother.

Jane silently dished out the food and carried everything over. Lunch was a subdued affair. Afterward, he settled Clara at the table with her slate and chalk, advising her to stay put while the adults spoke on the porch.

Outside, the clouds had multiplied. A stiff breeze teased her hem and threatened to dislodge strands from her neat twist. Leaning against the railing, she faced him.

"She misses her parents."

He took up the opposite railing, crossing one boot over the other. The breeze felt good, lifting the heavy humidity.

"She mentioned Jenny?"

"I believe what prompted her distress was a photograph we unearthed in the bottom of her trunk."

"Their family portrait." It had been taken shortly before his arrival at the ranch, which meant Clara had been about three years old.

"I wasn't sure what to do or say. I've spent time with my cousins' children, and I've watched friends' kids a time or two. But I don't have experience with a child who's dealing with grief."

Tom battled the impulse to hug her. "You were wonderful in there. I couldn't have handled it better. I knew you were the right person for the job."

She got that desperate look again, and when she opened her mouth, he held up a hand. "No need to remind me. I know it's not long-term. Still, any time you spend with her will be good for her."

Nodding, she turned her head to look out over his property, at the mountains, which had taken on a deep blue tone beneath the cloud cover. The grass appeared greener. The tree limbs shifted slightly in the wind, leaves rustling.

He studied her profile, the sweet curve of her cheek, straight, pert nose, determined chin. Even her ears were attractive. She was a prim and proper beauty. A refined lady. Much too serious for his liking. He longed to glimpse the old Jane. The one who laughed more than she frowned. The one with the ability to let go and join in his silly antics.

Was that part of her gone forever?

Chapter Nine

Friday afternoon, he was digging shallow holes in preparation for the squash seeds when Jane and Clara emerged from the cabin and walked over hand in hand, stopping at the outer row. He leaned his weight on the hoe.

"What are you pretty ladies up to?"

"We've come to help you, Uncle Tom."

He looked to Jane for confirmation.

"Where do you want us to start?" She inspected the work he'd done so far.

"You don't have to do this." Jane was already doing far more than he'd anticipated. "I'm paying you to keep Clara company, not restore my farm to working order."

She looked insulted. With a significant side glance at his niece, she said, "It's Clara's farm, too."

"Can I plant the seeds?" she piped up, eagerness in her high voice.

How could he deny her this small task? Jane hadn't voiced her thoughts, but he'd interpreted them, anyway. Clara needed to feel useful. This was her new home, after all.

And if Jane were his wife, he'd gladly accept her offer of assistance.

His gloved hands squeezed the hoe handle more tightly, and he switched his attention to the majestic mountains in the distance. What kind of crazy thoughts was he entertaining? Good thing she couldn't read his mind.

"Sure thing, birdie."

Waving them over to the sack of seeds, he explained his system, unable to hide a smile at Clara's obvious excitement. While he resumed his task, the girls each took a row and began dropping seeds into the holes. Clara's face screwed up in intense concentration as she carefully counted out the right number of seeds for the holes. Jane showed her how to cover them with dirt.

He met Jane's gaze and they shared a smile.

It didn't feel like work with her around. He listened as she patiently answered his niece's many questions. Clara seemed particularly fascinated by the fact that Jane was a twin.

When they reached the end and started on another section, he put Jane in the middle and his niece on her other side.

"You're a natural with kids," he said. "If you had your choice, how many would you have?"

Focused on the mound of dirt she was patting, red flags appeared in her cheeks. "Half a dozen sounds like a good goal."

He chuckled, easily picturing her surrounded by a gaggle of redheaded children. "You'd manage them wonderfully, I'm sure." Hacking at the hard earth, he ignored the throbbing that had set up behind his forehead. "Do you think you might have twins?"

"Hard to know for certain." Reaching into her apron

pocket, she extracted more seeds. "Mama didn't leave the house for a full month after we were born. Apparently, we were a demanding pair."

"You're not now."

Her green eyes hit on his before returning to her task, her color still high.

No, Jane was anything but selfish. In their circle of friends, she'd been the first one to see a need, the first to volunteer. That's why her initial resistance to watching Clara had confounded him.

Well, she's here now. That's all that matters.

Sweat trickled along his spine. The sun was unrelenting, the humidity closing around him like a tight fist. The pain in his head intensified. He'd been plagued by terrible headaches since his teens. Sometimes months would pass without one. When they hit, nothing but darkness and quiet and time could help.

He counted the remaining rows, confident he could finish before he was forced to quit.

"What about you?" Jane adjusted her cream-colored bonnet, ran a finger beneath the ribbon tied beneath her chin. He disliked when she wore hats because they hid her glorious hair. "How many children do you want?"

He glanced at Clara. "I'd like more than two, for sure. A couple of girls to keep Clara company. A couple of boys to keep the farm going."

Lips compressed, she nodded and continued down the row. Soaking in her beauty, her tranquil presence, he realized what a challenge it was going to be to find someone who fit in his family as effortlessly as she did. Clara was already attached. And he…

He'd always liked Jane. He just hadn't viewed her as anything more than a little sister.

That was quickly changing, and he didn't know how to feel about it.

A wave of nausea hit him. Spots danced before his eyes. Squeezing them shut, he massaged his temples in a vain attempt to slow the advancing discomfort.

"Clara," he heard Jane say, "please go inside and wash up. Your uncle and I will be there momentarily."

"Yes, ma'am."

Hearing the disappointment in her voice, he opened his eyes and tipped his hat up. "I'm okay."

"No, you're not." Jane stood and, brushing the dirt off her skirts, stepped over the row separating them. Behind her, Clara trudged toward the house. "How long has it been since the last one?"

He was surprised she remembered his ailment.

"Just before we left Kansas." He waved a hand over the untouched section. "I can make it a while longer. These seeds won't plant themselves."

"They can wait." The light of battle sparked in her eyes. Taking the hoe from him, she linked her arm through his and tugged. "Let's get you inside."

"I like it when you're bossy."

"Continue to be stubborn, and you'll see more of this side of me," she quipped.

In spite of his pain, a tiny grin formed on his lips.

She didn't release him until they reached the steps. The dimmer interior was a welcome relief from the bright sun. While he removed his boots and gloves, she washed up and directed Clara to the table to practice her letters.

Then she was in front of him, her bonnet discarded on the coffee table, upswept hair slightly disheveled. She handed him a glass of water. When he'd drained the contents, she pointed to the sofa.

"Lie down."

"Yes, ma'am." He settled on his side, the only position that would allow his feet to fit on the too-short sofa. She disappeared into the kitchen and returned with a cold compress, draping it carefully over his forehead.

Staring down at him, concern creased her brow. "Is there anything else I can do to make you comfortable?"

"You could sit here with me."

Her lips parted. Old memories sparked between them.

He recalled those instances when he'd been sidelined by these headaches, often in the middle of an outing with the O'Malleys. While Megan had expressed sympathy, she hadn't ministered to him like Jane. Uncaring that she was missing the fun, Jane always found a quiet, shady spot for him to rest, taking his head in her lap and stroking his hair until he fell asleep. She'd remained with him until he woke, sometimes hours later.

Tom didn't realize he was holding his breath until she reluctantly nodded.

Gingerly sliding onto the end of the sofa, she situated a small pillow on her lap and waited for him to get comfortable. Her softness and fresh-berry scent wrapped him in a soft cocoon. The moment her fingers sank into his hair, he recognized his mistake.

She wasn't a young girl anymore. He wasn't an oblivious young man, blind to her many attributes.

Eyes shut, he held very still, careful not to let his fingers brush her knee where he anchored the pillow.

Jane stroked his damp strands with measured movements, fingertips brushing his temple and following the path behind his ear. The feathery touch sparked a tingling sensation across his skin. He couldn't recall the last time someone had coddled him this way. It felt amazing.

"You're wonderful, you know that?" he murmured, stuck in a nebulous place between comfort and pain.

Her hand curved around his nape, resting there, the weight and coolness soothing. "You shouldn't talk," she whispered. "Go to sleep, Tom."

Her fingers trailed up his scalp, and he did as she'd ordered, giving himself up to her ministrations.

It took him about fifteen minutes to drift off. His big body relaxed into the cushions, his hand limp on her leg.

Jane watched the slow inhale, exhale of his chest before turning her focus to his strong profile. Unable to resist, she skimmed the stubble covering his firm jaws and chin. He burrowed farther into the pillow, so she returned to stroking his soft waves.

The world could be a cruel, cruel place.

She'd lost count how many times they'd been together like this, usually on her cousins' property, him sleeping away a headache and her waving away flies and other insects and dreaming of what could never be.

Clara's soft humming ceased, her steps quiet as she came around to the living area. "Is Uncle taking a nap?" she said in a loud whisper.

Jane nodded. "His head hurts."

"He doesn't take many naps." Tilting her head, she wrinkled her nose. "Papa takes lots of naps."

"Oh?" Her hand stilled.

"He smells bad, too."

Tom had mentioned the constant drinking. How horrible for him to have to shield Clara from an ugly reality. Perhaps Charles's disappearance had been for the best.

"When he comes here, I hope he takes more baths."

Disquiet shimmered through her. "Clara, we don't know for sure that he will come."

"I've been praying for him, just like you said."

"That's wonderful. Keep praying. But, sweetheart, I want you to keep this in mind—God doesn't always answer our requests the way we want."

The proof of that was right here in front of her.

Twisting the hem of her dress, Clara said, "May I go play dolls now?"

Blinking at the sudden change in subject, Jane nodded. "Of course."

While she hated to dampen the child's hopes, she had proof that reality didn't always line up with dreams.

Chapter Ten

❧

Bottling up her true feelings was wearing on Jane.

She was now forced to spend not only her weekdays projecting a nonchalant attitude, but her weekends, as well. Her entire family considered Tom an honorary O'Malley, and after his long absence clearly felt compelled to include him in their activities.

She craved a respite.

When she'd overheard her aunt inviting him to Sunday lunch, she'd thought he'd spend the bulk of the afternoon with her cousins. Jessica had ruined that with her *inspired* idea for the four of them—her and Lee, Tom and Jane—to have their lunch outside, apart from the clamor and commotion inside the crowded cabin.

She couldn't even count on Clara to provide a distraction. The little girl had bonded with Amy and hadn't wanted to leave her side.

"Are you going to the Thompsons' barn dance, Tom?" Jessica asked.

Seated on a multicolored quilt spread out beneath the hickory tree's leafy bower, Jane sipped her tea, deliberately smoothing the curiosity from her face. She mustn't care. Or let on that she did, anyway. The pretense was exhausting.

Passing a napkin across his mouth, Tom laid it atop his empty plate and leaned back against the gnarled trunk. "It would give Clara a chance to get to know other families in the area."

"And you to get reacquainted with old friends." Jessica popped the last bite of chicken into her mouth.

Lee's grin turned wolfish. "You're both forgetting the most important parts. Dancing with beautiful ladies and moonlit strolls out of the view of chaperones." Above his piercing blue eyes, thick eyebrows wriggled suggestively.

Jessica playfully swatted his knee. "Just how many ladies are you planning on dancing with?"

"A slip of the tongue, my dear. I only want to dance with one woman."

Resting her weight on her palms, Jane angled her head to stare up at the tree branches crisscrossing above them. A light breeze danced across her heated skin, a brief reprieve from the humidity. She tracked a squirrel's progress, tuning out the man's coarse laughter.

Lee Cavanaugh was a difficult man to like. For her twin's sake, she'd tried to overcome her reservations. Outwardly, he was an attractive, strapping man who took pride in his appearance. He wore his black hair cropped short. His clothes were clean and pressed, shoes polished to a high shine. But his brash, overbearing demeanor grated on her nerves.

Some of his comments left her wondering if he truly followed the Bible's teachings or simply attended church for show. Like Roy, he hadn't grown up in Gatlinburg. Born and raised in Virginia, he'd moved to the area shortly after Tom moved away. Jessica had no choice but to trust whatever he told her was true.

Look where that got me.

Desperate for peace and quiet, she looped her satchel strap over her shoulder and stood. "I'm going for a short walk."

Tom sat up. "I can accompany you, if you'd like."

Jessica's eyes went dark with determination. "I recognize the look on her face. She's had her fill of company for the moment." Softening her words with a dazzling smile, she added, "I'd like to hear more about Kansas. What did you like most about ranch life?"

Not sticking around for his response, Jane strode into the woods she'd played and lived in her entire life. Searching for the rusty tub mill half-buried in the earth, she turned right when she found it, taking a diagonal course to the stream bordering her aunt and uncle's property. There was a tree there with a smooth trunk and a bed of moss surrounding the base, a perfect spot for writing in her journal.

Ten minutes later, she was settled near the trickling stream. Her pen flew across the page, dammed-up emotions pouring out in a torrent. At the core of it all was the question *why*. Why couldn't Roy have been the answer to her problem? If Laura hadn't been in the picture, she would be his wife right now. A life with Tom would've been out of the question. Impossible. And every tendril of hope would've withered and crumbled into dust.

She would've had no choice but to acknowledge the futility of her dreams.

But she wasn't anyone's wife. She was a free, unattached woman. Tom was a free, unattached man. And there was the tiniest portion of her heart—the naive, optimistic, stubborn part—that refused to give up.

Jane wasn't aware of how much time had passed when the crunch of twigs beneath boots registered seconds before a shadow fell over her.

"Here you are."

Her gaze traveled up Tom's long, sturdy legs planted far apart, the dressy green vest paired with a charcoal-gray shirt, landing on his handsome, expectant face. He gestured to the open journal, bright eyes knowing. "Still chronicling your thoughts, I see."

Alarm punched her in the middle. Contained on these pages were her most private thoughts, many about him. Only now realizing the danger of such an exercise— what if her journal were misplaced, lost, read by someone with a penchant for gossip?—Jane snapped it closed and shoved it in her satchel.

"I gave you an hour before I came looking. Are you up for company now?"

"Sure."

Half turning, hands gripping his hips, he assessed the dead tree trunk forming a natural bridge across a deeper portion of the stream. She didn't have to ask what he was thinking. He'd challenged her to cross it many times without success.

"Don't bother asking." Standing, she brushed off the back of her dress, a tight grip on her satchel. "We should start for the cabin. Is Clara sleeping?"

"Too much excitement. I think she and Amy are still in the barn admiring the latest litter of kittens." Twisting again to study the opposite bank, his vivid gaze swung around to probe hers. "When was the last time you visited the cave?"

She hadn't thought about the cave in a long time.

Tucked into the base of a steep hill about a thirty-minute walk from here, it was an interesting area to explore. "With you and Megan. Maybe a month before Lucian came to town."

Eager to spend time in his company, Jane had often tagged along on their excursions. He hadn't seemed to mind and neither had Megan.

"I remember that day." His lips curved ruefully. "You twisted your ankle on the trek home, and I had to carry you for miles."

"Don't remind me."

Did he have to bring up that awkward, embarrassing memory? He'd been forced to transport her like a monkey on his back, arms looped around her knees to balance her weight, with her clutching him around his neck while trying not to choke him. Next to her older, mature sister, Jane had felt unsophisticated and clumsy. That incident only served to underscore her inadequacy.

Tom, of course, had taken it all in stride. Careful not to jostle her injured foot, he'd kept up a steady stream of conversation to keep her mind off it. Her admiration for him had only deepened in the face of his heroic behavior.

"I'd like to see it again." He was looking at her with anticipation.

"What? Now?"

"Why not? Clara's in good hands, and the skies are clear."

Longing flared. She'd like to see it, as well, and who else better to accompany her?

You're spending too much time with him as it is. Tell him no.

As if sensing her impending refusal, he said, "Look, I'm a little desperate for some adult time. I haven't had that in what feels like forever." Tiny lines radiated out from his eyes. "Does that make me a terrible person?"

Compassion swept away any arguments.

"Not at all. Tom, you're a bachelor who's been thrust into parenthood. It's completely normal for you to want a break."

The slightly guilty air shimmering around him evaporated. "You'll come with me, then?"

She would regret this later. "How can I say no?"

Because Jane wouldn't cross the log and wasn't keen on getting wet by splashing through the thigh-high water, they had to walk about a quarter of a mile to find a spot where the water level was shallow enough for her to leap across. They walked in companionable silence as they traversed the spacious field with knee-high grasses, soaking in God's glorious nature. It was a lovely June day—low humidity and pleasant temperatures. Big, puffy white clouds hung in the cerulean sky above. Deep green mountains almost completely circled the valley.

At one point, Tom put an arm out to stop her, a finger to his lips as he directed her attention to a group of white-tailed deer grazing nearby. They shared a smile. Though they'd grown up in these east Tennessee mountains, and such sights were fairly common, they didn't take the wildlife or their impressive habitats for granted.

After a while, they reached the opposite tree line and entered the denser forest as the terrain became hilly.

"Tom?"

"Hmm?"

He was scanning the forest, alert to potential hazards. His gun belt hung low on his hips, the nickel handle of his Colt Lightning revolver peeking out of its holster. This far from town, they couldn't afford to be complacent. Danger could come in the form of black bears, wolves or even strangers passing through this part of the state.

"Why didn't Clara go and live with any of Jenny's relatives?"

"She didn't have siblings." Sidestepping a varmint hole, he said, "Her parents live in the same town and would've loved to have Clara if they were physically able to care for her. John, Jenny's father, is in particularly poor health."

"Does she talk about her grandparents a lot? Miss them?"

"Sometimes. Even though they lived close, there weren't as many opportunities to visit as Jenny would've liked. The ranch kept all of us busy from dawn to dusk."

A robin swooped out of a tree, startling Jane, who was watching the ground for obstacles. She had to avoid a repeat of their last trip out here.

"How long has Charles been gone?"

"A little more than six months."

"I can't imagine how you were able to cope."

He slowed. "I wasn't given a choice."

Jane moved ahead of him. "You're wonderful with her. She's adjusting well, considering all the changes in her life recently. And it's plain as day she adores you."

"You've played a big role in that adjustment." His voice trailed off.

Suddenly, she felt herself grabbed from behind and yanked against his hard length. "Don't move." His lips grazed her earlobe, sending massive tremors through her body. Her knees didn't want to support her.

"What—"

"Rattlesnake," he murmured. "See him?"

Jane searched the underbrush, stomach flip-flopping. In

the spot where she'd been about to place her boot slithered a healthy-size adult timber rattlesnake. The danger this poisonous creature posed couldn't be underestimated— loss of limb, incredible pain and even death.

They stayed locked like that for long moments until it was gone.

Spinning in his hold, Jane gave him a fierce hug.

"What's this?" he said against her hair, lips snagging the strands.

She didn't want to move from this spot. This...*this* was what she'd longed to do since his homecoming. Hug him. Hold him. Relish in the safety of his embrace.

Reluctantly pulling back to look into his dancing, inquisitive gaze, she said simply, "You saved my life."

He cocked his head to one side. "I did, didn't I? Does that mean I've earned a ribbon fruitcake at last?"

Jane became aware of his fingers curved about her ribs. Taking a backward step, she dislodged his hold and instantly regretted it. "Maybe."

One brow inched up. *"Maybe?"*

"Probably."

Whistling low, he shook his head in mock disbelief. "You're a hard woman to impress, Jane O'Malley."

If he only knew... He didn't have to exert himself to impress her.

Chapter Eleven

He couldn't get that spontaneous hug out of his head.

As they hiked the remainder of the way, his attention repeatedly strayed to her, soaking in her vibrant beauty as if he could internalize it.

Jane had come close to getting seriously hurt. His pulse sped up, residual fear entering his bloodstream. That fear had nothing to do with the fact Josh, Nathan and Caleb would've strung him up if he'd allowed her to be harmed. Bottom line was, he couldn't handle the thought of her in pain. He'd tried to mask it from her, adopting a lighthearted air, while inside he'd been as shaken as she. And when she'd launched herself at him, he'd wanted to anchor her to him and never let go.

She was quickly insinuating herself deep into his heart, staking claim to more of it than mere friendship warranted. It wasn't wise, he knew, but he was at a loss as to how to prevent it.

Tom looked her direction again, noting her dawning recognition. Up ahead, tucked in the base of the mountain, was the cave the O'Malley brothers had discovered as adolescents. They'd brought Tom in on the secret with the intention of keeping it from the girls. Months passed before the eldest sister, Juliana, overheard them talking and followed them. Unhappy at first, the brothers had eventually given up trying to keep them away.

"Looks the same, doesn't it?" he said as they neared the mouth.

"Except for that." Nose scrunched, she pointed to the intricate web strung across the top left corner and the huge black-and-yellow spider in the center.

Tom let out a laugh. Jane did not appreciate insects' roles in the world. "Aw, he looks mighty comfortable."

Stopping dead in her tracks, her obstinate streak made itself known. "I'm not going in there."

Locating a long stick, he approached the hapless spider. "Will it make you feel better if I transfer him to a new home?"

"There are probably plenty more inside."

"Stick close to me, darlin'. I'll protect you."

It took a bit of coaxing to convince the little guy to go where Tom wanted. He came and took Jane's elbow. "Ready?"

"I suppose." Her boots dragged the ground. "I don't recall it being quite so dark in there."

"Where's your sense of adventure?"

"You're confusing me with Megan."

He stared hard at her, unable to assess her mood. "Not possible, Janie girl. I distinctly remember you falling in with a number of my schemes."

"I was young and naive."

"And now that you're older, you're not interested in having fun?" He wanted to shatter that cool reserve.

A breeze stirred the skirts of her dove-gray dress. Peeling away a rogue tendril that had caught on her mouth, she dipped her head. "Let's just get this over with."

Side by side, they entered the dark space, dank, musty air shrouding them. Their eyes eventually adjusted. Enough light spilled in so that they could make out the wobbly table Josh and Nathan had crafted and a single dusty kerosene lamp. Memories rushed in, too many to riffle through them all. He'd passed many a summer afternoon here, playing pretend while his older brother tended to chores with their pa.

Here the cave's ceiling sloped down to about an inch from his head. In the rear, the opening narrowed to a tunnel too tight for a human to crawl through. Caleb had lamented not being able to explore deeper. He'd been convinced there was a cavern filled with treasure on the other side of the rock wall.

"Any sign of Mr. Batling?"

Smiling at the fictitious name the girls had dreamed up, he scanned the ceiling. "No little brown bats that I can see. He must've moved on to a bigger, better cave."

Funny how Jane couldn't abide spiders but didn't mind bats.

"One of my journals!" Jane snatched a small book from the floor. "I looked everywhere for this." Rubbing the grit from the cover, she opened it, wincing at the damp pages. Her eyes shone with the light of discovery. "I must've forgotten it the day I twisted my ankle."

"Our last day here. Makes sense."

Her fingers drifted almost reverently over the words. Shifting away, he attempted to shake the remembrance of her holding his head in her lap, stroking his hair with incredible tenderness until he fell asleep. If he were honest, he'd dearly like to repeat those moments. Not the headache, of course. Jane's ministrations had made him feel cared for, something he hadn't felt in a very long time.

Needing a distraction, he turned back and plucked the book from her hands. "You know," he drawled, "I've always wondered how you managed to fill so many of these things. What was so important you had to get it on paper?"

Her gasp echoed off the cave walls. "Give it back." When she lurched forward, he held it out of reach.

"Come on, Janie girl." Edging to the entrance, he fought laughter. "Let me read at least some of it." Presenting her with his back, he held the open book into the light. "What's in here? Poems? Stories? Secrets of national importance?"

"That's private," she gritted, clutching his arm with a surprisingly punishing grip. *"Tom."*

Swiveling around, he walked backward out of the cave, searching her face. The frantic slant of her mouth gave him pause. Closing the journal, he held it out to her.

He'd thought to tease her, not unnerve her. What was *in* that journal, anyway?

Even after she had it in her possession, practically adhered to her chest, apprehension came off her in waves.

"See what I mean?" he demanded, the slightest bit irked. "I was playing around, and you react as if I've killed your favorite cat."

Staring into the distance, her profile unreadable, she didn't respond.

He exhaled through his mouth. "Is it the situation with Roy?"

"What? No."

Snapping her head around, she looked surprised he'd mention her ex-fiancé, as if she'd already forgotten the man. Strange.

"Then what's bothering you?" Unable to stop himself, he traced his knuckles along the curve of her cheek. "I miss your smile, Jane. Your laugh. I can't promise I can fix the problem, but I can offer advice."

She started to speak, thought better of it, he supposed, because she leaned out of reach and hurriedly locked the lost journal in her satchel with her latest one.

"This problem can't be fixed, so there's no point talking about it."

She charged down the hill, and he had no choice but to follow.

What kind of problem didn't have a solution?

Tom worried the issue the entire way.

Jane wasn't talking. Lost in her own private world, she struck him as decidedly uninterested in having him join her.

Was it financial in nature? Few families in the area were wealthy, but he'd thought her family was doing fine, especially now that Lucian and Quinn had joined the fold. Neither man would let a need go unfulfilled. Perhaps he should approach Josh about it.

Not paying attention to his exact route, he discovered too late that he'd led them back to the spot where he'd found her writing. The only way across this deeper part of the stream was the log bridge.

Jane registered that fact about the same time as he did. Pensive, she pivoted in the opposite direction.

He caught her elbow and gently spun her around. "I don't know about you, but I'm not in the mood for an out-of-the-way detour. Cross the bridge with me. It's not dangerously high, and I'll be right behind you."

Indecision played across her expressive features. "I might fall. Twist my ankle. Break a leg. The possibilities are endless…" He could practically see what her imagination was conjuring up. "No, it's too risky."

"Or you might cross without a single mishap." He stopped her escape with both hands on her shoulders. "Sometimes risks are worth taking, Jane."

Her nostrils flared. And there, in the deep, swirling green of her eyes, he spotted a flicker of the spirited friend he missed.

Lips pursed, she averted her face to study this quiet, out-of-the-way section of the O'Malleys' property. He waited, knowing not to push her. Either she'd agree or she wouldn't.

In shadow, the stream had a brown-green hue, and in light patches, he could see straight through to the bottom where thousands of tiny pebbles littered the streambed. Minnows darted every direction. Close to where they stood, a black-and-red salamander scurried beneath a mossy rock.

"It is a very short span to the other side," she conceded.

"Less than ten steps, I'd guess. A whole lot quicker than the other route."

Touching the satchel resting against her hip, she frowned. "I'm not sure I can balance with this."

"Easy. I'll take it across and come back for you."

She stared at his outstretched hand as if it was the rattlesnake they'd encountered earlier.

"I'm not going to undo the clasp, much less try and read your journals. I have a feeling you'd find a way to get over there and punish me if I did."

A ghost of a smile graced her mouth. "You're right. I would."

He returned her smile. When she'd relinquished her precious belongings to him, he quickly traversed the natural bridge and left it on the opposite bank. He rejoined her.

"Want me to go first and you hold on to me?"

"I'll go first. That way you'll see if I start to fall." Raising her skirts to reveal a snowy-white petticoat, she climbed onto the medium-size log without his assistance. Graceful, spine stiff, shoulders set.

"Take it slow, okay? I'll be close."

Her arms held out at her sides for balance, Jane carefully placed one foot in front of the other. "This isn't so bad." Her voice was higher than normal.

"You're doing great."

Approximately five feet below them, pond skater insects rippled across the water's surface. This section of the stream came to about midthigh, and it was free of large rocks. Gaze returning to Jane, he noticed the slight tremor in her arms and wondered if he was right in pushing her to do this.

They were halfway to solid ground when her foot slipped. "Oh!" Before he could react, she teetered wildly to the left. "Tom!"

He snagged a bit of material between her shoulder blades, but it wasn't enough to halt her downward motion. She landed sideways in the water. He jumped in after her.

Jane came up spluttering, sections of sodden hair hanging in her face.

Tom steadied her, bracing himself for a stinging rebuke. Or a glare that could freeze his eyelashes.

What he didn't expect was a face full of water. Laughter burst out of her, an exuberant, carefree sound that enveloped him, tickling his ears. With a half growl, half laugh, he retaliated, and an intense water fight ensued. They scooped and splashed. Circled each other like warring animals, each trying to gain the advantage.

"Stop!" she panted minutes later, one hand pressed against her midsection and the other extended to ward him off. "I can't catch my breath."

He was suffering a similar condition. Water dripped from his wet hair, slid under his collar and along his spine. He was soaked clean through. His body hummed with energy and, in this moment, he felt more alive, happier than he had in years.

This was the girl he remembered. The one he'd missed.

The fitted bodice and scalloped skirts of Jane's dress bore evidence of their antics. Her hair hung in thick, wet ropes about her shoulders. Moisture sprinkled her forehead and cheekbones. Her plump lips were parted, sucking in air, and her eyes sparkled with vitality.

She was magnificent.

"Welcome back, old friend."

Without thinking, he reached for her upper arms and pulled her close, intending to kiss her cheek. Only his aim was wrong. He landed squarely on her mouth.

She stilled. He froze. His heart slammed against his chest cavity. Blood roared through his ears. Conscious thought went up in smoke…and just that fast, he was kissing Jane O'Malley.

It was a hesitant, tender exploration. Jane blossomed under his attention, meeting his advance with surprising willingness, fingers twisting in his sodden shirt. His hands slid up and into her hair to cradle her head.

Jane was sweet wonder and delightful discovery in one package. She yielded to him, soft and giving, not questioning his sanity or hers.

Until her palms went flat against his chest and shoved. Unprepared, he stumbled back.

"Jane?"

Stricken, she lifted trembling fingers to her lips. "I wish you hadn't done that." Her voice was an anguished whisper.

Jerkily gathering up her puffy skirts, she made for the bank.

"Wait!" He sloshed through the water. "I'm sorry!"

Are you? an irritating voice inside his head demanded. *Are you really?*

"It wasn't planned," he called after her, cringing at the way that sounded. "It didn't mean anything."

Up on the level ground, she whirled on him, bristling with anger. "That's right, Tom. It didn't mean anything to you. So why do it at all?"

Stunned, regret making him ill, he let her go.

He didn't notice Jessica until she emerged from the tree line. "Jess." Slogging up the slight incline, he shoved the hair out of his eyes and tried to gauge her mood. She could be a firecracker at times. But she struck him as more resigned than outraged. "I suppose you witnessed what happened."

"I saw enough."

"You know that I'd never intentionally upset your sister."

"Intentional or not, you have. She doesn't deserve anymore heartache on account of you." A sad sort of laugh escaped. "The thing is, Tom, you just don't understand O'Malley women. You messed up with Megan. And now you're doing it again with Jane."

Spinning on her heel, she left him there to stew over her parting words.

Chapter Twelve

Jane ignored her sister's repeated requests to stop. Jessica was nothing if not persistent, however.

"Jane, talk to me." Taking hold of her hand, she pulled her around, visibly worried. "I saw what happened. I know you're hurting."

"I don't wish to discuss it." Scanning the woods, she was relieved to find them empty.

"It might help to sort through your feelings. For what it's worth…" She trailed off, uncharacteristically reticent.

Jane studied her sister's face. To other people, the idea of having an exact copy of oneself walking around was eerie. Strange. Her twin was part of her, however. They shared a unique bond only other twins could understand.

"What?"

"Never mind."

"Say it."

Hands folded behind her back, Jess scraped the toe of her boot across the forest floor. "He looked to be as affected as you."

Jane shook her head, squashing the little leap of satisfaction her words elicited. "He said it didn't mean anything."

Jess didn't blink. "I don't believe him."

Closing her eyes tight, hands fisting at her sides, she fought to tamp down the emotions raging like a rain-swollen, out-of-control river inside. That kiss... His embrace...

She'd been too shocked to respond at first. Then her buried feelings for him had burst forth, sweeping away reason and caution. Being held in his strong arms, his firm lips pressed to hers, had fulfilled every wistful daydream she'd dared to entertain. Exceeded, actually. No daydream could ever match the delightful reality of his touch.

It didn't mean anything.

Pain licked at her like relentless, searing-hot flames, Tom's expression taunting her. Shock, as if he couldn't quite fathom that he'd kissed *her.* And worse, regret. He must've been so disappointed.

Another thought struck her. Was he comparing her to her sister? Megan had told her he'd kissed her once, right after proposing marriage. A brief one, because Megan hadn't responded, her heart full of love for Lucian.

Nauseous, she swept a hand down the front of her dress. "I have to change out of these wet clothes."

Jane wasn't surprised when Jessica fell into step beside her. They didn't speak for long moments. Sidestepping a tree stump, she glanced at Jess's profile. "Have you allowed Lee to kiss you?"

Her bark of laughter startled a pair of doves.

"What's so funny?"

"I'm surprised you have to ask. Does he strike you as the shy type?"

"Not at all," Jane said drily. "So…how do you know if he…" Hot color rushed to her cheeks, and she couldn't finish. Too embarrassing to voice aloud.

Bending to avoid getting swatted in the face by a branch, Jess arched a brow. "Believe me, Tom wasn't disappointed. A herd of elephants could've stomped through that stream, and he wouldn't have noticed."

What did it matter, anyway? He didn't plan on doing it again. And she had to make sure he stood by that. She was barely hanging on as it was.

Through the thinning trees, the main cabin came into view. Lee's wagon was still parked in front of their uncle's barn. Tom's, too.

Jessica put out a hand. "I'm not sure it's wise for you to continue working for him. It's not healthy. How are you ever going to be open to another man's love if you're spending most of your time with Tom?"

"I can't abandon Clara. Besides, he's searching for a replacement."

"Is he?" She cocked her head to one side, considering. "Has he mentioned possible candidates? Has he brought anyone over to introduce them to Clara?"

"No."

"The truth is, he's comfortable having you around. He's not going to be in a hurry to lose you."

Bracing her hand against a tree, she hung her head, the impossibility of it all weighing heavily on her shoulders. "Perhaps the best solution is to give him a time limit. I've been thinking recently that a visit to Aunt Althea would do me good."

Their mother's sister lived in the nearby town of Maryville. A childless widow, she sent frequent letters requesting her nieces' presence. It had been at least a year since they'd seen her.

Jessica sighed. "While a change of scenery would be beneficial, I worry that once there, you might decide to stay for good."

Keeping up this pretense with Tom was draining the joy and peace from her soul. While the prospect of permanent escape held appeal, she could never leave her family and friends and start over in a different town.

"Gatlinburg is my home. All I need is enough time to get my thoughts sorted out."

Far away from Tom Leighton.

Instead of lying in bed and shutting out the world as she longed to do, Jane climbed Tom's porch steps Monday morning and prayed she could pull off another believable performance.

But when the door creaked open, it wasn't Tom who'd answered her summons. Still in her nightgown, dark hair mussed, Clara bounced from foot to foot on the worn rug.

"Morning, Miss Jane."

Masking her confusion, she stepped quickly inside and shut the door. "Is your uncle in the barn?"

Up until today, Tom had always greeted her in the mornings. Was he avoiding her because of the kiss?

"He's in bed."

Anxiety instantly flared. Glancing at the closed bedroom door, she put her belongings on the table. "Is he sick?"

"His head hurts."

Flopping into one of the chairs, Clara picked up a half-eaten biscuit. Strawberry jam was slathered across the golden crust. A glass of milk had been poured.

"Did you help yourself to breakfast?"

"Uncle Tom doesn't like for me to be in the kitchen

alone." Her dubious look would've been comical if not for Jane's mounting concern.

"I'm going to look in on him while you finish eating, okay?"

"'Kay."

Slowly pushing open the door, Jane hesitated on the threshold of the dark room. When her eyes adjusted, she saw his prone form beneath the flower-emblazoned quilt.

She shouldn't disturb him. But he might need something to drink or medicine or her gentle touch in his hair.

"Tom?"

Her advance into his private space was tentative, halting.

His head shifted on the pillow. "Hey." Weariness wove through his voice. "Sorry I couldn't greet you."

She took up residence at his bedside, staring down at his taut features. "What's wrong?"

"Another headache." He tried to smile and failed. "Tried to push through it. Had to lie down before the dizziness overtook me."

Before she could stop herself, Jane placed her palm against his forehead. "No fever. That's good."

"I'm not ill," he murmured. "It'll pass soon enough, and I can get back to work."

Gingerly threading his dark hair off his face, she wished she could erase his discomfort. Tom didn't like to be idle. Considering the volume of chores awaiting him, it was no wonder he was displeased with this setback.

His lids drifted shut. "Is Clara still eating?"

"She is. You could've asked her to wait until I arrived. She wouldn't have minded."

"In case you haven't noticed, little girls with empty stomachs aren't exactly a pleasure to be around."

Jane folded her hands at her waist when she would've liked to continue stroking his hair.

Tom opened his eyes, and they gleamed up at her. "I wasn't sure you'd come."

Deliberately mistaking his meaning, she strove for a flippant air. "Why wouldn't I?"

He frowned. "We can't ignore what happened, Jane."

"We can talk about it later." Picking up the empty glass on his bedside table, she said, "I'll go and get you some more water. Is there any medicine you'd like for me to bring you? An herbal infusion to help the headache?"

"Not right now." He sighed, turning onto his side to face her, one hand slipping under his cheek. "I'm going to try and sleep it off."

"Call if you need anything."

His gaze was fixed on her face. "Thank you, Jane. It means a lot that you're here."

She reluctantly left him. Lingering at the table, Clara had her glass tilted up and was trying to get every last drop of milk. Jane noticed the brimming milk pail on the counter, the basket of eggs beside it. He'd done chores despite not feeling well. Pushed himself to the edge of his endurance. Seen to Clara's needs before his own.

Her heart melted. The admiration she had for him swelled to immeasurable proportions. This man she loved was special. One of a kind.

The kiss had been an aberration. His goal had been to get her to have fun. To forget her troubles. To recapture the adventures they used to share. He hadn't meant to upset her. He'd been as shocked as she.

His request for his favorite dessert replayed in her mind.

She could bake him a cake. It wouldn't make his

physical discomfort go away, but it would lift his spirits. Clara would be thrilled to be included.

Riffling through his drawers and cabinets, she located all the ingredients except for currants. Since leaving him to go to the mercantile was out of the question, she decided to double the amount of raisins.

She and Clara worked together all morning. Jane checked in on Tom every half hour, relieved to find him sleeping soundly. Clara was building a fort from a set of wooden blocks they'd unearthed, and Jane was stirring the chicken soup she'd put together for lunch when he emerged.

She looked up and there he stood, scruffy, sleep tousled and far too hug-worthy.

"How are you feeling?"

"Much better." His smile warmed her through and through. Padding closer in his stocking feet, he sniffed the pot's contents. "Mmm. Smells good. I didn't eat breakfast, so I'm starving."

Deliberately not breathing in the wonderful, woodsy scent that clung to his clothes, she retrieved a stack of bowls. Turning back, she saw that he'd noticed the rectangular cake in the middle of the table. His brows lifted. "What's that? Something for the café?"

Clara piped up from her spot on the center rug. "It's for you, Uncle Tom! Miss Jane and I baked it."

"For me?" Going over to the table, he studied it. Dipped a fingertip in the icing. "But it's not my birthday."

"Miss Jane said it's a 'just because' cake."

Jane smiled at his bafflement and, as he sucked on his finger, the comprehension lighting his eyes. Twisting around, he said eagerly, "It's the ribbon fruitcake, isn't it?"

"Your favorite."

Coming around to where she stood, he encircled her waist and twirled her around. She yelped. Clara giggled. "Tom, your dizziness will come back."

Chuckling, he set her on her feet and lightly tapped her nose. "You're the best, Janie girl."

She absolutely would not let him see how much those simple words affected her.

"Can I have my dessert first?" he said, cocking his head in boyish petition.

"Yes!" Clara ran over, blinking up at Jane. "Say yes!"

"That's not up to me," she said, laughing.

"It's settled, then," he declared. "We will all have cake before soup."

Carrying plates over to the table, Tom waited for Jane to bring a knife. Clara gathered the forks. They sat together eating the moist, fruity cake. His enjoyment made joy bubble up inside. If he'd let her, she'd bake for him every day for the rest of her life.

Don't spoil the moment with hopeless wishes, she scolded herself.

After lunch, Tom went out to the barn while Jane got Clara down for a nap. He'd promised not to do too much. When he returned to the house an hour later and found Clara sleeping, she could see he was determined to have the conversation she'd been dreading.

"The cake was delicious Jane. Better than I remember." Joining her in the kitchen, he watched as she cut up potatoes for the evening meal. "What I don't understand is why you made it for me, especially after yesterday."

If they were going to move past this, she had to convince him it meant nothing. Mimicking her twin's casual attitude, she shrugged and continued chopping. "I wanted to. You weren't feeling well, and I thought you'd appreciate the gesture."

"I do. Of course, it's just—"

"The kiss wasn't supposed to happen, but it did. I'm not losing sleep over it, and neither should you."

The look on his face was almost comical. He'd been expecting a different response. "You're not upset anymore?"

"I overreacted. If you'll recall, I'm still dealing with Roy's defection."

So far, so good. Leading him to think she was still mourning the loss of her fiancé was inspired. *It's not the truth, though. You're misleading him.*

"Another reason I should've been more circumspect." His low, rich voice riddled with self-derision bathed her in guilt. "I regret causing you distress. That wasn't my intention. Can you forgive me?"

He wanted her forgiveness for something beautiful and precious, a never-to-be-repeated moment she'd treasure in her heart forever.

"There's nothing to forgive. We got caught up in the moment, that's all. Let's just consider it forgotten, okay?"

Tom moved to stand beside her a respectable distance away. "More than anything, Jane, I don't want to lose your friendship." A sigh gusted out of him. In her peripheral vision, she saw him shove his fingers through his wavy locks, mussing them further. "I missed you while I was away. I can't express how much having you in my life again means to me."

Struck by his earnestness, she met his gaze. The deep green pools reflected anxiety. Her fingers itched to smooth the furrow between his eyes. "We're still friends. We always will be."

"I want you to be comfortable here. As comfortable as if this were your own home."

That was the very thing she could not allow. Inserting herself into this family, even temporarily, would widen the unhealed fissure in her heart, inviting in even more heartbreak.

She scooped up the diced potatoes and dropped them in the enamel bowl. "What matters is that my replacement is comfortable here. Do you have any prospects?"

He'd snagged a cube from the bowl and was about to pop it in his mouth. The sheepish tilt to his mouth gave her the answer. "I'm afraid I haven't given the matter my full attention."

Jessica's theory had been right. Jane didn't blame him. His and Clara's lives had been turned upside down. Made sense he'd crave routine and tranquility.

"I won't be here indefinitely." She started peeling an onion, deliberately not looking at him. "In fact, I'm planning an extended visit to Maryville soon. My aunt Althea would dearly love the company."

The air whooshed out of him. "When? How long will you be gone?"

Telling herself his anxiety stemmed entirely from how her absence would affect Clara, she focused on her task. "In a month. As for how long I'll be gone, I have no idea."

"One month."

His beautiful eyes dulled slightly, his lips turning down at the corners. Memories of how they'd felt whispering against hers awakened a yearning deep inside. Unnerved, Jane gripped the knife handle and chopped faster. The tears springing to her eyes were a result of the onion. Nothing more.

Both hands braced on the counter, dark hair sliding

forward onto his forehead, he appeared to be having trouble absorbing her news.

He'll accept your decision soon enough, she consoled herself. There were any number of eligible women, both young and old, who'd be willing to step in. Tom was a kind, considerate man, Clara an endearing five-year-old.

Who knew? Perhaps the woman he found to replace her would be the one to finally make him forget he'd ever wanted Megan.

Several days had passed since Jane's announcement, yet Tom was having trouble moving past his disappointment. He couldn't stop questioning the timing. Had she made up her mind to go before or after his shocking lapse in judgment?

Hitching his horse to an outlying tree, he surveyed the party in full swing. The massive cantilever barn set in the middle of rolling fields was lit up like a jar of fireflies, lanterns strung across the open interior that ran the length of the structure. Outside, a large bonfire threw sparks into the silken night sky. Those folks not interested in dancing mingled in small clusters around it. Lively music dominated by fiddles drifted on the breeze as he loped across the yard.

He normally enjoyed the chance to relax and catch up with neighbors. Tonight, his current troubles consumed him.

The doorless entrance gave him an unobstructed view of the crowd. Old and young women alike congregated on one side, chatting together and doling out the refreshments. The men lined the opposite wall, married ones no doubt discussing crops and farm business while the single ones searched for willing dance partners. In the wide, central area, couples twirled to the musicians' tunes.

Nathan and Sophie were among the dancers, as were Caleb and Rebecca.

Josh separated himself from the group of men he'd been conversing with and wound his way through the press of bodies to Tom's side. "I was beginning to think you weren't gonna make it." He raised his voice to be heard over the noise.

Scooting to stand against the wall, the uneven slats poking his back, Tom said, "I was late getting Clara to your ma's."

"Was Victoria sleeping when you got there?"

"No. Caleb's sister-in-law was reading her a story. She's a sweetheart, Josh. Once she reaches courting age, you'll have trouble fighting off the young bucks."

"Any man interested in her will have to go through me first," Josh declared, chin jutting determinedly.

Tom looked away, aware of his friend's instinctive drive to watch out for the females in his family. That protectiveness extended to Jane. He didn't want to think what Josh's reaction might be if he found out about that kiss.

I took advantage of her vulnerability. What should I expect?

He searched for a familiar flash of red hair. She hadn't said whether or not she was coming, but he'd sensed her reluctance. Jane was content with her own company or a small group of friends.

"Looking for anyone in particular?" Josh drawled with a trace of humor.

Tom ceased his survey at once. "Just curious how many people I recognize. Seems a number of folks moved into the area during my absence."

"Including attractive, available young ladies. You know, now that you have Clara to take care of, you might consider marrying one of them."

"I'm not in the frame of mind to think about that yet." He frowned at his friend, annoyed for some unknown reason. How could he court a young lady when he couldn't get Jane out of his head? "The farm's my top priority."

Couples whirled past in a colorful blur. As they parted, he spotted Jane near the refreshment table conversing with her best friend, Caroline Turner. Stunning in a square-necked satiny cream dress with maroon trim and lace cuffs, her cinnamon-hued tresses pinned up and interwoven with dainty white flowers, Jane looked like spring personified. Lush and vibrant. Her skin, he knew from experience, would be incredibly soft beneath his fingertips.

How could he entertain thoughts of marriage to anyone when memories of their embrace refused to leave him be? Every moment in her company this week had been a test of his resolve. He'd been forced to remind himself more than once that she didn't welcome his advances, didn't appreciate his actions. He'd found himself struggling to define his feelings.

Was this merely a normal male reaction to her beauty? Or was it something more? Something he dared not examine too closely? He'd ruined his friendship with Megan because he'd misread the signs, had allowed himself to believe she returned his feelings when, in truth, she'd loved another. He would not be repeating that mistake.

Loneliness was no doubt to blame in this instance. In Kansas, after Charles had disappeared and the ranch hands sought work elsewhere, weeks would sometimes pass without another soul to speak to besides Clara. Spending his days in Jane's company reawakened a need to connect. Her demure appeal drew him like a bee to honey, the way she looked at him made him feel invincible capable of great feats.

He liked her. He liked being with her.

Ruining their friendship over a stupid kiss was not an option.

He simply had to subdue the loneliness inside that demanded he get close to her.

Beside him, Josh expelled an irritated huff. Tom followed his gaze and scowled at the sight of Roy Crowley entering the barn, a petite brunette on his arm. A hasty glance in Jane's direction revealed she was as yet unaware of his arrival.

He pushed off the wall. "I'm going to warn Jane."

His mood unreadable, Josh tipped his head. "Thanks for looking out for her."

"No need to thank me."

Winding his way through the throng, he approached Jane and her friend. "Evening, ladies."

Soft color suffused Jane's cheeks. "Tom. You remember Caroline Turner?"

"I do." He smiled at the willowy blonde. "How have you been?"

"Fine. Jane told me you were home to stay this time. Is that true?" Caroline's answering smile had a wintry edge, and he wondered at it.

"That's the plan."

"Well...that's wonderful." Sounding anything but enthusiastic, she smirked. "Please excuse me while I go and speak to my mother. Jane, I'll see you at the quilting bee next week."

"Did I interrupt something?" He leaned close to Jane and was enveloped by her summer-fruit scent.

"Nothing of import." Flipping open a decorative fan, she slowly flicked it back and forth, the movement stirring the tendrils at her temples.

Watching the blonde's retreat, he caught her backward glance and accompanying smirk. "I get the impression she doesn't approve of me."

He didn't care, not really, but he didn't like to think of Caroline complaining to Jane about him.

"Caroline can't abide many men. She has a difficult relationship with her father."

"Are you sure it's not because of my friendship with you?"

"She's loyal and protective."

"And she knows that I hurt you with my immature handling of my absence."

"I thought we'd moved past that."

Her frank observation eased his anxiety on that front. He could detect no lingering accusation.

Someone bumped into him.

"Sorry, mister." A blushing girl of about twelve darted off to join her giggling friends.

"You don't normally enjoy this sort of outing," he said. "What made you come?"

"My sister said that if I didn't, everyone would assume I was hiding from Roy and Laura." Defiance kindled in her eyes, and her chin angled up. "I refuse to be a coward."

Astonishment angled through him. "You? A coward? Not possible."

Lowering the fan to her side, she didn't respond.

"He's here, you know," he said gently. "With her."

Her lips parted to release a puff of air. "I'm not surprised. They don't seem to be suffering any humiliation."

Over by the musicians, the couple in question was being greeted by a gaggle of folks, no doubt eager to hear Laura wax on about her fortuitous timing. The irritating woman wasn't shy about discussing the almost wedding. Annoyance filtered through him.

"Dance with me," he blurted.

"What?"

"It'll be like old times." He meshed his fingers with hers. "And you can show that fool what he's missing."

She hung back. "I can't remember the last time I danced."

"I don't mind if you step on my toes."

A tiny smile lifted the corners of her mouth. "You may regret saying that."

Chuckling, Tom led her into the fray, happy he could do this for her. It was just a dance between friends, he assured himself as he settled his arm about her waist and slowly pulled her close. Despite her protests, she was graceful on her feet, following his lead as if they were connected by an invisible string. Her fine-boned hand fit perfectly in his. As the melody wove through them, she relaxed, a small smile fixed on her face, mysterious green eyes lit from within.

The tension that had characterized their exchanges this week dissipated.

"You enjoying yourself?" he said, grinning at her.

The lamplight caught the sheen in her rich waves with every movement of her head. "As a matter of fact, I am."

He maneuvered a tight spin and, as he did, knocked into a solid form. He murmured an apology over his shoulder.

"Tom? Jane?"

Megan's lilting voice had him stopping midpivot, and Jane collided with his chest. "Hello, Megan," he said. "Lucian."

The dark-headed man's smile was gracious as he dipped his head. "Good to see you, Tom. You're looking lovely this evening, Jane."

"Thank you." Her eyes were downcast, her cheeks pale.

He noticed then that folks were staring. Jane wasn't the only one who'd set the grapevines ablaze with rampant rumors. Might as well show them the past was just that…the past.

Glancing at Lucian, he said, "Would you mind if we switched partners?"

He hesitated but a moment. "Fine with me. Ladies?"

Megan's smile didn't falter. "Certainly."

During that initial visit to her home, while Jane had occupied the children in the garden, he'd apologized for putting her in the position he had all those years ago. He shouldn't have insisted on her wearing his ring while considering his proposal. By doing so, he'd caused a rift between her and Lucian, who'd almost left Gatlinburg for good.

Not looking at Tom, Jane held out her hand to her brother-in-law. "I'd love to dance with you, Lucian."

As Tom swept Megan in his arms, he registered the loss of Jane's company with a resigned sigh.

Chapter Thirteen

"He's not in love with her anymore."

Jane's fingers flexed on Lucian's arm. Born and raised among New Orleans's high society, he was an accomplished dancer, deftly maneuvering her across the straw-strewn earth. She looked up into his warm brown eyes that radiated understanding and compassion.

"Megan told you about my…feelings?"

He inclined his head. "Your secret is safe with me, *ma petite*."

Against her better judgment, she allowed her gaze to stray to Tom and Megan, not surprised by the ache overtaking her. "How can you be certain? He looks happy to be with her. Really happy."

"I remember how he used to look at her, and it's not the same," he said thoughtfully, also watching the pair. "Tom's an intelligent man. He's accepted that she will never be his. Much time has passed, and now he regards her with fondness."

Jane wasn't sure she shared his conviction. She'd thought Tom was enjoying himself with her. So why draw attention to himself by dancing with the woman who'd spurned him?

The music faded. Tom was thanking Megan, preparing to return her to her husband's side. Jane slipped free.

"I, uh, would like some fresh air." She gestured to where the pleasant anonymity of darkness awaited. "Thanks for the dance."

Darting around couples, she escaped into the quieter, cooler air and hurried away from the noise with no particular destination in mind. Entering the woods cloaked in shadows, she slowed. A fat white moon hung in the inky sky, giving off sufficient light for her to make out shapes.

She hadn't progressed very far when Tom called out to her. He must've pursued her the instant he'd noticed her retreat. Turning, fingers splayed on a gnarled tree trunk, she saw his impressive form silhouetted in the moonlight. He hadn't yet entered the woods. His hair gleamed a rich chocolate, his forehead and sharp cheekbones visible while his eyes were not.

No use hiding. Entering a swath of muted light, she said, "I'm here."

The stiff set of his shoulders eased. Striding forward, he stopped short a few feet away. "I won't interrupt your solitude for long. Just wanted to check on you."

"I've been taking care of myself for a long time." She said the words without bite. "I don't need you to look after me."

He sidled closer. "I care about you, Jane. I know exactly how you're feeling right now. Megan's rejection may not have been a public spectacle, but everyone in town heard about it." His fingertips grazed her knuckles. "It must be difficult dealing with the attention. You were brave to come here tonight. I'm proud of you."

He had no idea of the true reason for her distress.

"I don't love Roy." She threw her hands up. "I was

marrying him because…" *Because I was desperate to get over you.* "We were well suited. But not in love. Not like my sister and Lucian."

He was quiet a long time. Then he tipped his head to one side. "You think I'm still crazy about her."

Glad of the cover of darkness, she folded her arms across her middle. "I think it's going to be tough for any other woman to measure up to her in your mind."

He let loose a surprised laugh. "We were close once upon a time, and I will always admire her. She's built a good life with him. I couldn't have made her happy. Not like he has."

Jane heard the conviction behind his assertion yet found it hard to fully accept. For years she'd told herself he'd never love anyone else, that no other woman stood a chance with him.

"For what it's worth, I'm relieved your feelings weren't engaged," he said quietly. "At least you were spared a broken heart."

Oh, her feelings were engaged, all right. Just not with Roy.

Laughter trickled through the foliage on their right. Whispers followed.

Tom stiffened, moved to block Jane with his body. "Who's there?"

They heard what sounded like a hushed male voice. Then unrushed footsteps.

Jane's jaw dropped when she recognized the approaching pair. "Jessica!"

Even in the faint light, she could make out her twin's sheepish expression. Holding tight to her hand, Lee had the nerve to grin, teeth flashing.

"Sorry to disturb you," he said. "Jess and I were enjoying a private conversation."

Unspeaking, Tom moved so that he stood shoulder to shoulder with Jane, his hand coming to rest lightly against her lower back. The contact both comforted her and left her wanting.

Jane wasn't sure what to say. The courting couple had surely been indulging in more than mere conversation. The deserted woods were the perfect place for a few stolen kisses. And that led her thoughts to that ill-conceived water fight and what had happened afterward.

"We're going to get some food," Jessica said at last. "Will you join us?"

"No." Jane wasn't ready to return. "The barn's stuffy and crowded. I'm staying out here for a while."

They didn't try to change her mind. As they passed hand in hand, Lee winked at Tom. "Enjoy your privacy."

Jane's cheeks heated. "Sorry about that. I don't know what she sees in him."

"Have you told her you have reservations?" He put distance between them, sliding his hand in his pockets.

"She's smitten with him. If I were to say something, her defense would be that we have different taste in men."

"Makes sense that she would be attracted to a charismatic man like Cavanaugh."

"What bothers me is that we don't know much about him. Like Roy, he doesn't have roots in Gatlinburg. There are no family members or friends of his around. Do you know she's never been to his home? He could reside in a tent, for all we know."

"Maybe he's slovenly." She sensed rather than saw his smile.

"You've seen how he dresses."

"Good point. Why don't you just ask her about it?"

"Don't you think it's odd that a farmer would have the money for such a wardrobe? Did you see his cuff links? They were gold with diamond studs."

"Maybe his family has money." With a soft laugh, he draped his arm about her shoulders, reminding her of how they used to be with each other. "Talk to her, Jane. You'll feel better."

"I'll think about it."

"Come on, let's go stand by the fire. I'll get you something to drink."

While Tom went inside to fetch them lemonade, Jane meandered past kids playing tag and young men tossing nuts into the fire. She found a secluded spot at the barn's far corner and studied the night sky. Several sturdy toolsheds flanked a grouping of outbuildings draped in darkness. Above her, stars winked in interesting patterns.

Movement registered in her peripheral vision. A big man moved between the horses and wagons and crossed the night-cloaked yard. She recognized his profile instantly. Where was Lee headed? The outhouses were in the opposite direction.

Sticking close to the outer wall, she stood very still in the hopes he wouldn't see her if he looked back. Intent on his destination, he hurried to the nearest shed and disappeared behind it. A match flared. She stretched her neck for a better view. There was another man, an elderly bachelor who lived alone on the outskirts of town and didn't often participate in town activities. Something small and shiny—coins, perhaps?—passed between the two. And then Lee pushed a mason jar into the man's hands.

What in the world?

The light flickered out. Seconds later, a large form separated from the shadowy buildings.

Jane sucked in a sharp breath and ducked around the corner. Had he seen her?

Not sure why her heartbeat was so out of control, she walked along the exterior in search of Tom, unaware of the activity around her.

Be reasonable, Jane. Lee's actions are likely innocent.

She had no cause to suspect him of wrongdoing. She couldn't let her poor opinion of him cloud her common sense. Still, worry lodged in her chest and refused to go away.

In the days since the dance, the strain between him and Jane had all but disappeared.

She'd apparently put the kiss behind her. He wished he could. The entire episode frequented his dreams, the memory of her response branded on his brain, replaying again and again.

She must not have been as affected as he'd originally thought.

He should be glad. Not miffed that his kiss had been so easily dismissed.

Tom let himself in the cabin midafternoon and was immediately enveloped by a rich, berry-sweetened aroma. Emitting a good-natured groan, he removed his boots and hat and, hands on his hips, soaked in the sight of his messy kitchen and the two females in the midst of it.

"Please tell me you have extra of whatever it is you're making."

Behind the high work surface separating the table from the cookstove and dry sink, Jane was helping Clara roll out dough. Flour dusting her nose, the little girl's grin was wide. The happiness in her eyes elicited a smile of his own.

Jane was responsible for that happiness. No question she cared about Clara. Watching the pair of them together, he wondered how she'd be able to bring herself to leave. *Admit it, Leighton. You're hoping she'll change her mind.*

"We're making cobbler," Clara announced proudly.

"What kind?" he said.

"Blackberry."

Jane's tender smile transformed her. He'd glimpsed a number of those smiles lately, and he rejoiced that her guardedness around him had receded. *See? This is a good thing.*

Tom walked across the worn floorboards toward her, consumed suddenly with the wish that she was a permanent part of their family. He had no trouble picturing her here every morning, noon and night, a nurturing and compassionate mother for his niece.

Get that crazy notion out of your head, he told himself. She didn't see him as husband material. Besides, he wouldn't be content with a marriage based on anything but true, abiding love. As for Jane, he was sadly lacking answers. While she didn't strike him as the type to settle, she'd admitted that she hadn't loved Roy. What, then, had been her motivation?

Quickly washing up, he moved closer to survey their work.

"I believe I should sample that one." He pointed to the golden-crusted dessert near the stove behind him. Deep purple juices were visible beneath the latticework.

Merriment danced across Jane's features. "That's for the café. You'll have to be patient."

He reached past her to snag a berry from the bowl,

a movement that brought their faces within inches of each other. "I'm not a very patient man when it comes to cobbler."

Grinning, he popped the fruit in his mouth and chewed. Her gaze snagged on the motion and stayed there. His grin faded, and all his nerve endings stood to attention. She was right in front of him. So close. And so beautiful his common sense fled.

He'd dipped his head a fraction when she sidled sideways, reached for the flour sack and flicked the fine powder at him with both hands. He glanced at the white dots peppering his shirt and, when he looked up, Clara's mouth formed an O.

"You want to play?" he said in a mock threatening tone. "We'll play."

Before Jane could react, he smashed a berry in his fingers and smeared it across her cheek. Her jaw dropped. "You didn't just do that."

He laughed and repeated the action, this time targeting her other cheek. A glob of mashed fruit hit the floor. Her luminous eyes flared, promising retaliation.

"Let's get him, Clara," she cried.

And suddenly he was ducking two pairs of hands tossing sugar and flour at him. He managed to fight back, getting flour on his niece's cheeks and in her hair. Jane succeeded in smushing berries on his shirt. He and Megan hadn't played like this. He'd been too busy trying to impress her.

Laughing, he seized her arms and pinned them to her sides, easily subduing her squirming.

"Now what are you going to do, Janie girl?"

White streaked her upswept hair, and tendrils had escaped to caress her cheeks. Breathing hard, she was laughing up at him, uncaring of her appearance and fully rooted in the moment—a poignant reminder of the lighthearted girl she used to be. Mystifying emotion locked him in its grip, more complex than fondness and far deeper than physical attraction. It jolted him.

Clara tugged on his wrist. "Let her go, Uncle Tom."

He did as she asked, thankful for the distraction. He tugged lightly on one of her curls. "I wasn't going to hurt her, birdie. You know that, right?"

"We were just playing," Jane added softly, already wiping the mess from her face.

Clara seemed to have trouble understanding. "Adults play, too? Like kids?"

"Not as often." Moistening a towel in the water pail, he crouched to her level and set about cleaning her up. "Adults have a lot of serious work to tend to. But we like to have fun, just like you."

She was too young to recall her parents' interactions. Charles had liked to tease Jenny and sometimes tickled her until she begged him to stop. Sadness barreled through him, erasing the frivolity of moments ago. Clara would never know her mother. And if Charles didn't come to his senses, she wouldn't know her father, either.

Quiet descended after that. They worked together to restore the kitchen to rights. When it was finished, he strode to the door and pulled on his boots.

"I'm going to work on the smokehouse." The rear wall had been damaged during his long absence, possibly due to a storm, and he needed to fix it so he could hang hams and other meats in there. "Do you need anything?" He smoothed out his hat's crown.

"No. I'll have your cobbler on the table in about an hour."

"Fine."

Closing the door behind him, Tom stopped at the window and peered in, observing the pair through the wavy glass. If he were to marry, Clara would benefit in many ways. She'd experience what it meant to have both a mother and father. Problem was, he couldn't picture any other woman in his life besides Jane.

Chapter Fourteen

"Will you stay for supper?"

Jane stirred the venison stew one final time and, setting aside the ladle, turned to Clara. "I wish I could, sweetheart, but Mrs. Greene's customers will be disappointed if they don't get dessert. Maybe another time."

"Tomorrow?"

Smiling, she untied her apron and tucked it in a drawer. "We'll see."

Tom waited by the door with her crate in his arms. To ease his niece's disappointment, he said, "After supper, you can show me the alphabet letters you practiced today. Jane told me your handwriting has improved."

"Will you read me a story after?"

"Sure thing, little bird." He looked at the mantel clock. "We'd better not keep Jane."

Jane noted his resignation. He'd been quiet since
spontaneous food fight, which was unlike him
saying goodbye to Clara, she gathered her th
followed him to the wagon waiting in the

He met her on the far side and would'
onto the seat if she hadn't stopped hin
ering you, Tom?"

"I've a lot on my mind, that's all." He reached for her waist. She placed her hand flat against his chest, and his eyes delved into hers.

"I thought you trusted me."

"I do."

"I've shared my troubles with you."

"Not all of them."

The excursion to the cave reasserted itself. He'd been teasing her about the journal, and she'd reacted out of sheer panic. Overreacted, actually. Still rattled, she'd referred to an insurmountable problem. What would he say if he knew *he* was the problem?

"I guess I deserved that."

Hands dropping to his sides, he frowned. "Guess I'm not used to having anyone willing to listen. I've been dealing with my problems alone for a while now."

"I don't like seeing you upset."

"I worry, okay? About Clara. About whether or not I can give her everything she needs." Pacing away, he sliced the air with his hand. "That scene in there today... She doesn't remember what her parents were like together. Doesn't remember having a mother who doted on her or a father who—" He hung his head. "Sometimes I get so angry at Charles I can't see straight. If he were here right now, I'm not sure I could forgive him."

Jane longed to hold him, to soothe away his hurt. "You've a right to be angry."

"I understand he's grieving. If you'd seen the two of them together..." Sorrow carved lines in his face. "She was a wonderful woman. I miss her, too. And Clara won't get a chance to know her. I just come home. She deserves better."

"ything he's done, he's still your brother."

He passed a weary hand over his face. "Yeah."

Unable to resist offering him comfort, she took his hand in between hers and held it. "You haven't been alone all this time, you know. God has been with you, giving you the strength to do whatever necessary to care for that precious child. You are not only providing her with a good, safe home, you're giving her what she needs most. Love. Acceptance. Guidance."

The muscle in his jaw worked. Jane lost herself in the swirling emotion in his beautiful eyes. When he dipped his head to rest his forehead against hers, his body coming close and radiating heat, she closed her eyes and reveled in the brief moment of rightness, of connection. More than anything, she yearned to be the one he turned to in times of trouble, the one he rejoiced with during the good times.

You're not the kind of woman he wants for a wife, she reminded herself. *You're too timid, too closed off. Too practical.*

"I have to go," she murmured, aching to remain here for the remainder of the day.

Pulling away, he nodded, countenance shadowed. "Thank you, Jane. You're a good listener."

"That's what friends are for, right?" Her voice shook.

His brows drew together. Before he could speak, she grabbed the springs and hauled herself up. "I'll see you in the morning."

He waved as she set the team in motion, a lonely, solitary figure that tugged on her heartstrings. Already it hurt to leave them every night. It had been difficult to refuse Clara's request. What she wanted was to join them at the supper table, hold hands with them as Tom said grace in his rich voice, listen as Clara regaled him with all they'd done that day.

Giving him a time limit had been a wise move. A visit to her aunt's was exactly what she needed to put her mind on something other than her thwarted dreams.

Mulling over their conversation, she drove into town and guided the wagon behind the row of businesses housing the café. Mrs. Greene noticed her distraction and commented on it. Jane apologized, citing fatigue. They briefly discussed her dessert order for the remainder of the week, and Jane exited out the kitchen door leading into the alley.

Male voices drifted from the trash barrels to her left. One of them she recognized as Lee's. Rushing to the wagon, she kept her head down, using the high seat as cover. Peeking through the space underneath the wooden bench, she saw him with a couple of middle-aged men who looked as if they hadn't bathed in weeks.

She watched as they handed him a handful of coins. In exchange, he gave them each a mason jar filled with clear liquid. Her stomach plummeted to her toes. Was that corn liquor? It wasn't uncommon for families in the region to make batches of moonshine and sometimes brandy for themselves and neighbors—small operations that mostly went unnoticed by the government's revenue collectors.

Jane's great-uncle hadn't escaped notice, however. Peter O'Malley had died in defiance of tax laws and in the name of independence. Not interested in giving up his property, he'd clashed with federal agents and gotten shot in the process. Illegal stills and trouble went hand in hand.

If Lee was operating one, Jessica needed to know.

The shortest man shook the jar and squinted at the contents.

"This batch is at least 115 proof," Lee said, glancing impatiently around.

Apparently satisfied with what he saw, he gave a hearty nod. The other one shook his jar, as well, similarly pleased. Pocketing the money, Lee doffed his hat and strode in the opposite direction.

Jane debated what to do. Accusing Lee without solid evidence would not sway Jess. She'd demand proof. Part of her hoped her suspicions were wrong. While she wasn't crazy about the man, her twin was enamored.

Waiting until Lee was out of sight, she stood to her full height and forced her feet to carry her across the alley. The pair gawked at her. The stench of sweat and cigar smoke made her stomach roil.

Knees rubbery, skin hot and tight, she exuded a false calm. "Can either of you gentlemen tell me where Mr. Cavanaugh resides?"

Lee had given her family the general area of his home, but no specifics. Now she wondered if this was the reason for his secrecy.

The shorter man's overgrown brows hung low over bloodshot eyes. "Why you askin'?"

"I have business with him." She gripped her reticule so tightly, the ribbons were beginning to cut off the blood supply to her fingers.

They exchanged a doubtful look. "How much it worth to ya?"

"Um…" They wanted money for information. Of course they did. Fishing out a coin, she dropped it in the first man's hand. "How's that?"

Examining the payment, he gave her directions. She thanked him and hurried to her wagon, not giving herself time to think about what she was about to do. Jessica was supposed to be at the mercantile right now fulfilling their order. That would take a while, since she'd probably visit with Nicole and maybe share a pot of tea. Plenty of time for Jane to ride out to Lee's and return home.

The wagon was too cumbersome, however, so she left the team at the livery, taking only her fastest horse. The road took her several miles past Tom's farm. The farther she traveled from town, the wilder the terrain. Cabins were set farther back from the lane, some obscured by untamed undergrowth. The mountainsides grew steeper, blocking the evening sun.

Doubt was kicking in with a vengeance when she noticed the turn. A ramshackle shed stood at the entrance, just like the men had said there'd be. Hitching her horse to a tree not visible from the lane, she set off on foot.

Every unexpected noise spooked her. If Lee happened upon her, what possible excuse could she give? This was too far from town and her own home to say she was out for an innocent jaunt through the woods. She had no plausible story and no weapon. This wasn't her brightest idea. But she couldn't ignore the possibility that Jessica might be involved with a criminal.

I'll just take a quick look around, then leave.

Fifteen long, nerve-racking minutes later, she spied a clearing and a rusty, ancient reaper to huddle behind. The tiny cabin, while not exactly ramshackle, would benefit from a new roof and chinking between the logs. The expansive barn was in better shape.

Jane started when Lee himself loped out of the cabin, followed by another man she didn't recognize. Dressed as neatly as Lee, he was perhaps a decade older. They disappeared into the barn for what felt like an hour, but was probably more like ten minutes, before they emerged, arms full of what looked to be five- or ten-gallon kegs.

Four massive dogs of unspecified origin trotted out behind them. Brindle coats, large paws, ferocious-looking teeth. Her eyes widened. Those were guard dogs, not pets.

Her great-uncle Peter had had guard dogs, too.

The men placed their burdens in the wagon bed, their conversation too low to make out.

Behind her, a disturbance in the trees caught the dogs' attention. Jane instinctively jerked, her boot heel snapping a twig. The sound reverberated in the silence. Even from this distance, she could see their ears twitching, their muscles bunching. One barked.

Father God, I really shouldn't be here, should I? I didn't think this through. Just reacted. Please, please help me get out of here without getting eaten.

The stranger put his hand on one of the guns at his waist. Lee's burly form swung around, jaw rock hard as he scanned the woods, and she ducked out of sight. Her breath came in short puffs.

Time to go.

Moving as stealthily as possible, mindful of the placement of her feet, Jane attempted to put distance between her and the dogs. Her body strained to break out into a full run. Minutes later, when she heard multiple dogs barking and Lee's booming voice, she did just that. The forest seemed endless, the trees blurring into one another, inciting panic. Was she going the right way?

Not seeing the rock jutting out of the uneven ground, she tripped and went sprawling, a jagged branch gouging deep into her arm as she tried to stop her descent. The moan couldn't be helped. She lay there for a moment, dizzy and queasy, staring up at the interwoven branches and clutching her arm to her chest.

I can't let him find me here. Especially now that I've run. He'll know I was spying on him.

Praying for strength, she pushed onto her knees and scrambled to her feet. The dogs sounded far away. Concentrating on putting one foot in front of the other, she almost wept with relief at the sight of her horse. She didn't inspect the wound until they were well away.

Her serrated skin smeared with blood, she couldn't tell how deep the injury was.

"Stupid move, Jane."

Tom was about to guide his team onto the lane leading into town when he caught sight of Jane astride her horse. Hunched in the saddle, red hair flowing down her back, her countenance was alarmingly pale.

"Clara, stay in the wagon."

Setting the brake, he vaulted down and hurried to intercept her. The animal had been moving at a snail's pace and heeded Tom's command at once.

"Tom." She sat up straight. Winced. "Where are you going?"

Eyeing the wounded arm she cradled against her body, he said, "Mercantile. What happened?"

"I fell."

"Your horse threw you?" Worry sharpened his voice. Head injuries were dangerous.

"No." Her lips went flat. "I was running and tripped."

He reached for her. "Come home with me. I'll get you cleaned up."

She came willingly, sagging against him when her boots hit the ground. He steadied her with his hands on her waist. "Are you hurt anywhere else?" When she shook her head, he scooped her up and carried her to the wagon bed. "Clara, Miss Jane has a sore arm. We're going to make her feel better, okay?"

His niece remained quiet as he helped prop Jane against the side. He hoped the sight of blood on Jane's clothing and skin didn't scare her. Or make her sick.

Jane braved a smile. "I was clumsy, but I'll be fine. Your uncle is going to patch me up."

"Does it hurt?" Clara clasped her hands tightly in her lap.

"Only a little."

An understatement, gauging from her demeanor. He tied her horse to the back and carefully turned the wagon around. At the cabin, he sent Clara to the bedroom to play with her dolls. Then he once again swept Jane into his arms.

"You don't have to carry me," she murmured, a little color returning to her cheeks.

"I don't mind. I carried you once before, remember?"

"I was twelve."

"We were playing a game with your cousins, and you didn't see the snake hole."

Her uninjured arm was slung about his neck, and her fingers tangled with his hair.

"My ankle started swelling immediately, and you insisted I shouldn't walk on it. You took me to my aunt's and stayed while she wrapped it. You even held my hand." Her gaze roamed his face. "You're good at taking care of people, you know that?"

The gratitude shining in her eyes, her confidence in him, made him feel invincible. "Most people like to feel useful." He shrugged off her praise.

Navigating the stairs, he went inside and set her on the nearest dining chair, hovering a moment to make sure she was steady. "Do you feel faint?"

"No."

"Tell me if you do."

She watched as he gathered the water bowl, clean rags and a mortar and pestle. "What's that for?"

"I have to make a paste that will hopefully prevent infection." Striding to the hutch in the corner, he sifted through the lower cabinet and, retrieving a scuffed case, took out a bottle of what looked like dried herbs. "Juniper leaves. Ma always used these for our cuts and scrapes."

He sniffed the contents. "Should still be good. I'll ask around tomorrow. Maybe your aunt has a fresh supply."

When he'd readied the paste, she extended her arm on the tabletop. He paused before cleaning her wound. "Sorry I can't hold your hand this time."

"Thank you for doing this. Jessica wouldn't be as gentle as you."

He cleaned the injury with care, hating that she was experiencing discomfort. "Who was chasing you this time?"

Jane jerked in her seat. "What do you mean?"

He twisted open the jar lid and set it aside. "Your cousins were chasing you when you twisted your ankle. What were you running from just now?"

Something very much like guilt passed over her face. "I...I feel a bit light-headed. Can we discuss this later?"

Holding her wrist, he set about applying the cream. Her pulse was rapid beneath the pads of his fingers. He got the impression she was hiding something from him. That wasn't like her. While Jane wasn't always forthcoming with her private thoughts, she was an honest person. Didn't have a deceptive bone in her body.

In the hushed stillness that had descended between them, Clara's conversation with her homemade dolls filtered in from the bedroom. Jane stared at her lap as he wrapped her arm in gauze.

"All done." Sinking against the chair back, he rested his hands on his knees and studied her. "Keep that wound clean and dry. As long as infection doesn't set in, it should heal relatively quickly."

With a quick nod, she pushed to her feet. "Thanks again, Tom."

He followed suit. "Let me take you home."

"No need. I can make it on my own."

"Jane." He skimmed her shoulder. "Look at me."

When she lifted her luminous gaze, his gut instinct told him she was keeping secrets. "You asked me earlier if I trusted you. Now it's my turn. Do you trust me?"

"Of course."

"Then you know you can tell me anything."

The light smattering of freckles across the bridge of her nose stood out against her pale skin. "I know."

Whatever was bothering her, she wasn't telling. Not tonight, anyway. Frustration warred with concern. "Be careful going home. If you need to stay in and rest tomorrow, that's fine. Clara and I will manage."

"That's not necessary. I'll be here shortly after breakfast."

Going to the bedroom door, she bid Clara good-night, patiently answering her questions and letting her examine the wrapping. Tom accompanied her out into the dusky evening and helped her into the saddle. She struck him as eager to escape his company. Worried he'd demand more information?

He remained in the yard and watched her retreating form with a heavy spirit. "What exactly are you hiding, Jane O'Malley?"

Chapter Fifteen

Jessica was spitting mad. Vaulting out of the rocking chair, she stomped down the porch steps and met Jane in the yard.

"Do you have any idea what time it is?"

"Not really." After leaving Tom's, she'd had to hurry to the livery and retrieve the wagon before Mr. Warring closed up for the night. The climb down was awkward with one arm.

Her twin's ire faded the instant she caught sight of her blood-splattered dress. "What happened to you?"

"I fell and scraped up my arm."

One sleek eyebrow quirked. "Were you and Tom playing tag?"

"No."

"Then what?"

"Not now, Jess. I have a splitting headache. I'm going to bed as soon as I get the horses situated."

Concern flared. "I'll see to them. You go on inside and lie down. I'll fix you some hot cocoa once I'm finished here."

"Are you sure?"

"I don't mind. Truly." She gave her a tiny nudge. "Go."

"Thanks, sis."

Inside, multiple lamps cast the living room in a cozy glow. Good thing her ma wasn't here. Jane wouldn't have been able to avoid a confession in the face of Alice's persistence. She'd been so close to confiding in Tom. Only the knowledge that doing so could put him in danger had prevented her.

Federal revenue collectors had turned their attention to this area in recent years, determined to enforce the excise tax, but that hadn't halted the production of homemade moonshine. The sale of alcohol was a lucrative business. Not everyone was willing to give that up, even if it meant dealing in illegal activities and risking jail time.

Those who dared snitch on neighbors or family members were dealt with harshly. Property damage was one outcome—burned barns and homes. Personal violence was another. She'd heard of at least four deaths connected to the hidden stills...innocent people who were murdered for alerting the law.

She couldn't put Tom's life on the line. Or her sister's.

The only solution was for Jane to handle this herself. Somehow, she had to find out what Lee was up to. If he was involved in criminal activities, Jessica could be at risk.

By the time she'd changed into her nightclothes, her arm throbbed with a deep, unremitting ache and her headache had increased to an almost unbearable point. Trying to come up with a plan would have to wait. She'd climbed beneath the covers when Jessica came to check on her.

"The milk is heating." Sinking onto the mattress edge, she folded her hands in her lap. "Are you going to Tom's tomorrow?"

"Clara needs me."

"That's what I thought. Well, don't worry about the café order. I'll take care of it."

"That's three pound cakes. Oh, and we're supposed to make the almond cake for Mrs. Liverton's party."

"I'll get an early start tomorrow." She lifted a shoulder. "Oh, I forgot to tell you. I invited Lee for supper tomorrow night. Do you mind?"

Jane worked to keep her tone nonchalant. "That's fine."

She must not have been convincing, because Jess's face fell. "Tell me the truth, Jane. You don't approve of him, do you?"

At the sight of her twin's uncharacteristic vulnerability, she covered her hand to stop her from worrying a stray quilt thread. "I'm worried that what happened to me might happen to you. We don't know anything about Lee except for what he tells us. Just like with Roy."

"Lee doesn't have a wife hidden away somewhere."

"Maybe not. But there could be other secrets. Dangerous ones." Jane bit her lip. Had she said the wrong thing?

Jessica laughed. "You read too much, sister of mine."

"Maybe you're right." Oh, she hoped and prayed she was wrong.

Jess squeezed her hand, wide eyes growing unexpectedly earnest. "Lee's a wonderful man. I'm beginning to care for him a great deal. If things keep progressing as they are now, there's a good chance he'll propose. You're the person who knows me best in this world, and I want you to be happy with my choice."

Speechless, Jane sank into the pillows. She'd had no idea her sister's feelings were this far gone. Deeply troubled, she strove for an even tone. "I only ask that you take your time in deciding if he's truly the man God has chosen for you. I failed to do that with Roy, and I suffered for it."

She'd taken her own path instead of the Lord's.

"Lee's different. He's a faithful church member, has good standing in the community and is able to support himself." She ticked off his attributes. "Most importantly, he makes me laugh."

"Church attendance doesn't mean his relationship with God is what it needs to be."

Leaning over, Jess kissed her forehead. "There's nothing to worry about, sis. Promise me you'll give him a chance. Please."

"Fine."

"Thank you." Her smile bright, she hooked a thumb toward the doorway. "I'll go prepare your cocoa."

When she'd gone, Jane closed her eyes, a soft groan slipping out. How was she supposed to view Lee Cavanaugh as a potential brother-in-law when she suspected he was a bootlegger?

"Thanks for coming tonight," Jane told Tom. "Your presence lent the dinner respectability since Ma is out of town."

A plausible excuse for her invitation, especially since she couldn't reveal the real reason…that she felt extremely uncomfortable around Lee. Having Tom there had provided the buffer she'd needed. The only truly tense moment had been when Lee questioned her about her injury. He'd appeared to accept her mumbled explanation, however.

Lounging against the porch post, flipping the lid of his pocket watch open and closed, Tom quirked a single eyebrow. "Is that the only reason you invited me?"

"It wasn't romantically motivated," she rushed to say. "Our kiss didn't give me fanciful thoughts about you and me." That wasn't a lie. She'd entertained thoughts of that nature long before their embrace.

He tilted his head slightly, attention on the moon-washed flower beds flanking the steps, leaving his forehead and straight nose in sharp relief. "I know you didn't think that. I'm practically a brother to you."

Jane hugged her sore arm to her chest. Had she imagined the dissatisfaction behind that statement?

When she remained silent, he lifted his head. "I'm assuming only Jessica is aware what occurred that day?"

"I haven't told anyone else. Why?"

His mouth curled in a rueful half grin. "Because if you had, I'd have had three irate O'Malleys on my property, all with the intent to throttle me."

Pushing out of the rocker, she went and leaned against the opposite post a couple of feet from him. "My cousins consider you part of the family. Why would they object to you and me?"

His eyes glittered shades of emerald and peridot green. Sliding the watch in his pocket, he folded his arms across his chest and regarded her with open scrutiny. "Because, my dear Jane, it's their duty to protect you. They wouldn't approve of me making advances when you and I don't have a future together."

His words dug into her like flaming arrows. *No future.*

She stared at her rounded boot tips until they blurred. This was not a new revelation. Hadn't she told herself the same all along? Way back when she was fifteen and he was twenty-two and in love with Megan, she'd accepted her chances were very slim. Guess the stubborn

O'Malley streak ran deeper than she'd thought. A part of her refused to give up hope.

What will it take to finally purge it? Purge him?

As long as she stayed in Gatlinburg, and as long as he remained unwed, a part of her would cling to hope for the impossible. Better to leave than to prolong the agony. Perhaps Jessica had been right—her stay in Maryville might become a permanent one.

"Coffee's ready." Jessica emerged from the cabin bearing a tray, Lee following behind with the desserts. They set them both on a low table, careful not to topple the candles flickering there.

When everyone had been served, Lee and Jessica took the rocking chairs flanking the door. Tom and Jane sat on the top step, using the solid posts as supports.

Cradling her mug in her hands, Jane blew on the hot liquid.

Lee forked a bite of coffee cake. "This is delicious, as usual. You two shouldn't waste your talent on the café. Have you ever thought of opening up a bakery?"

The clink of utensils against the dishes punctuated the silence. Somewhere nearby, an owl hooted.

Jessica looked as surprised as Jane felt. "What would Mrs. Greene do?"

"Hire someone else. Of course, they wouldn't be as talented as you. Her customers would become your customers. Now that they've tasted your fine baking, they'll follow you anywhere."

"I don't know," Jess said doubtfully.

"Don't you want all the profit for yourselves?"

Jane sipped her coffee, troubled by his utter lack of empathy for Mrs. Greene. Not only had she lost her beloved husband of twenty-five years, but she'd struggled with health problems all last year. The café gave her purpose. Jane didn't want to contemplate becoming her competitor.

Across from her, Tom's attention was on the plate in his hand. The candlelight glinted in his dark hair. If he let it grow any longer, it would begin to curl.

"I haven't thought about it before, but I'm not sure either of us is ready for such an undertaking. What's your opinion, Jane?" Jessica said.

Tom's watchful gaze lifted to hers. It frustrated her not to know what he was thinking.

"I'm content with our current arrangement."

"Ambition isn't a bad thing, ladies." Lee polished off his slice and returned the empty plate to the table. "And neither is making money." His teeth flashed in the low light.

"Spoken like a true businessman." Balancing an arm on his bent knee, Tom shifted in order to see the other man better. "Have you ever managed your own business?"

Lee hesitated. Humor fading, he resumed his seat. "As a matter of fact, my family owns a general store back in Virginia. The largest in our town. It's quite successful."

Jessica lowered her cup to her lap. "You never told me that."

"Not something I like to talk about. My father and I...well, we don't exactly get along."

"Is that why you left?"

"He didn't think I was capable of running things."

His frustration was understandable. The bitterness etched on his features gave Jane pause, however.

"He couldn't be more wrong," Jessica announced. "You're the most enterprising man I know."

He snapped his fingers. "See, I knew there was a reason I fancied you."

Her soft laughter spoke of her affection.

"What brought you to Gatlinburg?" Tom gave voice to the questions pestering Jane. "And why farming and not business?"

"Friends of mine traveled through these parts and had only glowing reports about the landscape and people. I'm an adventurous man, and I was looking for an excuse to leave. Tennessee sounded like a good place to start fresh. As for farming, it's a challenge for the current season. Will I make it a lifelong vocation?" He spread his hands. "I can't answer that one."

"You're not planning on moving away, are you?" Jessica's countenance clouded.

Lee shifted uncomfortably.

Tom abruptly gained his feet and extended his hand to Jane. "I'd like more coffee. Care to assist me?"

His grip was sure and careful as he helped her up. Once in the dimly lit kitchen, she glanced in his mug. "You've only drank half of that."

"They deserved some privacy. Besides, I should fetch Clara from your aunt's. It will soon be past her bedtime."

"I'm glad you came."

Draining the contents, he left his cup in the dry sink and came to stand before her. "Me, too."

She sensed the resignation in him and wondered at it. So gently she almost didn't register the touch, he trailed his fingers down the length of her bandage.

"How's the pain this evening?"

His husky voice beckoned her nearer. Breath hitching, she braced herself against the pie safe ledge. "Not as bad as before."

"Good." Time seemed to slow, and Jane thought she

glimpsed a surge of longing that matched her own. "I'll change the gauze for you in the morning."

Hardly believing her daring, she placed her hand against his chest. "What do I owe you for your doctoring services?"

Beneath smooth cotton, sleek muscle and bone, his heart pounded strong and steady. His woodsy scent swirled around her, and she inhaled deeply. He covered her hand with his, imprisoning it. "Since you're an old friend, I work for free."

The golden light from the lone lamp in the middle of the table highlighted the angles of his cheekbones and jawline. His mouth hovered just above hers. Memories of the water fight flooded her—the fun-filled abandon she'd experienced and later the joyous sensation of being in his arms. She desperately wished to relive those moments.

"Free, huh?" she murmured. "I'm a fortunate girl."

Somehow, his other hand had found her back, and he was slowly drawing her into him. She didn't resist. Although there was no question she'd pay dearly for this slip, she couldn't find the strength to stop it.

"Jane…" His voice issued a warning and a promise.

From the living room, the sound of the main door opening jolted them apart. Lee and Jessica's quiet conversation drifted in.

Tom's expression shuttered. "Good night, Jane."

He strode from the room, leaving her weak-kneed.

Chapter Sixteen

He was beginning to think Jane's trip to visit her aunt would be a blessing. Not one he welcomed, but one he needed if he hoped to maintain their friendship.

Lowering the pruning shears, he surveyed the procession of peach trees he'd just released his frustration on. His shoulders and upper back testified to the handful of hours he'd spent cleaning up the orchard. Parched, he gathered his tools and headed for the shed.

Thunder rumbled in the near distance. Above him, thick clouds stretched across the sky like cotton batting, effectively blocking the sun. There was no activity around the cabin.

The girls had spent much of the day inside. He'd stayed outside. Except for lunch, an unavoidable and predictably stifled affair. Thankfully, Clara hadn't noticed either adult's unusual silence. That morning, shortly after Jane's arrival and without his niece's peppy chatter to distract them, he'd made good on his promise to tend to her wound—and she hadn't uttered a single voluntary word as he applied a fresh layer of ointment to her cut and wrapped it in clean gauze.

He'd made absolutely no mention of last night.

Hadn't had to. Their almost kiss hung between them, a reminder of his foolishness.

What galled him was this weakness where Jane was concerned, his inability to hold tight to sound judgment. He was keenly aware of the consequences of such actions. That didn't seem to matter when she was near, however.

If given another opportunity, he didn't trust himself not to take advantage.

Jane had to go. Soon. He cared too much to continue in this manner.

Half an hour later, he was still tinkering in the toolshed when thunder pealed directly overhead, rumbling through the ground beneath his soles. He went to the doorway and peered out. The wind had picked up, the sky darkened to pewter. Clara didn't like storms. As much as he dreaded going in, he had no more cause to delay.

The clouds opened up as soon as he ducked beneath the porch's overhang, the torrent drenching the yard and obscuring his vision. Lightning lit up the sky in a spectacular display. Jane wouldn't be going home for a while. He had mixed feelings about that.

Letting himself in, he found them on the couch with a book. Jane looked past him to the view beyond the window glass.

"Come and read with us," Clara said.

Clara's short legs didn't quite reach the floor. Her curls formed a shiny halo about her bright face. Seeing her relaxed and happy sent a trill of thankfulness through him. Having Jane around these first weeks in Gatlinburg had made the transition smoother than it might've been otherwise. He'd have to be very careful to choose the right woman to take her place.

Isn't it about time you started searching for said woman?

Unable to deny his niece's beseeching look, he hastily removed his boots and rid his hands of grit and grime before joining them. He motioned for Clara to scoot over. She was tucked against the far end, with Jane occupying the middle.

Shaking her head, she pointed to the empty spot on the other side of her caretaker. "Sit there, Uncle Tom. That way you can see the pictures while Miss Jane reads."

A telltale blush climbed Jane's slender throat and invaded her cheeks.

"Fine."

This isn't a big deal, he told himself as he sat beside her. The worn sofa had seen better days, and the springs inside weren't all that supportive. Without meaning to, he began to shift closer to her.

Her fingers gripping the book tighter, she flicked her luminous green eyes to his, questions in the mossy depths.

"Sorry." To halt his sideways slide, he braced his arm along the sofa back behind her. "Guess I should see about replacing this old relic."

It wasn't a perfect solution, because now he had to concentrate on not brushing against her neck or shoulders. A whiff of strawberries filled his nostrils. It clung to her hair, her skin, her clothes. He yearned to wrap his arm around her—something he wouldn't have hesitated to do before—and pull her close. Tuck her head beneath his chin, stroke her silky hair and just enjoy being near her.

He closed his eyes and prayed for fortitude.

"Read this page again, Miss Jane." Clara tapped the

drawing. "Uncle Tom won't know what happened to the princess if you don't."

Lifting his head from the sofa, Tom listened with his attention fixed on the pages.

"How did you like this one?" Jane asked Clara when she'd finished.

"I like princesses." Hopping down, she scooted in front of him and put a hand on his knee. "Did my mama read to me?"

He nodded, his throat suddenly thick. "Almost every night before bed."

Questions like this were to be expected. She deserved to know about Jenny. That didn't make answering them any easier. Charles should be the one telling her about her mother, not him.

Big green eyes full of innocence, Clara blinked up at Jane. "Will you be my new mama?"

Surprise ricocheting through him, Tom couldn't resist a glance at the woman beside him. A mixture of sadness and regret weighed down her features.

"Oh, sweetheart," she breathed. "It doesn't work that way."

"You could marry my uncle. Then you wouldn't have to go home every night."

Tom bit back a groan. This wasn't helping ease the awkwardness between him and Jane. He pushed to standing and paced to the window. The storm outside mirrored the one inside him.

His back to the room, he didn't see Jane's reaction.

"One day, your uncle is going to find a special lady whom he l-loves and wants to marry." She seemed to have trouble voicing the solemn words. "She will be your new mother."

He was having trouble picturing wooing a nameless, faceless woman.

"But I like *you*."

Another intense rumble of thunder punctuated the silence. Tom twisted around to see Jane hugging Clara. "I like you, too," Jane whispered. "Very much."

Over Clara's shoulder, Jane was looking at him. Her gaze was not only pained, but a turbulent mass of longing. He wasn't fool enough to believe that longing was directed at him. Marriage and family had been within her grasp before they were cruelly and publicly snatched away. All of the O'Malley cousins had married and were starting families, save for the twins. And from what he'd seen, Jessica wasn't far from that state, which left Jane.

Clara's naive request had stirred those dreams to life.

Unable to handle her anguish, he knew he needed to lighten the mood.

Jane instantly recognized Tom's determination. It reminded her of the time Caroline had accused her of going to the boy she liked, Larry Winston, and telling him of her infatuation. Jane hadn't, of course, but Caroline had refused to believe her. Hurt, she'd confessed the entire story to him. He'd ignored her protests and went directly to her friend's home to sort things out.

She hadn't thanked him then for his interference. Right now, though, she desperately needed to *not* think about her problems. "The storm isn't letting up, is it?"

On the other side of the window, the rain was coming down in sheets. A mixture of water and mud splattered onto the steps. The road would be a muddy morass by the time it was over.

He clapped his hands together. "I have an idea to pass the time. Let's play charades."

"Yay!" Clara jumped up and down. "Me first!"

Seeing her excitement, bittersweet emotion swept over Jane. One innocent question was all it had taken to demolish the barrier she'd erected the day they met. *Will you be my new mama?*

She'd been so careful not to give in to fruitless imaginings. How easy it would've been to pretend she could have a permanent role in Clara's life. All those afternoons baking together, teaching her to write, untangling her curls, washing the smudges from her sweet face, comforting her when Jenny's absence became too much…everyday moments that added up to motherhood.

The dream of becoming Tom's wife was joined by another, futile desire—to be a mother to Clara.

Tom sat on one end of the sofa. Leaning into the cushions, long legs extended and hooked at the ankles, he gestured to the opposite end. "You have to play, too, Jane. Won't work with just two players."

Father God, all I want is to disappear with my journal and pencil and put my feelings to paper. But I'm stuck here for the duration. Help me, please.

Fingers closing over the cross pendant in the dip of her collarbone, she crossed the room and assumed her seat. Clara was an expressive child. Watching her move and wriggle and make funny faces in an attempt to get her point across served to distract Jane from her darker thoughts. Then it was Tom's turn. Clever and funny, he wasn't afraid to look foolish. Bit by bit, the rigidity in her body seeped away, and she found herself able to smile. When she took her place before the stone fireplace, her self-consciousness faded in the face of Clara's enthusiasm. Her giggles, and the absence of sadness in her big eyes, made the effort worthwhile.

Jane chose not to dwell on Tom's frank admiration.

When they'd finished, he insisted on frying up the ham and potatoes she'd sliced earlier, leaving her and Clara to set the table. The lingering rain gave her no choice but to join them. Thanks to Tom's concerted efforts, the experience was nowhere near as trying as the noon meal had been.

His sensitivity and kindness only made her love him more. Her past feelings, she was quickly recognizing, had been those of an immature young girl. Sure, she'd witnessed the goodness in him and responded to that, had thought him dashing, like some storybook hero. Dealing with him on an adult level, she saw so much more, beyond the obvious to his generous, selfless nature.

He would be a loving, attentive husband. A fine father, too. All she had to do was observe him with his niece to be convinced of that.

The rain finally abated around the time they finished cleaning up the kitchen. Jane eagerly took her leave, grateful for the solitude, even if she did have to concentrate extra hard to navigate the mucky lanes.

Jessica was relieved to see her.

"I don't suppose you heard the news," she said over her shoulder as Jane followed her to the kitchen.

"I didn't leave Tom's all day. What happened?"

"I went to the post office this morning, hoping to find a letter from Ma, and Main Street was abuzz with the news that Mr. Huffaker discovered a dead body on his property."

Jane froze. The Huffakers' farm was situated about a mile east of Lee's. "That's horrible. Who was it?"

She shrugged. "No one local. Sheriff Timmons seems to think he was a drifter."

"Do they think it was an accident?"

"He was shot to death, Jane. Four bullet holes to the chest."

She shuddered at the graphic mental image. "Isn't that near Lee's place?" Her casual tone belied the rapid pounding of her heart.

"I hadn't thought about it. I mean, I haven't been there, but it sounds like the general vicinity."

"Why haven't you?"

Jessica's eyes widened at her abrupt manner.

"You said yourself things are getting serious," Jane said. "Don't you think it's a bit strange he hasn't invited you to see his home at least once?"

"Since when did you become Miss Sally Sleuth?" Her hands fisted. "I've never known you to be the suspicious type, Jane. The fact of the matter is, you don't like him. You're searching for reasons not to."

"Hold on—"

"You're being so unfair. When I think how I supported you through the Roy fiasco—"

Jane's composure slipped. "Excuse me? You call analyzing my every decision supporting me? You made it clear from the start that you didn't like him."

"I was right, wasn't I?" she retorted. "Maybe if you'd listened to me, you wouldn't have been humiliated in front of the entire town."

She felt the color drain from her face.

Jessica immediately looked contrite. "I'm sorry. I shouldn't have said that."

Weariness cloaked her. "Let's just forget it. It's been a long day." Turning away, she said, "I'll be in my room for a while."

Her twin didn't move to stop her. Once in her room with the door closed, she sank onto the low bed and dropped her head in her hands. No matter how irritated she got with Jessica, she wouldn't stop worrying about her.

The clandestine trip out to Lee's had frightened Jane. After coming close to being dog food, she'd decided to abandon her amateur investigation. But now someone was dead. Murdered. A stranger close to Cavanaugh property. Coincidence?

A chill skittered along her spine. Could it have been the man she'd seen at Lee's barn?

She had to find out the truth. Before her sister got caught up in something she'd never be able to escape.

Chapter Seventeen

This was a dumb idea. The worst ever.

Tiny drops of sweat beaded her brow, and her midsection was one giant knot of tension. Three times now she'd almost turned around and returned home. She hadn't. Jessica's stubborn refusal to consider Lee might not be who he appeared kept her on her current course.

If her deception were discovered... No, she couldn't consider such an outcome.

Holding the thin white shawl tightly about her shoulders, she forced her feet to continue along the boardwalk. The midmorning temperatures didn't require a shawl. She had to have it in order to hide her wound. If Lee spotted the bandage, he'd know at once she wasn't Jessica.

What makes you think he won't guess, anyway? her voice of reason chided. *You're not the most skillful actress even in the best of times.*

The fact she'd managed to keep Tom from guessing her true feelings had to count for something, didn't it?

Customers passed in and out of the post office entrance. Fridays were the busiest days because they were closed for the weekends. She'd learned from Jessica that

Lee came into town every Friday morning to post letters and check for packages. Jane was counting on him sticking to his usual schedule.

Before leaving Tom's yesterday, she'd mentioned having an errand to tend to this morning and not to expect her until lunchtime. He hadn't questioned her. Why would he? Assuming her twin's identity was so far out of character he'd never suspect her of it.

That's what she was banking on to carry this off. They hadn't switched identities since they were kids. No one would expect it of them now.

Jane flinched when a hand clamped on her sore arm.

"Jessica! I've been calling for you to stop." Megan stepped into her path, slightly out of breath. "Didn't you hear me?"

Oh, no. Fooling Lee was one thing. How was she supposed to trick her sibling?

Her tongue stuck to the roof of her mouth.

Megan's brow creased. "Are you okay?"

"I'm fine."

When Megan cocked her head to one side, considering her, Jane reminded herself to think and act like Jessica.

"I simply didn't hear you." She flipped her ponytail— Jessica's signature style—behind her shoulder. "No need to make a fuss, sister of mine."

"Where are you going in such a hurry?" Megan said.

"Post office. I have a lot to do today."

If she wasn't careful, she'd miss Lee. She couldn't let that happen. Not after all the effort she'd put in. It had taken quite a bit of maneuvering to sneak one of Jessica's dresses out of her wardrobe without her being aware, not to mention slipping out of the house without Jessica seeing her wearing it.

"Listen, I wanted to ask your opinion on something."

"What is it?"

"I'm worried about Jane."

Her stomach sank. This was wrong on so many points. "What about Jane?" she said slowly.

Glancing around at the bustling street, Megan moved closer and lowered her voice. "Do you think she's upset with me?"

"Why would she be?" Guilt suffused her cheeks in a searing blush. Guilt for ever feeling jealous of Megan. Guilt for standing here pretending to be Jessica while she confided in her about *her*.

"Things have been strained between us since Tom's return. If you'd seen her when he asked me to dance…" Biting her lip, she blinked away the sheen of moisture. "What she doesn't know is why he did it."

Jane's heart slowed in her chest. The sounds of wagon wheels rolling over the packed earth, horses' hooves plodding by and townsfolk greeting each other faded to a low hum. Lee was all but forgotten. She couldn't stop the question from forming on her lips. "What do you mean?"

"Just like Jane and Roy, Tom and I have been under scrutiny ever since he came home. Folks have long memories. They're waiting, and maybe hoping, for some tragic scene. He did what he did to show them that we're still friends. That the past is no longer an issue for either of us."

It took every ounce of her self-control not to press for details.

"I'm sure Jane isn't mad at you. But you should really discuss this with her. Not me." She tacked that last part on because it sounded like Jessica.

"You're right." She sighed.

Jane wanted nothing more than to hug Megan right there in the middle of town. But that wasn't something her twin would do.

"I'll talk to you later, okay?" Jane hoped her expression didn't betray her.

"Thanks for listening, Jess. See you soon."

Fingers gripping the ends of her shawl, Jane didn't notice the passersby as Megan walked the other direction. Soon she'd have to have a talk with her older sister. As herself.

With a shaky breath, she pivoted and, pulling her mind to her task, searched the area around the post office for a sign of her target. She went inside, disappointed when she didn't see him. Might as well make this trip look legitimate. While she was standing in line for mail, another customer entered. She twisted and her gaze clashed with Lee's.

For a split second, he looked disconcerted. Then he flashed his bold grin and winked.

I can't do this.

A tremor worked its way up from the soles of her feet. *Think of Jessica. Isn't her safety worth it? Besides, this is your chance to prove to yourself that you can be brave. You can do whatever is necessary to protect her.*

Smiling what she hoped was a cheeky smile, she excused herself and joined him at the back of the line. "Hello, handsome."

His intense blue eyes sparkled. This close, she realized they were quite stunning. When the elderly lady in front of them frowned at Jane, no doubt due to her greeting, he chuckled. His fingers wrapped around her upper arm, and she struggled not to react.

"Hello, beautiful," he murmured very near her ear. "This is a nice surprise."

"I agree." Her smile felt plastered on.

He pointed to the long line. "Unless you're waiting on something important, let's go talk outside. I can come back later."

Perfect suggestion. The quicker she got this over with, the better. Jessica hadn't mentioned plans to come to town, but plans sometimes changed.

Lee guided her into the deserted alley between the post office and bank. She wished he hadn't. Her nerves were already frayed without him isolating her, out of direct sight of pedestrians. This was her first time alone with the man and, forced to deal with him one-on-one, she was belatedly noticing his muscular build and the fact he was a good three inches taller than her.

She'd never seen him angry and prayed she wouldn't. *Please don't let him act too familiar.* There were certain lines she refused to cross.

"I'm actually glad we ran into each other," she rushed out, eager to be done.

"Is that so?"

"I've been thinking how nice it would be to have a picnic."

"I won't turn down a chance to spend time with my girl." He winked.

"Great. Can we have it at your place?"

He hesitated. "My place?"

"Sure. Why not?"

"It's not as orderly as yours or your cousins'. I'm still learning this whole farming thing."

"I don't mind. Please, Lee? I haven't ever been there. I'd like to see where you live."

Folding his arms, he rocked back on his heels. "That's never bothered you before."

Jane tamped down a surge of unease. She couldn't appear too eager. *Think like Jessica.*

Praying he wouldn't detect her shakiness, she ran her fingertips over his thick biceps and smiled up at him. "We've gotten to know each other well these past months, but I feel as if there's more I can learn about you."

He studied her for a long moment. When one corner of his mouth tipped up, she released her pent-up breath.

"Are you looking for an excuse to get me alone, Jessica O'Malley?"

"I—"

Bending at the waist, he brought his face near. Too near. His cologne, too pretentious for her taste, clogged her airway.

"All you had to do was say so, sweetheart. When did you have in mind?"

"Tomorrow?"

"Can't. I'm meeting with a man about a horse I'd like to buy. How about Sunday?"

"No."

His forehead wrinkled at the slightly desperate edge to her response.

"I mean, we have family plans that day." And the real Jessica would be free to discover her perfidy. "How about today?"

He hesitated.

"I'll bring your favorite." As soon as she asked Jessica what that was and somehow got her out of the house.

"Fried chicken?" His smile had a strange twist to it.

"Yes. Fried chicken and all the fixings."

"Then I accept. I'll pick you up."

"No. I, um, will meet you right here at noon." Already

scooting sideways along the notched-log exterior wall, Jane moved toward the boardwalk.

He dipped his head, his blue eyes more piercing than ever before. "See you then."

Tom knew instantly that the woman entering his yard was not Jane.

It wasn't her hairstyle or outfit that set her apart. It was the way she carried herself. Jane comported herself with grace and understated dignity. Jessica, on the other hand, practically oozed confidence.

Long strides carried him to her side. "Is something the matter with Jane?"

Reaching far into the wagon bed for her crate, she tossed him a sidelong glance. "Good afternoon to you, too. I'm fine, thanks. How are you?"

His shoulders bunched. "Jessica."

"She's fine." Rolling her eyes, she slid the crate to him and snagged a second one. "She simply needed a chance to rest. I agreed to come and watch Clara. You don't mind the switch, do you?"

Yes. He did mind. He'd been expecting Jane. The morning hours had dragged, the place too quiet without her humming a tune or practicing letter sounds with Clara.

What did it say about him that he'd missed her when he saw her nearly every day?

"I appreciate the help," he said at last, earning him another speculative look.

When they'd taken her things inside and he was confident Clara would be content to stay with her, he returned to the fields and the backbreaking task of cutting hay. The scythe sliced through the stalks with a soft thwack. Wasn't long before he was drenched in sweat, his back and arm muscles protesting the repetitive movements. As demanding as farm work was most days, he didn't regret his choice to sell the barbershop. The land and livestock demanded a lot from him, both mentally and physically, and he relished the challenge.

He continued to work through the lunch hour, not interested in sharing a meal with Jessica. It wasn't that he didn't like her. He found it strange to be in her presence, though, because she looked exactly like Jane and he was disappointed when she didn't speak and act like her.

Hunger drove him to take a break sometime after two o'clock. Jess and Clara were in the kitchen scarfing down cinnamon cookies when he finally went inside. She didn't ask him any questions, just pointed him to a bowl of vegetable soup and a thick slice of corn bread.

When he'd finished, he announced his intention to visit Jane. Jess contemplated him with eyes that saw too much.

"Take your time. We'll be fine, won't we, sweet pea?"

Clara nodded, still a little in awe of the woman. Tom ducked out of the cabin and hurried to the barn to saddle his mount. By the time he reached her place, he regretted the spontaneous decision. What if she were napping? She'd told Jessica she needed rest.

But he felt responsible. She wouldn't be exhausted to the point of needing a day off if he hadn't pressured her into helping him with Clara.

I'll stay long enough to make sure she's truly all right. Then I'll give her the space she requires.

At his knock, there was no sound inside signifying anyone was home. He tried again, louder this time. When she didn't come to the door, he strode around to the rear and peered in the window. The kitchen was empty.

He didn't know whether or not Jane was a sound sleeper, but he wasn't about to invade her privacy by peeking in her bedroom window. No harm in checking the barn stalls, however. What he discovered confounded him.

A single horse occupied the barn. Jessica's palomino. Jane's horse, Rusty, was gone.

Returning to the cabin, he pounded on the door until it rattled. No way could she not hear that. Turning to scan the terrain, he shook his head. Where could she be? And why wasn't she at home resting as she'd told her sister?

Chapter Eighteen

"**M**mm… This fried chicken is mighty tasty."

Jane wouldn't know. Nothing she'd consumed had registered in her haze of nervousness. Fanning herself with Jessica's black-and-white-striped fan, she said, "I can't take the credit. I was running short on time, so I picked up an order from Plum's."

Lee took stock of the long-sleeved jade blouse she'd snatched from Jessica's wardrobe. Not because it was a good choice for a steamy spring day, but because it hid her bandage.

"You look uncomfortable." After wiping his hands on a cloth napkin, he tucked a stray lock behind her ear, large hand lingering on her neck. "Your skin is flushed."

"I, ah, didn't realize how hot it was going to be." Casually but deliberately moving out of reach, she began to pack up the remaining food "You live quite a ways from town. The isolation doesn't bother you?"

They'd chosen the nicest spot in the yard, a grassy knoll beneath a weeping willow tree, behind which trickled a shallow creek. The cabin stood about twenty steps away. She'd glimpsed multiple outbuildings behind the barn.

She'd seen no sign of the dogs.

"I had my fill of nosy neighbors in Virginia."

"On the other hand, neighbors can help guard against criminals. Town's abuzz with the news of the unidentified man murdered not far from here."

Jane's hopes of getting a reaction were dashed. His lips twisted. "Are you worried about me, Jess?"

Something in his manner set her teeth on edge.

"Not really." Lifting one shoulder, she continued to wave the fan in a lazy back-and-forth motion.

He arched a brow. "No?"

"You know how to take care of yourself."

"That's right. I do."

The glitter in his eyes made her uneasy. "I'll have to be getting home soon. Will you take me on a tour of your property?"

"There's nothing special to see, really. If you've seen one barn, you've seen them all."

Jane bit down on her frustration. How was she supposed to find out if he was engaged in illegal activities if she couldn't look around? He wouldn't have a still here close to the main residence. Most stills were located high up in mountain hollows, hard for revenue agents to find. But there'd likely be other clues.

Lee edged his powerful upper body closer, his manner predator-like. And she certainly felt like prey. "I'd much rather spend the remainder of our time right here with the most beautiful woman in the Smokies."

Suddenly his mouth loomed close. Tom's face flashed in her mind, followed quickly by Jessica's. At the last second, she turned so that his kiss landed on her cheek.

He went still. Jane was certain he could hear her heart thundering against her rib cage, see the guilt written across her face. *He's going to confront me. Right here. Right now.* She had no clear notion of how he might react to her deception.

If he had something to hide, probably not well.

His hand cupped her cheek, the restrained strength in him unsettling. Jessica might trust this man, but Jane didn't. For the hundredth time that day, she wondered what on earth she'd been thinking to go through with such an outrageous plan. This was why she was the practical twin. Impulsiveness usually got a girl into trouble.

"What's the matter?" His thumb scraped over her cheekbone."

"N-nothing."

Lee studied her with an enigmatic expression that didn't so much as hint at his thoughts. Touching the ribbon restraining her hair, he closed his hand over the mass and ran it down the length of it. "Why don't you ever wear your hair up like Jane?"

The question threw her. Licking her dry lips, she said, "It's less time-consuming this way."

Jessica wouldn't ask whether or not he liked it or if he'd rather she fix it another way. So Jane didn't.

"You know, I never imagined I'd be courting a lady with an identical twin sister. Guess it's fortunate for me you two wear your hair differently. I'd hate to get the pair of you mixed up."

Jane swallowed hard. Did he know? Was he playing with her like a cat played with a mouse before pouncing and tearing it to pieces?

"Can I use your outhouse?" she blurted.

Several heartbeats later, his hand fell away. He got smoothly to his feet and helped her up. "I'll have to escort you. My dogs are penned behind the cabin, and they'll go a little crazy if a stranger comes around without me there to reassure them."

This whole outing was a spectacular failure. He wasn't going to give her even a minute alone! They were nearing the cabin, Lee holding her elbow the entire way, when the rumble of an approaching wagon reached them. He stiffened.

"Were you expecting company?" she asked.

"No." He began to stride away. "Wait here."

"I don't think I can." Blushing fiercely, she jerked a thumb toward the corner of the house. "You go greet your guest. I'll stay away from the dog pen, I promise."

A deep frown carved grooves on either side of his mouth. With a sharp nod, he went to intercept the lone man swinging his wagon round near the barn entrance.

Finally. A chance to do some snooping.

Hurrying out of sight, she quickly peered into the cabin's rear windows, not expecting to see anything unusual but checking all the same. The interior looked similar to every other farmer's cabin. As soon as she skirted around the outhouse, the dogs pressed against the enclosure's outer fence, ears flat and canines bared. Her skin pricked with apprehension. They did not look happy.

Praying their chains held, she ignored their warning growls and pushed into the first shed she came to. She blinked to get her bearings in the darkness. Nothing here but the usual tools hanging from nails the length of the walls. Buckets and crates littered the dirt floor.

Outside again, she scanned the remaining structures, dismissing the smokehouse and corncrib outright. That left a second shed and the barn, the latter being the logical place to store crates of the mason jars she'd glimpsed both at the dance and behind the café.

Hesitating, she debated whether or not to search the other shed.

This is what I came for, right? Can't waste this chance.

Bending low, she dashed toward it. The distance seemed endless. Breathless by the time she got there, she had to shove her shoulder against the worn wood several times to get it to budge. The smell hit her with the truth before her sight adjusted to the gloom.

Four large barrels were crammed inside, brimming with fermented corn ready for distillation. Bulging sacks lined the far wall. Maneuvering between the barrels, she looked inside the sacks. They contained cornmeal, which was used to make the mash inside these barrels. Too much for personal use. This was a large-scale operation.

Her heart a heavy weight in her chest, not at all pleased to have her suspicions confirmed, Jane emerged into the bright light. The absence of sound didn't immediately register. When it did, her legs nearly gave out. Where was Lee?

Almost jogging in the direction of the dog pen, where the animals were barking viciously, Jane rounded the far corner of the cabin and crashed into a solid chest.

Hands curved about her upper arms. "Whoa. What's on fire?"

Jane jerked her face up to Lee's. "I got spooked. You were right—those dogs didn't want me around."

"They don't cotton to strangers, that's for sure." Stepping away, he gripped her elbow and guided her in the direction of their abandoned picnic. "I've had some unexpected business come up. I'll escort you home."

"That's not necessary."

Although Jessica would still be at Tom's, and there'd be no chance of discovery, she was more than ready to be away from his disturbing presence.

"I insist." His tone brooked no argument.

Cold seeped into her bones.

While she rid the blanket of crumbs and folded it into a neat square, he readied his wagon. As they were leaving, Lee's visitor emerged from the shadowed barn opening, his watchful gaze pinned on her. Two things stood out about him—striking silver hair that didn't mesh with his unlined, youthful face, and a crescent-shaped scar disappearing into his top lip.

She debated asking Lee about him much of the ride home, ultimately deciding against it. His former good humor had vanished. His silence had a brooding edge, and she didn't know him well enough to try and guess the reasons behind it.

Relief cascaded over her when her cabin came into view. Soon she'd be safe inside.

Of course he wouldn't allow her to make her own way to her door. His hold on her was unrelenting.

What if he tries to kiss me again? He'd expect Jess to eagerly welcome such displays of affection.

On the porch, she turned to him with a strained smile. "Thank you for today. I'll see you Sunday morning."

"Thank you for gifting me with your presence. In hindsight, I should've invited you to my home long ago. We'll do it again very soon."

Blue eyes glittering, he dipped his head and brushed his lips across her cheek. It took a will of iron not to flinch.

"Until next time, my dear." With a brief tug on his hat brim, he left her on the porch.

Legs like jelly, Jane hugged the post for support, remaining there until his wagon turned onto the lane and the forest swallowed him up.

A pair of boots hitting the floorboards behind her made her jump. Gasping, she spun around and would've fallen had she not grasped the rail behind her.

"Tom! Wh-what are you doing here?"

He knew. Somehow, he knew what she'd been up to. And he was livid.

He stalked closer, fury radiating from him in waves. Jaw like granite, the skin across his chiseled cheekbones stretched taut, his eyes burned emerald fire.

Unease skittered along her spine. In all her years of knowing him, not once had she seen him like this.

"What am I doing here?" His lips thinned. "I was worried when Jess showed up instead of you. Feeling responsible for your *exhaustion*, I came to check on you. Imagine my surprise when I arrived to find you gone."

"I—"

"Just answer me this—what were you doing with Lee? And why were you pretending to be your sister?"

Chapter Nineteen

Due to the disbelief and anger clouding his judgment, Tom didn't at first register the alarm flickering in her eyes. All he could focus on was the image of Lee's hands on Jane. Of him kissing her…

Teeth grinding together, he rolled his shoulders to try and unknot the muscles. Using a tree for cover, he'd observed the pair, his tension intensifying with each passing minute.

"Kindly explain what you were doing with Jessica's beau."

The smattering of tiny freckles stood out in stark relief to her milk-white skin. Arms crossing to shield her body, her lashes lowered to skim her cheeks. "I had a good reason."

"Tell me." He started forward, and she flinched. That was when he realized he needed to calm down. She'd never seen him lose his composure. What would she have thought if she'd seen him and Charles fighting?

"Look at me, Jane."

She did, albeit reluctantly. "I know this looks bad."

He worked to gentle his tone. "So tell me the truth."

Somewhere beneath the roiling emotions lay a deep well of hurt. He hadn't thought her capable of deception.

"The night of the barn dance, I saw Lee slip away from the festivities and sell someone what looked to be a jar of alcohol."

Jane haltingly related the sequence of events leading up to her decision to impersonate her twin. Tom could scarcely believe what she'd done.

"You mentioned a man with silver hair. He saw you?"

"Yes."

Groaning in frustration, Tom buried his fingers in his hair.

"Lee will tell him who I am. Or rather, who Jessica is. I—I don't think there's cause to worry."

"You put yourself in grave danger, you know that?" Pacing before her, he threw up his hands. "If Lee *is* involved in bootlegging, and he discovered what you were up to—" He broke off, unwilling to entertain the possibilities. "We don't know how he or his business associates might react to meddlers. Something tells me they'd go to great lengths to protect their interests."

Twin red flags seared her cheeks as determination settled across her features. "He didn't. And to be clear, I'd do it again if it meant protecting Jess."

"You could've come to me or any one of your cousins. We could've handled this the right way. The safe way."

How could she be so sensible about everything else and yet so reckless in this one area? She and Jessica shared a unique bond. Perhaps it was that deep connection that had spawned Jane's uncharacteristic behavior.

"You know what happens to snitches," she said. "Going to the authorities carries immense risks."

"A bigger risk than you out there alone? If you'd been

discovered, no one would've known you were in trouble. I wouldn't have been able to help you."

The image of Lee and Jane standing close together on this porch not twenty minutes ago sent a shudder through his body. He didn't know how Lee might've punished Jane for her snooping.

Apparently no longer intimidated by his foul mood, she approached and lightly touched his wrist. "I'm fine."

In a flash, he'd captured her hand and drew her close. "I saw him kiss you, Jane."

He caught sight of her grimace before she bowed her head. Dark emotion surged. Caging it, he tipped her chin so that his gaze was free to roam her upturned face. "Did he do more than what I saw? Back at his house, when you were alone with him?"

Her lips parted. *Please say no*, he silently begged. Jessica wouldn't be the only one to feel betrayed. No matter that he had no claim on Jane, it would kill him to know she'd accepted another man's advances.

"I'm surprised you have to ask. I wouldn't have let that happen—wouldn't have hurt her like that."

"I never thought I'd doubt you, Jane." It hurt to admit. Hurt to see the resulting dismay crumpling her features. "You deliberately maneuvered the both of us in order for you to assume her identity."

"I did it to protect her!" Fingers digging into his upper arms, she beseeched him. "You know how stubborn she is. Going to her with my suspicions wouldn't have been enough. I may not have seen the actual still, but the items in that shed are exactly what's used to make moonshine. I can go to her with reasonable proof now. She'll have to accept Lee isn't who he's portrayed himself to be."

He exhaled slowly. "I wish you'd gone about this differently."

"It wasn't the wisest plan. For once in my life, I just…" Lips pursing, she shook her head.

"You what?"

"I wanted to be the brave one."

Her voice was barely audible, but he heard more than what she was saying. He heard the wistfulness, the wish to be more than what she was.

Lightly massaging her shoulders, he rested his forehead against hers. "You *are* brave, Janie girl. Everyone else can see it in you. Why can't you?"

"I'm sorry I deceived you," she whispered. "And I'm sorry I d-disappointed you."

He closed his eyes tight. More than anything, he yearned to be close to her. To feel her respond to him, to show her what he was feeling. But that would only confuse them both.

Lifting his head a fraction to peer into her sad eyes, he said, "The thing about friends is this—they fight sometimes. They don't always see eye to eye on things. That doesn't mean they don't still care about each other."

Worrying her lower lip, she nodded. "I won't violate your trust again. I promise."

Unable to resist caressing her cheek, he gave her a small smile. "I believe you."

A shaky sigh escaped. "I would never willingly hurt you."

"You love your sister, and you want what's best for her. I can relate."

"I dread telling her. I wish I hadn't found anything. She's going to be devastated."

"Irate, too, I imagine," he drawled.

"That, too."

Gold glinted around her neck, and Tom went numb.

Extending a finger, he tapped the cross pendant visible atop the first button of her blouse. "Did Lee see this?"

Understanding dawned, and she clutched her throat. "I'm not sure. I forgot to remove it."

"Promise me you'll stay far away from him until we sort through everything."

"That's one promise I don't mind making."

Jane did not immediately confess.

Before returning home, Tom had promised not to breathe a word, agreeing that Jessica should hear the news from her. But she'd been unprepared for the sting of her guilty conscience, had found it impossible to utter the necessary words in the face of Jessica's concern. Her sister had arrived home about an hour after Tom's departure, eager to check on her and surprisingly upbeat about her afternoon with Clara. She'd even teased Jane about Tom's obvious devotion.

Having sought refuge in the barn once they cleaned up the supper mess, she sat on a hay square cradling one of their rabbits in her lap and stroking its downy fur in a rhythmic motion. The familiar sounds of the animals bedding down for the night, the pungent odor of fresh hay mingling with the dust motes in the still air, did little to soothe her troubled spirit.

She would never forget Tom's look of utter disappointment. His suspicion had been hard to handle, but the disappointment...that was another story altogether. She felt as if she'd failed him. And, while he'd said he believed she wouldn't repeat her actions, deep down Jane wondered if he'd ever fully trust her again.

Her head sagged against the wall. *I messed up, Lord.*

Just like with Roy, I didn't seek Your guidance in this. I may have had Jessica's best interests at heart, but I also wanted to prove I could be bold like her. I'm not sure if she'll forgive me for what I've done.

Jane prayed to the God who'd created her, who knew her better than she knew herself. The friend who would never forsake her. She asked for strength for both her and Jess. They'd certainly need it in the coming days.

When she finally opened her eyes, she nearly suffered an apoplectic seizure.

Not three feet away stood Lee, menacing in head-to-toe black, his black hair windswept and gaze hooded as he stared down at her.

"Good evening, Jane." He cocked his head. "Or it is Jessica?"

Her hold tightened a fraction on the poor animal in her grasp, and it wriggled in protest. Fear glued her lips together.

"The dress you had on earlier belongs to Jessica. And the ponytail is hers, too."

He bent at the waist, hands outstretched, and she flattened herself against the wall. One sardonic brow inching upward, he plucked the now trembling rabbit from her. A protest half formed on her lips.

"Jessica isn't the nervous sort, though, is she?" He addressed the animal, which looked incredibly vulnerable in his large hands.

"How did you guess?" she pushed out, fingers digging into the logs at her back, unheeding of the splinters. Inside her chest, her heart flailed wildly about.

"For one thing, fried chicken is not my favorite," he replied dryly.

"Oh."

Tucking the rabbit to his chest, he mimicked her movements from before. He wouldn't hurt it, would he?

"For another—" he leveled a dark stare at her "—Jess doesn't shrink from my touch."

Jane couldn't suppress a shiver. "I suppose you'd like an explanation."

His fingers stilled. "Like? Oh, no, my dear Jane, I demand one."

Scraping up her courage, she staggered to her feet. "Let me put him away first."

"Not yet." He stepped away. "Not until I get what I came for."

"Fine. I saw you the night of the dance. And the other day, behind Plum's."

His carved features turned forbidding. "And?"

"And I decided to investigate. I should tell you that I saw what was in your shed…all the makings of home-made moonshine." Anger at *his* deception and how it would affect Jessica fueled her candor. "You've a still somewhere on your property, I'm sure of it, and you're selling your wares to the locals."

"I see." Lee surprised her by returning the rabbit to its hutch. A part of her wished he hadn't, because now his hands were free to strangle her if he chose to. He looked as if he'd like to do just that. "May I ask what you plan on doing with this information?"

"I'm going to tell Jessica, of course."

"You probably don't believe me, but I care for her. More than I'm willing to reveal to you before speaking to her." His earnest manner took her by surprise.

"If you cared for her, you'd free her to be with a man she can respect and trust. Our great-uncle ran an illegal still. Made life for our great-aunt extremely difficult. Every time he was out making 'shine, she'd have to stand watch in order to warn him of approaching visitors. Everyone, including family members, became the focus of their suspicion. Possible informers. It's not a life I want for my sister."

"I'm not planning on doing this forever. Just long enough to ensure our future. One worthy of her."

"Jess has never been one to aspire to riches. Once she learns of your involvement, she'll want nothing more to do with you."

"You won't tell her or anyone else." He erased the space between them. "You remember my friend from today? He's not as civilized as I am, and he doesn't take kindly to snoops."

"He can't hurt me if he's behind bars."

"This thing is bigger than us, Jane," he scoffed. "Way beyond Gatlinburg. He and I have people we answer to. Don't think they won't retaliate in the worst way if you do this."

She couldn't refute his statement. "That man who was killed. Did you know him?"

"The less I say about that, the better."

Disquiet gripped her. Lee might not have known the victim personally, but his response told her the crime was somehow connected to their business.

His hands came down on her shoulders, and she yelped.

"Heed my advice, Jane. Keep what you've learned to yourself, and no one gets hurt."

Pivoting away, he swept out of the barn and disappeared into the night, leaving her with an impossible decision to make.

Chapter Twenty

❧

"Please say you'll accept my invitation, Tom. We have lots to catch up on."

Patricia Vinson had cornered him at the base of the church steps right after service. Willowy and blessed with golden-haired beauty, she did nothing to hide her interest. Quite the opposite. She stood so close he could practically see down her throat each time she laughed. She did that a lot—laughed at nothing in particular.

Tucking his hands behind his back to avoid more of her "accidental" grazes, he strove for a regretful tone. "Thanks for thinking of me, Patricia, but I can't today. I have other plans."

At least, he hoped so. The idea to invite Jane to lunch had popped into his head during the ride to town. He couldn't stop replaying Friday's conversation. Now that he'd had time to assess matters rationally, he was aware he'd come down on her too hard.

Scanning the churchyard, he spotted her in the shade of a dogwood tree. She was alone. And watching him and Patricia with pinched features.

When the blonde's cool palm cupped his cheek, urging him to return his attention to her, he fought a surge of annoyance. The woman was far too forward.

"How about next Sunday?" she said. "I'll prepare whatever you'd like."

Removing her hand, he tried to be civil. "I don't think so. I spend most of my Sundays with the O'Malleys. Thanks, anyway."

With that, he left her to make his way through the dispersing crowd to Jane's side, checking first to make sure Clara was still with her friends beside the building.

Jane's appearance concerned him. Normally neat as a pin, there was a crease in the bodice of her butter-colored dress and her cameo brooch was pinned on crooked. Most disturbing was her hair. Like the day of her nonwedding, the shiny locks streamed down her back and curved over her shoulders, not a pin or ribbon in sight. Most unusual.

When he reached her, he noted the dark circles under her eyes. "Jane. Are you okay?"

Hands clasped tightly at her waist, she nodded jerkily. "We need to talk."

"I agree. Will you join Clara and me for lunch? It's nothing fancy, mind you—"

"No."

"You have plans?"

"No, I—I just can't." Her gaze darted around the yard to where folks were preparing to leave. "Listen, I've come to the conclusion that there's no reason to mention my charade to Jessica. I was no doubt mistaken about what I saw."

Tom wasn't stupid. He might not be an expert on women, but he wasn't blind. Something had occurred between Friday afternoon and today to make her change her mind. Something had spooked her, and he intended on discovering what that was.

"Are you afraid to face Jess's wrath? I will gladly be there to offer support when you tell her, if that's what you want."

Her chin came up. "I'd own up to my actions in a heartbeat if I thought it would accomplish anything. But it won't. Let's just forget it."

She made to brush past him. He curved a hand about her upper arm, halting her escape.

"Let me go, Tom."

Her eyes were huge in her face. The pleading in her tone knocked him for a loop. There was more to this than mere reluctance to admit to poor choices.

"What happens if Lee mentions the picnic Jessica never went on?"

She went as white as a sheet. "I suppose I'll deal with that when and if it happens. Hopefully it won't."

Concern and frustration at equal levels, Tom was tempted to toss her over his shoulder, whisk her away to a remote location and refuse to take her home until she told him the truth.

She stiffened in his hold. He followed her line of sight to the church entrance, where Jessica and Lee were shaking hands with the reverend.

Prying his fingers loose, Jane didn't look at him as she sidled away. "I'll see you in the morning."

Returning his attention to the couple, he was unprepared for the blistering heat that pooled in his gut. Lee's bright smile had vanished, his brooding focus on Jane's retreating form. Jessica couldn't see it as she was still conversing with the reverend. But Tom could.

Mystery solved.

Collecting Clara, he rode out to Sam and Mary

O'Malley's farm. Josh, holding a sleepy Victoria, was about to enter the main house when he arrived. Spying Tom, he transferred his daughter to Kate's arms.

Tom set the brake. "Got a minute?"

"I've got as much time as you need." Josh rounded the wagon and waited for him to descend. He glanced at Clara. "Would you like Kate to take her inside? Food's likely already on the table."

"That would probably be best."

With a wide smile, Kate beckoned and ushered her inside. As soon as the door closed behind them, Josh gestured to the orchard. "Walk with me."

He fell into step beside his old friend and tried to decide the best place to start. He supposed the logical point was the dance. As he related the sequence of events, the other man's scowl deepened the closer they got to the orderly rows of apple trees.

"I don't know what Jane was thinking." Ripping his Stetson from his head, Josh whacked it against his thigh. "We have to get Jessica away from him."

"That won't be easy." Tom stopped short, taking no notice of the branches poking into his shoulder blades. Fingernails biting into his palms, he struggled to maintain his equanimity. The object of his ire wasn't around to release it on. "Lee discovered Jane's pretense and coerced her into keeping his secret."

"She told you that?"

"Didn't have to." Her pale, strained countenance flashed in his memory. "She was rattled. I'm going to talk to her. Based on Jessica's upbeat manner today, Jane hasn't confessed yet."

"If Jane refuses, I'll talk to Jess myself. She can't remain with him."

His voice was tight with displeasure.

"Agreed." Tom said. "Are you interested in joining me in a bit of surveillance?"

"I most certainly am. Lee Cavanaugh will be made to pay for what he's put my cousins through."

Jane's pencil scraped across the page, not fast enough to keep up with the words bursting to break free. Jessica hadn't questioned her desire to slip away for a couple of hours. There was nothing unusual about a solitary sojourn in the woods behind their home. What was unusual was the Colt Cloverleaf revolver strapped to her calf. Lee's warning still fresh in her mind, she hadn't felt comfortable coming out here without protection.

One more thing her sister wasn't aware of.

Engrossed in her writing, she didn't immediately register Tom's presence. Who knew how long he'd been standing there before he nudged her boot with his.

"Hey there."

Her pencil slid from her grasp and toppled into the clover. "Hi."

Normally, the sight of his handsome face lifted her spirits. Not this time. Not now that she was deceiving him again, something she'd promised never to do.

Better to lie to him than to put him or Clara in danger.

Sinking onto the boulder jutting over the rippling, crystalline stream behind him, he pointed to the book on her lap. "How many of those have you filled up?"

"I haven't counted."

She hadn't tossed a single one, however. They were stored in the hayloft. Three trunks full. Jane liked to think of her future children and grandchildren reading them some day after she'd gone...an intimate glimpse into her ordinary life.

"Did you pen an account of Lee's clandestine visit in there?"

His unwavering scrutiny, while free of accusation, demanded the truth.

Skirting that truth did not come easy. "I'm not sure I know what you're talking about."

"You underestimate me, Jane. Fail to acknowledge how well I know you." Movements fluid for such a tall man, he was soon sitting beside her on the mossy bed, his muscular leg pressing against hers and upper body angled toward her.

"You don't know everything about me."

"I know you'd go to any lengths necessary to safeguard the ones you love." His voice deepened. "When did he confront you?"

Averting her face, she belatedly closed the book and stuffed it in her satchel.

"Ignoring me won't make me go away," he said without heat. "I'll keep you here until nightfall if need be."

He meant what he said. She could see it in the unyielding line of his jaw, the determined set of his chin.

"Why can't you accept that I was mistaken?" she demanded.

Lifting his hand, he very gently smoothed his thumb over her trembling lips. Jane sat immobile, dread and fascination warring with each other. If only she could snap her fingers and wish away her problems, then she could sit here and bask in his closeness, let his soft-as-velvet voice wrap her in a cocoon of safety.

"You're frightened." Taking in her unbound hair, he smoothed a section of it over her shoulder. "Anyone can see you aren't yourself."

The tender caress was her undoing. She'd slept very little in the nearly forty-eight hours since Lee's visit.

Light-headed from lack of sleep and appetite, she'd barely made it to church that morning. Dread of seeing Lee, combined with the prospect of lying to the man she loved, had left her feeling weak and sick to her stomach.

She was not cut out for subterfuge.

"I caught him watching you this morning. When did he figure it out?"

"I—" The words clogged in her throat. "I never should've started this. How stupid could I be to think I could pull this off? I'm not a professional. He is. He's had everyone fooled, my sister most of all. What am I going to do, Tom?"

She glimpsed his frown a second before he pulled her against his chest, arms holding her fast. She resisted at first. What had she done to deserve his compassion? Nothing but lie to him. But his reassuring heat and latent strength, the rhythmic movements of his fingers through her hair, had her surrendering to his ministrations.

"I don't want you to worry." His breath stirred the strands near her ear. "We'll figure this out."

Beneath her cheek, his heart beat slow and steady. "He's dangerous, Tom." Plucking at his sleeve, she spoke quietly. "He said that turning him and his associate in wouldn't accomplish much. Others in their organization will take their place. Unscrupulous men who will repay our actions."

He left off stroking her hair to rub circles on her lower back. "Josh and I have a plan."

Pushing upward, but not leaving his embrace, she met his intense perusal. "He knows?"

"When I saw Lee's reaction to you today, I knew he'd figured out what you'd done. Because the danger involves our family, Josh and I are going to gather a bit more information before going to the sheriff." He stopped, brows knitting in confusion. "Why are you smiling? Not that I'm complaining, mind you. I happen to adore your smile. Just not sure what I said to earn it."

"You said *our* family."

His mouth tipped up in a rueful grin. "Yeah, I guess I did." He tucked her closer. "I do consider myself a part of the O'Malley clan. You, your sisters and cousins mean the world to me."

Family. Friend. It was the most she could hope for. Tom would never discover her biggest lie of all.

"I—"

"Jane? Are you here..." Emerging from the underbrush, Jessica stopped short, eyes going wide at the sight of them. "Oh, I'm sorry."

Jane reluctantly pulled out of his arms. He seemed equally loath to release her.

Lithely gaining his footing, he helped her up, surprising her when he briefly cupped her cheek. "I believe you and your sister have some important things to discuss. Want me to stay?"

"Thank you, but no."

"I'll wait for you at your house."

Mouth going dry, she nodded. "Okay."

He left the way her sister had come.

Jessica picked her way over exposed roots, her brows quirked, the set of her mouth a tad smug. "I seemed to have interrupted something. What's going on, Jane?"

"We have to talk. And you're not going to like what I have to say."

"About you and Tom?"

"This has nothing to do with us. It's about Lee."

Chapter Twenty-One

"I don't believe you."

The ache inside Jane grew as she watched her twin grapple with what she'd told her. Perched at the tree base, she hugged her knees to her chest as Jessica paced in fits and starts along the bank, her anguish like a roiling black cloud hovering over her.

"Lee is loyal, hardworking and trustworthy. I would know it if the man was a liar and a criminal. I would know it in here." She thumped her chest, eyes blazing.

"I know this isn't easy to accept—" Jane ventured.

"There's nothing to accept! You're wrong. You've misconstrued things." Stomping over, she jammed a finger at her. "You're jealous of what Lee and I have. You've pined for Tom Leighton half your life, and since you can't have the man you love, you set out to destroy my happiness."

"That's not true." The outrageous accusation stung. "You don't know me if you think I'd do something that low. I was trying to protect you, Jess! Bootlegging is a serious offense. If the regulators are called in and they think you've been protecting him, you could be charged with a crime."

"I *thought* I knew you." The pain and betrayal twisting her features was like a dagger plunging into Jane's heart. "I still can't fathom that you pretended to be me. How would you feel if I did that with Tom?"

"Like clawing your eyes out." Shoving to her feet, she held her arms out at her sides. "So go ahead. Have at it. I deserve whatever you mete out."

Her lip curled. "I'm not going to hurt you."

Jane's shoulders drooped. This rift, the one *she* had created, was killing her. They'd had their share of arguments and petty disagreements, but this had driven a wedge between them she wasn't sure could ever be healed.

"I'm sorry, Jess. So very sorry. When I saw Lee's activities first at the dance, and later at the café, all I could think about was you. I had to find out."

"I won't believe it until I've heard it from Lee's mouth."

Jane gripped Jessica's elbows. "You can't tell him you know. He warned me not to say anything."

"I'm not leaving him. I love him."

The vulnerable light in Jess's eyes ate at her. "For what it's worth, I believe he truly cares about you."

Throat working, Jess wrenched free and presented Jane with her back. "Your secret is safe. For now. But I won't stay quiet forever."

"Jane? Are you listening?"

A hand passed in front of her face, and she shifted her focus from the little girls playing pretend tea party in the parlor across the hall to Caroline's slightly irritated visage.

"I'm sorry. What were you saying?"

"I was asking when you'd like to get started on the

decorations. We've a lot to accomplish before the celebration."

China clinked amid the female-dominated conversation in Caroline's parents' home. One of the largest in Gatlinburg, it was used for numerous gatherings, the Independence Day planning committee being one of them. Jane and Jessica had taken part for three years now.

At the thought of her twin, Jane's stomach did that uncomfortable tightening thing again.

"We can work in the evenings and on Saturdays until I leave for my aunt's."

Caroline worried her lip, blue eyes clouding. "I wish you weren't going. It's all because of *him*."

Her friend hadn't been thrilled about Tom's return and even less thrilled when Jane had agreed to watch Clara.

"A change of scenery will do me good."

"Not a permanent one, right?" She caught her hand. "I couldn't stand it if you left for good."

Jane's response was interrupted by Caroline's mother, Louise. An elegant, reserved woman who was involved in many of the town's activities, she and her daughter had a strained relationship.

"Jane, dear. Where is Jessica? I'd assumed she would be helping to coordinate the games again this year."

She squeezed the dainty cup between her hands. "She couldn't make it today, but I'm certain she plans to help."

Louise patted her shoulder. "Glad to hear it. Tell her to come and see me at her earliest convenience."

"I will."

She wasn't sure if her twin would give her an opportunity to speak. Jessica had frozen her out, had refused to even listen to her these past few days.

You have only yourself to blame for that, an inner voice prodded.

"Caroline, you should've worn the lavender dress as I suggested. That drab color doesn't complement your skin," Louise said.

She bristled. "I happen to like this color, Mother."

The woman's mouth pursed in displeasure. Jane knew if guests hadn't been within earshot, she would've launched into a lengthy speech about respecting one's parents. She commiserated with her friend, wished things were different.

As Louise was gliding away, the doorbell buzzed, and she changed direction.

"No matter what I do, she's never happy." She rolled her eyes.

"Enough about me. Are you and your sis having a spat? I noticed she didn't look your way once at church the other day."

"Know why you're such a dear friend, Car?"

Her fine blond brows wrinkled. "Why?"

"Because you know me so well. And because you respect my frequent need for privacy."

"So there is something going on, but you don't wish to speak about it."

"Precisely."

"That is an irritating trait in a friend, you know that?" She sighed dramatically.

Jane smiled, grateful for her understanding. "You could come with me to Maryville, you know. Aunt Althea wouldn't mind."

"Mother would never agree. You know how she is… I can't go to the mercantile alone without her dictating my every move."

Louise's heels clacked on the floor, signaling her return. "Jane, you have a visitor. Mr. Leighton is waiting for you on the porch."

Caroline's mouth compressed. "Go ahead. I'll keep an eye on Clara."

Tossing her a grateful look, Jane deposited her cup on the credenza and hurried outside. Tom pivoted at her approach, black Stetson clenched in his hands. A black kerchief hung about his neck, and his midnight-blue shirt was rolled up at the sleeves.

"I apologize for interrupting."

"Has something happened?"

"I received a letter." Voice sounding odd, he lifted a wrinkled envelope. "It's from my brother."

Sinking onto the porch swing, she gripped the chain connecting it to the ceiling. His features were carefully controlled. His eyes were another story.

"He says he's finally come to his senses and that he's ready to be a father to Clara."

"Does he expect you to return to Kansas?"

"He's coming here. What he'll decide to do after that is anyone's guess."

The metal chain bit into her palm. "I can't fathom what you're feeling right now."

Guilt flashed. "I want to believe he's changed." Tread heavy, he joined her, the wood creaking under his added weight. "What if seeing his daughter resurrects his grief, and he can't handle it? What if he fails her again?"

Jane covered his hand, throat thickening at the thought of them suffering. *Please, God, spare them that.* "Then you'll be there to help her. Just like you've always been."

"I'm her uncle, not her father," he said at last, defeat and confusion darkening his eyes. "I'm not supposed to feel as if Charles is intruding on my family."

"Tom, listen to me." She gave his hand a little shake. "You've been her substitute father for a long time. You moved her back here with the intention of raising her all on your own. It's only natural for you to feel that way."

"I *want* to trust him."

"You have reason not to. Perhaps it would be wise not to let him take Clara anywhere until he's proven to you he's capable of being the father she needs. He owes you that much."

Jane's own reservations were rising to the surface. Charles couldn't take Clara away. Tom wouldn't be the only one crushed.

The door opened, and Clara rushed over. "Uncle Tom! Marianne stole my doll and won't give it back." Tears pooling in her eyes, she looked at him, fully expecting him to fix her problem.

Her chest constricted. How would Tom cope if Charles took her away? How would Jane?

Caroline appeared in the doorway. "I tried to stop her, but she was insistent on seeing you."

"It's all right." Tom waved off her apology and tucked the letter in his pocket.

The blonde shot Jane a piercing look before going inside.

Thumbing away Clara's tears, he said softly, "Did you ask her to give it back?"

She nodded vigorously, dark ringlets bobbing. "Three times." She tried to arrange her short fingers to show the number but couldn't quite manage. "She still didn't."

"How about we go and talk to Marianne? I'm sure if we explain how important your doll is to you, she'll understand why you're so upset."

She looked doubtful. "Okay."

Tom turned his head to look at Jane. "If you're finished here, we could go the mercantile together. Your sister has completed the last of Clara's wardrobe."

Aware he shouldn't be alone right now, and eager to support him in any way he'd allow, she stood and smoothed her skirts. "I'd like that."

His obvious relief told her she'd done the right thing. After righting the situation with Clara's friend and bidding Louise and Caroline goodbye, they loaded into the wagon and set off for town. The adults remained attentive to Clara's account of her afternoon. While they commented in all the right places, Jane was certain Tom was as preoccupied as she.

When he'd parked the conveyance by the boardwalk and assisted them down, Clara skipped ahead, no doubt excited to see her new clothes as well as the mercantile's assorted goods.

Jane walked close beside him. "How long until…"

"I'm not sure. Possibly a week or two, if I've calculated the dates on his letter right."

She might not be here. From the moment of Tom's return, he'd comforted her through Roy's betrayal, supported her during this fiasco with Lee. He'd been a true friend. Her entire being rebelled at the thought of abandoning him in his time of need.

Inside the bustling store, Nicole spotted them at once. She rounded the counter and, after greeting Tom and Jane, bestowed a bright smile on Clara. "I've something for you, Miss Clara. Want me to show you?"

She looked to Tom for his decision, smiling when he nodded.

"We'll be in my shop." Taking her hand, Nicole led her into the hallway connecting the mercantile with the office, storeroom and her seamstress shop in the rear.

At the sound of raised voices behind them, Tom placed his hand against Jane's back and edged closer to her.

"What's going on?" she said.

"No idea."

In front of the wall where town notices were posted, Quinn was attempting to placate the group of onlookers. "I don't know the details, ladies and gentlemen. Please take your questions to Sheriff Timmons."

Working his way through the curious patrons, Quinn's frown grew more pronounced as he neared.

"What's all the fuss about?" Tom said.

"Jed Hamilton was found dead early this morning, sprawled in the middle of Main."

Dread settled like a weight in Jane's midsection. Jed wasn't known for being sober.

"Do they know how he died?"

"Timmons is of the opinion he was run down. They found a half-consumed jar of moonshine next to his body. There's talk of bringing in federal agents."

Her insides turned to stone. As if he sensed her unease, Tom curved his fingers about her side. No wonder the townsfolk were up in arms. Revenuers meant serious trouble. Not everyone in Gatlinburg and the surrounding areas shared the same views on home distilleries. Some families considered it an inherent and important part of their heritage and culture. Others argued the money they made allowed them to pay their property taxes and support local businesses. Still others were completely against it, citing the ills of alcohol.

"Has Timmons officially decided to bring them in?"

"I honestly don't know. He's being tight-lipped about the whole situation." He gestured to the counter and the line of customers. "I've got to go."

Tom maneuvered her to an empty corner. "We have to talk to the sheriff."

The prospect of repercussions frightened her. "Shouldn't we wait? You and Josh have been monitoring Lee's place and haven't seen anything incriminating."

"You don't call frequent visitors incriminating? Outsiders who have no legitimate business in town?" He kept his voice low. "And what about the mash barrels in his shed?"

"Nothing good will come of this."

"I know you're in a difficult position right now—"

"Jessica despises me," she whispered hotly.

"She may be hurt and angry, but she still loves you." His mouth softened. "What would you rather have happen? Shane Timmons investigating Lee's activities? Or total strangers—government agents—bent on wiping out tax defrauders?"

"I guess there's nothing I can do at this point to make her hate me more."

Chapter Twenty-Two

~~❦~~

He couldn't get Charles's words out of his head.

I'm ready to make things right between us and provide the life Jenny would want for our daughter.

Tom was grateful his brother had at long last gotten a handle on his grief. His apology, while sincere, was just words on paper. They couldn't begin to make up for his poor decisions. His neglect. And ultimately, his abandonment.

He needed to see his brother in the flesh. See his eyes, his expression, his mannerisms when he apologized.

Surrounded by sewing machines, spools of thread and needles, and frilly things that made him uncomfortable, Tom crouched to Clara's level.

"Jane and I have business to tend to here in town. Miss Nicole is going to keep you company until we return."

She looked past his shoulder to where the sisters conversed in the hallway. "I like her. She's nice. Like Jane."

"They are both very nice," he agreed.

When he'd arrived at the post office and recognized the slanted scrawl on the envelope Mr. Ledbetter placed in his hand, his first instinct had been to find Jane. He'd craved her comforting presence and sound advice. Hadn't thought twice about barging in on the planning committee's meeting. He'd had to get to her.

His brother's impending arrival wasn't the only thing troubling him.

Jane's trip was drawing nearer. His attempts to get a clear understanding of how long her visit would be had failed. She insisted she hadn't decided. And now that she and Jessica were at odds, he feared she would delay her return.

He had no idea how he was going to cope with his brother's homecoming and all that might entail without her.

"You look sad, Uncle Tom."

He blinked. "I do?"

"Uh-huh."

His niece had inherited traits from both parents. Green eyes like Charles's, which were also identical to his own. Chin and nose like Jenny's. Such a pretty child. More importantly, she'd been blessed with the same kind spirit her ma had possessed.

Lord Jesus, I was finally getting used to this whole fatherhood thing. I don't know what I'll do if Charles decides to take her back to Kansas.

There was more, so much more on his heart. Fortunately for him, he didn't have to utter every single thought and emotion. The Lord saw into the depths of his soul and understood without him having to explain.

Clara braced herself against his shoulder and popped forward to buss him on the cheek.

"What was that for?" He looked at her, bemused.

"To make you feel better."

A reluctant smile broke through. "It's working."

"Candy works, too."

At the impish dimple gracing her cheek, he chuckled and tapped her chin. "If you're really good, Miss Nicole might give you a piece."

Pushing upward, he turned and addressed Jane. "Ready?"

"I suppose."

Despite her misgivings, she looked composed. Determined. That was his Jane. She didn't hide from responsibility, didn't postpone unpleasant tasks. She did what needed doing without thought to her own well-being.

Since his return, his admiration for her had grown by leaps and bounds, deepening to such a degree he found himself wondering if what he felt for her was more than mere friendship.

The notion was a disturbing one. Even if she were receptive to his suit, she'd never accept that he could care for her. In her mind, Megan was his ideal woman. Anyone else would be a poor substitute. Stubborn as she was, he wasn't sure he'd ever rid her of the conviction.

Pushing those thoughts aside, he offered his arm and led her through the mercantile and onto the noisy boardwalk. Folks hurried to the bank and post office. A few men gathered outside the livery, pipes dangling from their mouths. A young lady emerged from Josh and Kate's business, a wrapped parcel that looked to be a framed photograph held protectively to her chest.

When they'd traversed the dense traffic on the street, he stopped with his hand on the jail door. "I can speak to him alone, if you'd prefer."

Peeling away a flame-colored strand from her cheek, Jane squared her shoulders. "No. I can do this."

He allowed her to precede him into the jail's front room, a tight space big enough to house Shane's desk and a couple of hard-backed chairs. Stationed behind his desk, the sheriff's rugged features were inscrutable as a group of men blasted him with questions regarding Jed Hamilton's death and his plans for involving the federal government.

Tom didn't envy him his job. Shane would be forced to walk a precarious line with this bootlegging business.

He held up a hand for silence. "There are a lot of unanswered questions surrounding Jed's death. My deputy and I will be putting all our energy into solving what happened. As for bringing in federal agents, I haven't made a decision about that yet."

The men tried to talk over each other in an effort to voice their opinions. Tom and Jane remained close to the exit. Shane put a finger to his lips, and a piercing whistle bounced off the walls.

"Enough," he barked. "I'm aware of the arguments against bringing in outsiders, and I'll take them into consideration. For now, you need to go on about your business and let me do my job."

Grumbling, the men shuffled out, many of them remaining on the boardwalk outside the jail. Shane sighed and lowered his large frame onto his chair.

"What can I do for you folks?"

Waiting until Jane had seated herself, Tom followed suit, propping his hat on his bent knee.

"We've got some information that might aid your investigation."

Shane leaned forward and propped his arms on the desk, interest flaring. "Not exactly what I expected you to say." Glancing from one to the other, he said, "I didn't realize you were acquainted with Jed Hamilton."

"We weren't. But we know where he likely got that moonshine." Jane threw Tom a desperate look. Reaching over, he threaded his fingers through hers, meeting Shane's pointed glance without flinching. He was offering her nothing more than friendly support. That's what he'd tell Josh if the sheriff decided to mention it.

But would it be true?

He scraped his thumb over her knuckles. "Start from the beginning."

With a jerky nod, she explained everything she'd seen and done.

"You impersonated your sister?" Shane's usual reserve fell away, jaw dropping. "I'm impressed."

At Tom's glare, he backtracked. "Not the wisest course of action, of course, but that took courage." Propping his arms on the desk, he studied Jane. "I suppose the reason she's not here is because she isn't speaking to you?"

Her hand tensed in his hold. Tom gave it a gentle squeeze.

"Unfortunately not. She's agreed not to mention this to Lee."

Somber once more, Shane scooted his chair back and, standing, reached for his hat. The gold star winked on his chest.

"I'll head out to Cavanaugh's now." His eyes shouted a warning. "Keep this to yourselves."

Tom shoved his own hat on. "You need my company?"

"Nah. I'll round up my deputy."

Tom held the door for Jane. "Be careful out there," he said over his shoulder.

Shane's grin was more of a grimace. "Always."

They weren't five steps from the jail when Jane went rigid beside him. Her startled gasp was nearly drowned by the rustle of harnesses as a wagon rolled by.

He took her arm. "What's wrong?"

"That man on the corner. Do you see him?"

Not sure whom she was referring to, he scoured the crowd, stiffening when his gaze encountered that of a man staring right at them. "The one with the scar?"

"And silver hair. Tom—" her fingernails bit into his skin "—he's the one who came to Lee's the day of the picnic. He knows I was there. And he knows I got a good look at him."

The blood pulsing through his veins turned sluggish. "And he just saw us exiting the sheriff's office."

She turned frightened eyes on him. "He'll know we told."

The man in question pivoted sharply and, dodging in and out of the throng, made for the rear alley.

"He's leaving. No doubt on his way to warn Lee."

"He won't make it in time."

Moments later, pistol shots rang out in the direction he'd gone. Unease flowed through those around them. Farther down the boardwalk, a mother hauled her young child into the café, worried face visible through the glass. A pair of men ahead of them drew their weapons, turning in circles to scan the street.

Tom's frown deepened. "He will if he creates a disturbance to delay Shane." Taking her arm, he hustled her in the opposite direction, toward the mercantile. "We're not sticking around to see what happens. I'm getting you and Clara away from here."

He had a sinking feeling that they'd started something big, something they couldn't reverse, and there were no guarantees he could keep them safe.

The ride to her cabin was a quiet one. Even Clara was subdued.

Tom had thought it best to bring her straight home. Jessica needed to be told the news.

As she was about to disembark, he stalled her. "I'll pick you up in the morning. Seven o'clock sharp."

"That's not necessary. I have a weapon, and I know how to use it."

"Indulge me, Jane."

There'd be no skirting his resolve. "Fine."

"See you then."

She waved. "Drive safe. Bye, Clara."

Holding on to the side, the little girl smiled a farewell, her head bobbing as the conveyance rolled over uneven ground.

Jane remained in the yard long after their departure, head full of all that had happened. Charles was on his way to Gatlinburg. No one knew how that would impact Tom's future. Shane and his deputy were on their way to investigate Lee, or soon would be. How that would affect Jessica's future Jane was afraid to venture a guess.

When she grew tired of batting away mosquitoes, she trudged inside, her spirit burdened.

Jessica sat at the table, hunched over a bowl of pinto beans, her disinterest plain. Her features were drawn, the worry line between her brows threatening to become permanent. Jane's heart squeezed into a painful ball.

"What are you doing here so early?" Jessica said, her spoon clinking against the bowl.

Jane discarded her reticule on the nearest chair and, continuing into the kitchen, called over her shoulder. "I could use a cup of coffee. Want some?"

The scrape of the chair and clipped footsteps punctuated the silence.

Pulling the golden tin from the top shelf, she plucked the kettle off the back stove plate. She grabbed two mugs and shot Jessica a questioning glance. "Well?"

Anger and something like anguish churned in her

green eyes as she stood there, arms folded and chin out. "Why not?"

"Good. Can you grab the milk?"

They worked without speaking, gathering the sugar bowl and a pair of stirring spoons. The fire in the box was already hot, so it didn't take long for the coffee to boil.

"Why did Tom bring you home?" Jessica burst out.

Inhaling a bracing breath, Jane waited until she'd poured the steaming liquid and slid one mug across the work surface before answering.

"I'm afraid the news isn't good."

Jess paused in dumping sugar into the dark brew. "What news?"

"A man was discovered dead this morning. Because he had moonshine on him, there was talk of bringing in federal agents."

Her hand crept up to grip her throat. "Oh, no."

"Tom and I decided to go to Shane with our information."

"What?" The spoon clattered to the counter, and sugar spilled across the surface. "I have to warn him." She dashed for the rear door.

Slow to react, Jane tripped after her. As she was rounding the far corner of the cabin, she seized her wrist. "Stop! You can't go over there!"

Jess tried to yank free. Jane held on tight.

"I most certainly can," she cried, distraught. "Let me go!"

"No." As much as it was killing her to see Jess like this, she had to make her see reason. "He's on the wrong side of the law. What will it look like if you go rushing over there?"

"I don't care. I won't stand here and do nothing while he's in danger of being hauled off to jail!"

Stunned, Jane released her. "Are you admitting he's done wrong?"

"I haven't seen any evidence. But who knows what Shane will do now that you've planted seeds of suspicion in his mind?"

"Shane's a fair man. He won't arrest Lee without solid proof." She jammed her hands on her hips. "Hold on a second, how do you know where he lives? You haven't been there."

"As a matter of fact, I have." She marched toward the barn. "I asked him to take me, and he did."

Jane followed on her heels. "Let me guess—he wouldn't let you inside any of the buildings besides the cabin."

"So he's messy. I never said he was perfect."

"If you go there, you could get yourself killed."

She stomped into the barn. "Lee wouldn't hurt me. He loves me. He admitted his feelings."

Dismayed, Jane sank onto the nearest hay square and dropped her head in her hands. She couldn't force her to stay here.

"What? Aren't you going to try and convince me he was lying?" she huffed, boosting a saddle onto her palomino, Caramel.

"I don't think he is." Her words came out muffled. "Not about his feelings for you, anyway."

The barn got quiet. One of their cats wound its way between Jane's legs, its tail brushing her knee.

"What did you mean when you said I'd be in danger?"

Jess stood before her, wariness and hurt warring in her features.

"The silver-haired man I told you about, the one we

believe is Lee's main associate, saw us leaving Shane's office about an hour and a half ago. Not long after he disappeared into the crowd, we heard gunshots. No doubt he was creating a disturbance in order to give him time to get to Lee's."

Jessica shook her head, lips parted in anguish. "This can't be true."

Jane slowly gained her feet, extending her hands, wanting nothing more than to take away her grief. "I wish it wasn't."

She cupped her forehead. "I—I have to go."

"But—"

"I'll stay on our property. I just need—"

"Privacy." Time to process these revelations alone. "I understand."

For a second, Jessica didn't look angry anymore, and the bond they'd shared since childhood once again became tangible. Then, as if a wall slammed down between them, she hung her head and escaped into the woods.

Chapter Twenty-Three

Jane busied herself cleaning up Jessica's abandoned meal and setting up her work space with the ingredients for boiled custards. Time dragged. Almost an hour passed before Jessica returned and, without a word, barricaded herself in her room.

By seven o'clock, the silence became too much.

Jess didn't respond to her first or second knock. Finally, she answered. "Go away."

"I've made cheese toast."

"Not hungry."

"You didn't eat your lunch." Flattening her palm against the wood, she said, "I used Aunt Mary's special blend."

Their aunt and uncle operated a small-scale dairy, and Mary liked to experiment with various dried herbs. She gave them enough cheese to feed a family double their size. That made her twin happy—Jess's love of cheese had started early. Their mother liked to recount how she'd found dried bits of it in their room when they were little.

"No, thanks."

Sighing, Jane returned to the kitchen and ate standing up. She was midchew when there was a knock on the front door. Untying her apron, she draped it over a chair and hurried to the living room window. Tom had indicated he might stop by tonight if Shane had an update.

Behind her, she heard a door creak open. "Who is it?" Jess called.

"Tom and the sheriff."

Swinging the door wide, Jane waved them in.

Shifting a drowsy Clara to his other shoulder, Tom came in first. An exhausted-looking Shane entered and discarded his hat, running his fingers through his hair in a vain effort to smooth it. He observed Jessica standing in the hallway watching them all.

"Everything okay?" he asked softly.

When Jessica remained tight-lipped, Jane jumped in. "We're managing."

Tom started to lower Clara to the sofa.

"Why don't you put her in my bed? She'd be comfortable there while we discuss…matters."

He straightened. "You sure?"

"Of course. Follow me." Passing Jess, she said, "Would you mind putting a kettle of coffee on?"

Not waiting for her reply, Jane hurried into her room on the right, turned down the covers and stepped back to give them space. Tom laid Clara on the straw-filled mattress, removed her shoes and tucked the quilt about her small body. Then he brushed the curls away from her forehead.

"Get some rest, birdie."

The sweet smile uncle and niece shared melted Jane's heart.

Would Charles be as attentive to her needs as Tom? As loving and gentle?

After lowering the lamplight on the bedside table, she waited for him near the doorway.

His glance took in her bedroom's modest furnishings. "I believe this is my first time in your room."

"It's nothing much."

"It's cozy." He nodded at the red, white and blue quilt with the log-cabin design. "Did you make that?"

"My grandmother gave it to me a couple of years ago."

Spying her journal on the bedside table, he grinned. "Do you record your dreams at night?"

She poked him in the stomach. "You're awfully nosy all of a sudden."

"Can't help it. Being in your inner sanctum awakens my curiosity."

Low voices and the clink of plates drifted in from the living area. Tom's humor vanished.

"How did she take the news?"

"Not well. I think she's beginning to accept that what we've been saying is true."

Massaging the back of his neck, he shook his head. "I hate it for her."

"Did Shane arrest Lee?"

"No."

Her relief was followed by a stab of guilt. The law must be upheld and those who broke it held accountable. This wasn't a faceless criminal, however. It was Lee. The man Jessica loved.

He gestured for her to precede him into the hallway. "Let's go hear what he has to say."

Cradling his cup in his large hands, the sheriff occupied a single chair kitty-corner to the worn sofa. Jessica stood at the fireplace, hands twisted together at her waist.

Tom and Jane sat together on the sofa, tension seizing her body the moment Shane opened his mouth.

"We didn't find the still. I suspect it's on a part of his property, far up in the hollows. We did, however, discover the mash barrels you told me about, Jane. They were empty. The barn looked as if it had been cleared out in a hurry. No kegs or mason jars. There were a couple of containers of mashed fruit. If they're making brandy, they're likely transporting it to Knoxville. Locals can't afford that stuff."

"So you can't arrest him," Jessica exclaimed.

"No." His unwavering gaze held a world of understanding. "This isn't over. He's going to continue until he slips up. Money is a powerful motivator. If it's not me there to catch him, it'll be someone else. In my experience, revenuers target the big operations. The federal government doesn't like being cheated out of what's theirs."

Folding in on herself, Jess stared out the window at the darkening sky. Jane restrained the impulse to go to her. She'd only be rebuffed.

"What of his accomplice?" Tom said. "We spotted him as soon as we left your office."

"I suspect he's the one responsible for stirring up the townsfolk this afternoon. By the time we made our way through the crowd, he was gone." His attention lingered on Jessica. "Now that they know we're on to them, it's best you all steer clear."

Head bent, Jess stalked to the door. "I'll be in the barn."

Jane started to get up. A hand on her arm stopped her. Tom's green eyes sad, he said, "Give her some time."

How much time? she wanted to demand.

Jane had had years to purge her feelings for Tom,

with no success. In fact, they were stronger than ever. How long would it take for her sister to recover? And would she ever forgive her for her part in the destruction of her dreams?

Tom didn't trust the complete absence of activity.

In the four days since Shane's visit to Lee's, things had been quiet. Too quiet, in his opinion. He couldn't help wondering if they were using the time to plot revenge. If Jane had noticed his somber mood, she hadn't remarked on it. Nor had she protested his insistence on sticking close, picking her up every morning, escorting her to the café and back home each evening.

But, then, she was preoccupied with her own issues.

From what he'd been able to gather, the twins still weren't on speaking terms. Jessica refused to discuss Lee, and Jane didn't know if she had broken things off with him or not. She was worried. Her unhappiness went soul-deep, and he struggled with a feeling of helplessness.

Trampling the ferns covering the forest floor, he kept his gaze trained on her crouched form as she plucked berries from a bush and dropped them in the pail at her feet. Not far from her, Clara was curled up on a blanket asleep, her tiny mouth stained from the blue-black berries.

Charles would be here any day. Anticipation mingled with latent anger. He was going to have a serious talk with his brother. No way would he stand by and allow him access to Clara if he thought for one second he'd hurt her again.

Jane looked up at his approach, a sad sort of smile curving her mouth. His breath caught. How many times had he looked upon her face? Thousands? Millions? Not until his homecoming had her beauty truly registered. The way she looked at him sometimes, with open admiration and confidence in him, both humbled him and had his chest expanding with pride.

He found himself searching for ways to make her smile, make her laugh.

A startling thought entered his mind, and he nearly stumbled.

Could she be happy with him?

If the past wasn't an issue, if his former relationship with Megan didn't stand between them, could she trust in his feelings for her?

Heart beating fast, he knelt close. "What are these for?" His voice was muddy. Thick. "More pies for the café?"

"I'll be making this batch into jam for you and Clara." She held out her cupped palm filled with the fruit. "Want some?"

He took her offering, popping them one by one into his mouth, relishing the burst of tart flavor. "Thank you."

"You're welcome."

"Not just for the fruit," he clarified. "For everything. We're going to miss you while you're gone. And, of course, things will be different once you get back."

She didn't want to resume her care of Clara once she returned. He understood. Sort of.

Her smile wobbled as she continued her task. "I'm not sure I should go just yet. Ma wrote that she's fine with me leaving before she returns from Juliana's. But Jessica needs me right now, even if she won't admit it."

He didn't voice that he and Clara needed her, too. Wouldn't be fair to pressure her.

"She'll come around eventually," he said.

"I hope you're right."

The overcast weather lent the forest a vibrancy not visible on sunny days. The leaves were greener. The berries a deeper purple. Jane's skin had a pearl-like cast, her deep red hair lustrous in the whitewashed light.

After a while, she stopped what she was doing to stare at him. "Why are you looking at me like that?"

Taking her hand in his, he gently unfurled her fingers and skimmed the stains on her fingertips. "Have I ever told you how extraordinarily lovely you are?"

Her sudden inhale echoed through the understory.

Feeling daring, he lifted her hand and pressed a kiss to the middle of her palm, gaze locked on hers. "I don't know why things altered between us. All I know is they did. Please tell me I'm not alone in this."

He thought he glimpsed a flare of longing in the green depths before her lashes swept down, blocking his view. "I can't tell you what you want to hear," she whispered on a ragged breath.

Razor-edged disappointment scraped his insides. He released her hand.

How could he have been so misguided?

He stared at the ground. "I shouldn't have said anything."

When she placed her trembling hands to his cheeks, he jerked his chin up.

"You are one of a handful of people who truly knows me. I couldn't bear to lose your friendship."

The well of sadness in her eyes threw him. He didn't understand. Was *he* the source of her distress?

He didn't have a clue about women. Jessica had been right when she'd accused him of repeating his mistakes. Just as Megan had been satisfied with a platonic relationship, so was Jane.

The ache inside had nothing to do with rejection and

everything to do with how badly he wanted a chance with her. *I love her. Not just in a friendship way, but a passionate, all-consuming, I-want-her-as-my-wife way.*

The revelation should've stunned him. He'd been moving toward this point since his return.

"Tom?"

Her hands fell to her lap, and he stifled a protest. She was close enough to touch, yet far above his reach.

"I'll always be here for you, Jane."

Was it his imagination, or did her shoulders slump a little? He was distracted by Clara's stirring. On her blanket, she stretched, lids fluttering. She'd wake any minute.

Angling her face away, Jane picked up her pail. "I have enough for now."

"You go on ahead," he said. "I'll carry her home."

"Good idea."

Tom watched her leave, regret a bitter taste in his mouth.

Leading him to believe this particular lie was the hardest thing she'd ever done.

Broken inside, Jane couldn't bear to face him. So she'd left a note saying she had to fetch something from town and left on foot.

A strong wind rushed through the surrounding woods, the leaves seeming to whisper the same message over and over. *Coward. Weakling. Useless.*

She shivered in spite of the stifling heat. How badly she'd been tempted to confess everything...her schoolgirl crush, her despondency after he left, the feelings that had matured into love.

His desire to be near her, while flattering, had been

borne out of loneliness. He didn't want her, specifically. She just happened to be the convenient choice.

Without intending to, she wound up on Megan's doorstep. Lucian answered her summons and took one look before ushering her into the library and going off in search of his wife.

"Jane!" Closing the door behind her, Megan crossed the room with hands outstretched. "Lucian said you looked peaked. Here, have a seat."

Jane allowed her to guide her to the chair by the window. Perching on the edge of the ottoman, knees pressing into hers, Megan searched her face for clues. Pale ringlets framing her face, she looked as fresh and stunning as ever. Her happiness, her confidence in Lucian's love and the strength of their marriage, enhanced her beauty.

"Have you had a letter from Ma? Are Juliana and the children all right?"

"They're fine. I don't really know why I'm here."

Hurt flashed in Megan's blue eyes. "We used to be close, you and I. Remember?"

Jane nodded miserably. After their run-in last week, she should've cleared the air.

"I miss it," Megan said.

"You spoke to Jessica about me."

"She told you about our conversation? You never said, and I wondered if she'd chosen not to involve herself."

"You weren't actually talking to Jessica." Fiddling with the pearl buttons on her bodice, Jane grimaced. "It was me."

Her jaw went slack. "But…you were wearing her clothes. And your hair…"

"I was pretending to be her."

"Why would you do that?" she demanded, brows knitting.

The story spilled out in a jumbled rush. Megan's reaction volleyed between fascination, horror and disbelief.

Jane answered her many questions, belatedly realizing she probably shouldn't have revealed quite so much. "You can't tell anyone, Meg."

"I won't keep secrets from Lucian."

"Fine. Tell him, but no one else. Promise?"

"You have my word."

"Why did you tell him about my feelings for Tom?"

She looked startled. "That was very long ago. Before we were married, in fact. Did he say something to you?"

"At the dance." Hands on the chair rests, she propelled herself up, plodding to the window and staring out at the sloping side yard. "He said Tom wasn't in love with you anymore."

"Ah." She came to stand behind her. "And you can't accept that."

"That's not the problem."

"What, then?"

Whirling, she threw her hands up in defeat. "Don't you see? I'm not like you, Meg. I'm not outgoing. Crowds make me skittish. I like children, but not enough to throw on a costume and perform for them. What kind of person refuses to bring pleasure to children? A self-centered one, that's who." Pacing over to the ceiling-high shelves, she gave the rolling ladder a little push. "Unlike you, I don't view the world as a place of limitless possibilities. I can be quite cynical at times."

Megan came to stand in the middle of the plush Oriental rug, hands folded serenely at her waist. "Lots of people find attention nerve-racking. That doesn't make you self-centered. Look at how you've cared for Tom's niece, despite the great personal cost."

"It took her nearly breaking her leg for me to agree."

"You were merely trying to protect yourself from further pain. The Lord has blessed you with a sensitive, compassionate soul. You possess many fine qualities. If Tom can't appreciate you for who you are, you don't need him."

"He hinted that he'd like us to be more than friends."

"What?" Coming over to where Jane leaned against the shelves, Megan gripped her arms. "Why are you here then? You should be with him, exploring what this means for your relationship."

"I told him I wasn't interested."

Her forehead creased. "I am thoroughly confused. The man you love wants to court you, and you rejected him?"

She stared at the tips of her shoes peeking out from beneath her hem. "I can't be the woman he truly wants."

"You're not giving him or yourself enough credit." She gave her a tiny shake. "You have to be honest with him. You have to tell him how you feel."

Pretending to be Jessica and facing Lee alone was one thing. Revealing her heart to Tom? She didn't possess that kind of courage...not when he'd be trading one O'Malley sister for another. Once he discovered what a poor substitute she was for Megan, he'd reject her.

She could handle a lot of things. Having Tom only to ultimately lose him was not one of them.

Chapter Twenty-Four

Rifle in hand, Tom left the cabin with the order for Clara to stay put. His hogs' squealing was probably nothing, but he couldn't let it go unchecked.

Jane's note crinkled in his pocket, irritating him anew. He understood that he'd messed up. His admission had embarrassed her. And while he dreaded another awkward exchange as much as she must, it wasn't safe for her to go gallivanting around Gatlinburg alone right now.

Passing the barn, he entered the woods where his hogs liked to root around for grasses and mushrooms.

He wished he'd kept his mouth shut.

No, that wasn't true. He wished her response had been different.

Memories pressed in, one after another, all of them featuring Jane. The day he'd discovered her in her wedding dress, beautifully broken, shocked and furious with him. The day she'd ordered him about and he'd let her, soaking up her attention like a lonely little boy and falling asleep under her touch. Then there was the food fight. Dancing with her. Arguing with her. Kissing her.

He wanted more memories. More dances. More kisses. He yearned to have it all with her.

The unnatural stillness sank in right about the time the coppery stench of blood assaulted his senses. Hand curling over the gun's forestock, he lifted it, turning in a slow circle. The hairs on the back of his neck stood up, and he had the distinct impression he was being watched.

Creeping toward the smell, he rounded a thick bush and felt his muscles turn to stone.

There, laid out across the forest floor in methodical fashion, were his hogs, ten in all, necks sliced open from ear to ear. A twig snapped behind him, and he whirled, prepared to sink a bullet into whoever was there.

"It's just me." Palms up, Josh stared grimly back at him.

"I could've shot you," Tom growled, anger over the senseless crime bubbling to the surface.

His friend stalked closer. "Sorry. I was too focused on that to announce myself." He jerked a thumb at the gruesome scene.

Searching the surrounding woods, he said, "Did you see anything strange?"

"I came the same way you did. Stopped by the house first. When Clara mentioned hearing the hogs, I figured I'd come looking for you." Going closer to the carnage, he scanned the ground.

Tom slowly lowered his weapon, still not sure if they were alone.

"Won't get much meat from these," Josh said, shaking his head in disgust. "What a waste."

Hogs foraged freely in the woods, their diet supplemented with corn until they'd fattened up for the slaughter in late fall. If he tried to process and cure it now, the meat would spoil.

"Who do you think did this?"

He hadn't had a chance to tell Josh they'd gone to the authorities. He was not going to be pleased once he found out he and Jane were in the sights of a criminal.

"You may as well tell him the truth." Both men spun at the feminine intrusion.

"What are you doing here, Jessica?" Tom said, concerned. She hadn't set foot on his property for days.

"I came to see Jane. I had a question about our order."

"Jane's not here."

Tom took a single step closer to Jessica. "Are you okay?"

Her eyes had a haunting quality...flat, devoid of emotion, lifeless. And because she looked exactly like Jane, their appearance troubled him.

"Why wouldn't I be?" Her voice dripped sarcasm. "My dear sister assumed my identity and discovered that the man I love is a criminal. Then she turned him in to the authorities. No big deal, right?"

Josh moved between them. "Hold on. You talked to the sheriff? When? How does Lee know?"

Tom outlined the events leading up to Shane's investigation. Jessica didn't interrupt once. Just stood there, head drooping, arms wrapped tightly about her middle. His heart went out to her.

Jane was right. Her twin desperately needed someone to lean on.

"Your sister regrets hurting you," he said at last. "If you could move beyond your anger—"

"Don't you dare lecture me, Tom Leighton!" she sneered, emotion finally flaring to life. "You think you know Jane. You think you see the real woman beneath the reserved veneer. Well, you don't. You don't have a clue!"

A muscle in his jaw worked. Her accusation lodged in his chest like an arrow, surprising him. Was what she said true?

Picking up her skirts, she ran in the opposite direction.

"Should we go after her?"

Josh shook his head, looking as if he'd like to murder someone. "How are we supposed to keep those two safe?"

He buried his hands in his hair. "If I could have them locked up until this business is over with, I would. If anything ever happened to Jane…" He clamped his lips together.

Folding his arms, Josh pinned him with a direct stare. "When are you going to admit you have feelings for my cousin?"

"Excuse me?"

"Jane?" His brows shot up. "You know, the cute redhead who's pined after you since she hit puberty? I've been waiting for you to admit it. My patience just snapped."

Tom gaped. "Jane doesn't *pine* after me. I'm like a brother to her. And how did you guess…about me? My interest?"

Amusement eased the severity of his features. "I've watched my brothers succumb to the love of good women. I know the signs."

"I thought you'd be angry."

Clapping an arm about his shoulders, Josh said, "Angry about my best friend and my cousin together? Not a chance."

"We're not together."

"Not yet. Trust me on this, if it's meant to be, things have a way of working out."

* * *

Tom was leaving the sheriff's office an hour and a half later when he caught sight of Jane and Nicole outside the mercantile. He didn't immediately go to her. Jessica's strange accusations, along with Josh's startling—and no doubt faulty—theory prevented him.

A pair of middle-aged women came around the corner, tossing him curious glances, and he backed closer to the building to give them room. His hat in his hands, he debated whether or not to tell Jane about the hogs. Shane had agreed that it had likely been done in retaliation and had warned him it might not be the end.

The sisters hugged, preparing to part.

He stuffed his hat on his head and, instead of crossing the street to speak to her, continued down the boardwalk.

Jessica's wrong. You do know Jane, he told himself. He might have misread her reaction to his kiss, his touch, but he knew the woman she was inside. *Pure. Good-hearted. Loving. Exasperating at times. Blind to her own strengths. Stubborn.*

Years ago, when he'd set his sights on Megan, the feeling that he was trying to meet impossible requirements had been constant. In his mind, he'd foolishly set her on a higher plane, one he'd been desperate to join her on. His feelings had been genuine, but skewed. Not based in reality.

Megan had done him a huge favor. If she'd agreed to his proposal, they would've both been miserable, condemned to a loveless marriage.

Risking a glance across the way, he saw Jane waving goodbye to her sister, her unhappiness a tangible thing. He faced forward before she could catch him spying.

Tom had been witness to his brother's blessed marriage, the evidence of a real, shared love based on mutual respect and appreciation. He'd seen it but hadn't experienced it for himself. Until now.

The love he had for Jane was based on truth. He was fully aware of her faults and strengths, her quirks and preferences. He saw her as she was, not how he wished for her to be.

But Jane didn't want a future with him. Friendship was all she required, and, no matter that it would slowly destroy him, he had to be satisfied with that.

"Mr. Leighton!"

Pivoting sharply, he waited for the young man he recognized as the postmaster's son to catch up.

"My father saw you passing by and asked me to give you this telegram. From a sheriff in middle Tennessee. I'm afraid it's bad news."

The passersby flowing around him, the shouts of the kids playing marbles in front of the blacksmith's, the single riders clopping along Main faded as Tom accepted the slip of paper. He took no notice of the man's departure. Stomach knotting up, he read the brief message.

Charles was dead. Killed in a barroom brawl.

He stood there for who knew how long, reading the words again and again until they blurred.

His brother had changed his ways. He wouldn't have been in a saloon. He'd been serious about making up for lost time with his daughter.

"Tom, what's wrong?"

Jane's voice seemed to come from far away. Her cool fingers encircled his wrist, forcing him to meet her worried gaze.

"My brother's gone." The words didn't want to come. "He's dead."

Dismay swirled in the fathomless depths. Glancing about, she twined her fingers with his. "Where's Clara?"

"At your aunt's." He hadn't told her about Charles's intent to return, and now he was glad he hadn't.

"Come with me."

"I need to see Clara."

"You need a moment to sort through this first," she implored.

He allowed her to lead him into Plum's. Most of the tables were unoccupied, so he was surprised when Jane asked the girl if they could use the office. Holding tight to his hand, she directed him through the spacious kitchen, briefly greeting the cook, and into a tight corner room with a single desk, a pair of scuffed chairs and makeshift shelving overflowing with papers and books on the wall.

"Have a seat. I'll be right back."

Dropping into the chair, he rested his elbows on his knees and stared unseeing at the floorboards. His only brother was dead. Gone, like their ma. It was just him and Clara now.

His insides roiled.

Jane returned and, depositing a large cup of coffee on the desk, took the chair opposite. "It's freshly made."

Sitting up, he ran a finger around the rim, not interested in food or drink. "I don't understand what he was doing in a saloon. He sounded sincere about changing his ways."

"What happened exactly?"

"Don't have details. Only this." He handed her the telegram.

"Perhaps you could write to this Sheriff Olsen."

"Yeah."

Placing the paper between them, Jane laid a hand on his forearm. "I'm so sorry, Tom."

"Clara's going to be devastated. She still talks about him, you know. Has this crazy notion he's coming back."

"You're going to help her through this." Sorrow darkened her eyes. "And I will, too."

Jane had good intentions. The truth of the matter was she was leaving. And by the time she returned, she expected him to have found someone else to take her place.

Yearning to hold him, Jane instead clasped her hands tightly in her lap.

The strain around his eyes, the way he held his body unnaturally still, bore testament to the intense blow he'd been dealt. She could hardly grasp the news. For Tom, Charles's death must be especially difficult. They'd been cheated out of a chance at reconciliation, and he'd been left with nothing more than unpleasant memories. And—knowing him—regrets.

Pushing away the untouched coffee, he lumbered to his feet, back bowed as if bearing the weight of a mountain. "I can't put off telling her."

She stood, as well. "I'll go with you."

"No."

Hurt flared at the harshness of his response. She tamped it down. He was in the grip of grief.

"I'll come by your place later tonight, then. Check on you both."

His eyes were a turbulent storm. "I don't think that's a good idea."

"But—"

"Clara's my sole responsibility now. Leaning on you,

expecting you to shoulder her care, was a mistake. I shouldn't have asked it of you."

Scarcely believing what she was hearing, she seized his hand. "Don't say that. These last few weeks have been—" She bit her lip, unwilling to share her deepest feelings.

"What, Jane?" He sounded soul-weary. "They've been what?"

Tom dipped his head, studying her with an intensity that made her feel exposed.

"I'm glad I got the chance to spend time with her. I wouldn't trade that for the world. I don't regret my decision, so please don't wish that you hadn't asked."

"Understood." His despondency nearly felled her.

She squeezed his hand. "I'm here whenever you need me."

With a final nod, he snatched his hat off the desk corner and strode out without inviting her to join him. As his footsteps receded, she had a sinking feeling he wouldn't reach out to her again.

Chapter Twenty-Five

She woke the next morning with a slight headache. The memories of the day before rushed in, and she pulled the covers over her head as bone-deep sadness spread like an illness through her system.

The hours between her conversation with Tom and bedtime had stretched endlessly. Half a dozen times she'd gotten her reticule and gone out onto the porch, fully intending to go to him. The need to offer comfort had been eclipsed only by the knowledge he didn't want her around.

Groaning, she dragged herself out of bed and got dressed, the mundane motions of brushing and arranging her hair doing little to detract from her misery. Outside her window, the first streaks of dawn chased the darkness across the sky. A quarter moon hung suspended above the mountain peaks.

How was she supposed to get through the day, knowing he was grieving his brother while also trying to comfort a sad little girl, and yet somehow stay away?

Tying her boot laces, she trudged into the cold, dark kitchen and started a fire in the stove box. She would bake the day away, she decided. What she couldn't sell to Mrs. Greene, she'd sell at the mercantile or donate.

After downing several cups of coffee, she rechecked the time. There'd been no stirring from the vicinity of Jessica's room. Now that she thought about it, she couldn't be positive she'd heard her return from the barn last night.

Unease tugging her skin taut, Jane strode through the cabin and banged on her door. "Jessica?"

Pushing inside, she stared at the made-up bed in dismay. Her twin must have risen extremely early.

Trying to hold on to her equanimity, Jane explored the upstairs and all the outbuildings.

Normally, they were diligent in sharing their plans, letting the other know when they were leaving and the general time they planned to come home. However, Jessica was still furious with her and communicated only when absolutely necessary.

What if she'd gone to see Lee and something terrible had happened? Jane trusted he wouldn't do anything to harm Jess. His business partner would have no such qualms.

She entered the barn last, stopping short at the sight of the empty stall. Jess's horse was gone. A sense of urgency seizing her, she retrieved her weapon and the ankle holster Josh had fashioned for her years ago from her room before saddling her own horse and making her way out to Lee's.

The trip passed in a haze of stark fear. Her mind had taken over, playing out endless scenarios, each more grisly than the last. She prayed she'd overtake Jessica, that they could talk things out and head home.

That didn't happen. Leaving Rusty tethered near the lane, Jane trekked through the forest, impatient to locate her sister but also aware how foolish rushing into the unknown would be. She had to stay clearheaded. Not let her emotions rule.

On the edge of the clearing, she hid behind the reaper and strained to listen for evidence the guard dogs were out of their pens. She had four bullets, but she wasn't a quick shot. The thought of their sharp teeth sinking into her flesh sent her pulse tripping into heart failure territory.

"Get a hold of yourself, Jane," she said, her grip on the gun handle growing slippery.

She waited there for what seemed an eternity. Not a living thing stirred.

Screwing up her courage, she traversed the expanse and began systematically searching the buildings, weapon held close to her side. The second she exited the cabin's rear door, ferocious barking shattered the silence. Squealing, she jumped back, the cabin wall blocking her escape. Any second now, she was going to be ripped to shreds.

It took her fear-frozen brain a full minute to realize no animals were materializing.

Gun outstretched, Jane crept forward, passing the outhouse and coming face-to-face with the beasts. Saliva dripping, gums curled back to reveal razor-edged teeth, they surged against the enclosure.

Movement in her peripheral vision had her whirling to the left, arms trembling so badly she doubted she'd be able to pull the trigger, much less aim.

The large form shifted restlessly. Jane lowered her gun and took a halting step forward.

Jessica's horse had been tethered to the hitching post behind the barn. Her worst nightmare confirmed. She was here. Somewhere. Or had been at some point.

Where was she now?

* * *

"When will we see Jane?"

Tucking Clara closer against his side, Tom glanced down. "Soon. Five more minutes."

Mired in shock and grief yesterday, he hadn't given thought to how much Clara had come to depend on Jane. Nor had he anticipated how sticking to her usual routine would help her cope with the fact her pa wasn't ever coming home. She'd woken up expecting to see her caretaker and, when she'd learned she wasn't coming, burst into tears.

Tom had plenty of experience soothing her hurts, but having Jane by his side offering support and encouragement would make it a whole lot easier to bear.

The moment he'd arrived at Sam and Mary's and looked into this little girl's face, he'd regretted not asking Jane to accompany him. Clara needed her. So did he.

He just wasn't sure how he was supposed to handle the fact she didn't want him.

"She will come home with us, right, Uncle?" Tears shimmered in her red-rimmed eyes. "I wanna bake a cake. A big, tall one with icing. Do you think Miss Jane will let me?"

Reins in hand, he guided the team onto her property. "We'll ask her, okay?"

"I hope she says yes."

Tom was fairly certain Jane would do anything in her power to cheer the child. He'd seen the loving glances she bestowed on her charge, her contentment whenever she and Clara were together.

"Stay in the wagon."

"Yes, sir."

Tom fully expected to find her in the midst of household chores. He was forming an explanation in his mind when he climbed the steps and noticed the front door standing ajar. His calls went unanswered. After surveying the woods, which stood infuriatingly empty, he went inside. The stench of burning food accosted his nostrils.

In the kitchen, he discovered a skillet on the front cook plate, eggs scorched to a black lump. A half-empty cup of coffee was still warm, and baking supplies were laid out. If Jane realized she was missing an ingredient, she wouldn't have simply up and left. She would've sent Jessica. And she wouldn't have left breakfast to burn.

Foreboding niggled at the base of his skull. Shane's warnings pulsed through his mind.

They'd slaughtered his hogs. What if the women were the next targets?

Striding out to the wagon, he hauled himself up and whipped the team around.

Clara blinked up at him, confusion creasing her forehead. "Where's Miss Jane?"

"She's not here. We're going to Miss Mary's to see if she paid them a visit."

"What if she's not there?"

"Then you and Amy will play together while I look for her."

"Amy has school."

He glanced over at her. "You can entertain Victoria. I'm sure Kate would love to have you visit. How does that sound?"

With a shrug, she watched the passing forest without uttering a word. Her profile looked so much like Charles's. A pang of regret struck him low in the gut.

I'll be the best pa I know how to be, brother. With the Almighty's help, I'll love her and guide her to the best of my abilities.

Fighting off the rising tide of sorrow, he settled Clara

at the O'Malley farm. Sam shared his concern and went off in search of Josh and Caleb, who had gone hunting on their property. Tom didn't heed the older man's urging to wait for them. He couldn't afford to wait. His gut told him something wasn't right.

His first stop—Lee's cabin.

Jane contemplated the steep mountain hollow, nearly impassable with brambles and rhododendron bushes, and holstered her gun. She'd need both hands and all her concentration to traverse this trail. It was the most obvious location for the still. Difficult for revenuers to find. More importantly, the stream trickling down the incline provided a constant source of water for the process of turning mash into liquor.

If she hadn't seen her great-uncle's still she might never have known to investigate this place. Jane, her sisters and cousins had overheard the adults talking about Uncle Peter's involvement and, curiosity sparked, had explored his property and discovered the location of his still. Of course, their folks weren't happy when they found out. They'd been relegated to mucking stalls, washing windows and other more unpleasant chores for the remainder of the week.

The climb wasn't pleasant. Branches got caught in her hair and occasionally poked her neck. Cobwebs with fat spiders hovered too near her head, and she was certain she'd have a tick or three stuck to her once she emerged. Three-quarters of the way up, the brush cleared, the terrain evened out and she was able to walk upright.

Following the stream, she stopped short at the wisps of smoke curling into the sky.

Crouching low, she kept close to the ground as she

rounded the slope, heart leaping into her throat. A pair of stills occupied the small clearing. Behind them, a weathered shack was situated close to the rushing water. Lee paced the short distance between it and the bank, his normally even-tempered demeanor gone. His big body radiated tension.

Feeling as if she might come out of her skin, Jane scoured the area for a clue as to Jessica's whereabouts. Could they be keeping her in the shack? What if she was tied up and gagged, unable to call for help?

The thought was cut off the instant a beefy arm snapped around her midsection. The breath whooshed from her lungs. Terror trickled into her veins as a knife's thin blade pressed into her throat.

"I don't recall inviting you up here." A gravelly voice grated against her ear.

Instinct urged her to fight, to struggle against her captor. Jane disobeyed her body's commands. She didn't move. Didn't speak. Was afraid to swallow as a stinging sensation radiated from the blade and a single drop of blood slid beneath her collar.

One swipe, and she'd be dead.

She'd never see Jessica or her family again. Tom would never know he meant everything to her. Unless he read her journals, she thought inanely. Then he'd know.

"Move."

The knife fell away, and a sharp shove low in her back had her stumbling forward into the clearing. Lee's head shot up, and the expression of disbelief was replaced by a grimness that frightened her more than the knife had. He wasn't going to fight for her.

"How did you find us?" he said.

"Where's Jessica?"

Apprehension slithered through his eyes. "Not here."

"Her horse is at your cabin. If she's not here, where is she?"

The stranger grabbed her arm, his grip brutal. He pointed to the shack. "Get a length of rope."

Jaw jutting, Lee planted his boots wide. "What are you going to do with her, Farnsworth?"

"What do you think? We can't have her snitching to the authorities again." Fingers digging into her skin, he told her, "You saved me a trip, you know that? You were next on my list."

"I didn't sign up for this. I'm a businessman, plain and simple," Lee said. His hand sliced the air. "Look, we can relocate to another area. They suspect us now. It's only a matter of time before they find this place."

"When obstacles get in the way of profits, we take action. We can't have a witness walking around free to testify against us. Get the rope. Now."

Lee shifted his weight, fists opening and closing. Clearly a battle waged inside him. Hope sprang up in Jane. Would his love for her twin push him to do what was right?

But then he turned on his heel and stalked into the leaning structure, returning within a minute with the requested rope. Anger mingled with fear. Once they tied her up, there'd be no way to reach her gun.

"I don't know what Jess ever saw in you," she exclaimed. "You don't deserve her."

"That may be true. Not for you to say, though, is it?" The skin around his right eye twitched. "If you'd kept your pretty little nose out of my business, I could've gotten out eventually. Made a good life for ourselves."

"Don't you dare blame Jane."

Jane gasped as Jessica materialized from the woods, gun drawn and leveled at Farnsworth.

"None of this is her fault."

"You shouldn't be here, Jess," Lee spit out, shock written across his face. "You should've stayed far away."

"I had to see this for myself," she retorted. "And I'm glad I did." Her narrowed gaze bounced between the rope in Lee's grasp and Farnsworth's hand practically glued to Jane's arm. "Release her, and you won't get a bullet lodged in your brain."

In a flash, Farnsworth had her pinned to his front, the blade digging into her throat again. Jane's eyes watered as it lightly pierced her skin.

Jessica went white. The color even leached from her lips. Her eyes were tormented pools of darkest green.

"If you don't wanna watch your sister bleed, you'll place the gun on the ground."

Lee lifted his hand in supplication. "Jess, do as he says."

She didn't move for long moments, her indecision playing out across her features. Jane swallowed thickly against the despair lodging in her throat. The stuttered prayers half forming in her mind hardly made sense.

God knows my need. He sees.

"All right." Slowly pointing the barrel toward the sky, she bent at the knees and laid the gun on the ground. "Just...don't hurt her. Please."

"Move closer to the fire."

Stepping over the gun, she did as he instructed.

The pain around Jane's wound increased a second before her captor lowered his weapon and shoved her against Lee, who caught her awkwardly. "Tie her up." Whipping a gun from where he'd had it tucked into his waistband, he pointed it at Jessica. "Over here, little lady. You're next."

When she'd reached their spot, she glared at Lee as he

bound Jane's wrists in front of her. "I trusted you." The words were ripped from her. "I thought you loved me."

His fingers fumbled on the rope. Was he deliberately tying it loosely?

When he didn't respond, Jess's face blazed. "I guess I was wrong."

"Now's hardly the time to discuss our relationship," he said at last, sounding morose.

Lips quivering, Jessica's lashes swept down, but not before Jane caught the anguish shining there.

Lee was apparently taking too long for Farnsworth's liking. Stalking past them, he fetched another length of rope and proceeded to tie Jess. Gauging from her wince, he wasn't as gentle as Lee.

"I say we leave them here." Lee faced his partner. "We'll take our money and supplies. Relocate where no one knows us."

"That's not an option." Turning away, he studied the coiled copper tube and the alcohol dripping steadily into the container below.

"At least ask Bryce. I'm sure if you explain—"

"I'm not asking Bryce anything. He's already aware of the situation."

"And he expects us to stay here?"

"He's got ways of handling problems like backwoods sheriffs." His focus shifted to where Jane and Jessica had edged closer together. "And I have mine."

Lee scowled. "What are you planning?"

"A little trip." He waved his weapon. "Start walking, ladies. Oh, and if you even think about making a sound, you'll discover just how creative I can be with a knife."

"I can't let you do this." Without warning, Lee tackled his partner, and a gunshot rang out.

They scuffled on the ground, Farnsworth slamming the butt of his gun against Lee's back.

"Jess, get my gun!" Jane cried, limbs shaking from terror.

Dropping low, she tried to shove Jane's skirts aside, but her hands were at an awkward angle.

Out of the corner of her eye, Jane saw Lee go down, blood trickling from his temple. He let out a frustrated groan of defeat.

Her hope withered and died then and there.

Chapter Twenty-Six

He'd found Jane's horse first. Then Jessica's.

Jane had come looking for her twin, putting them both in harm's way.

The sound of a single gunshot reverberated along the mountain walls. The fear Tom had been battling became a living, breathing, formidable foe, driving calm and reason from his mind. He had to get to them before it was too late.

Gun drawn, he was about to follow a barely discernible path at the southwest edge of the property when he heard voices. His muscles were primed for a fight. Sweat slid beneath his collar. Seeking shelter behind the nearest tree, he pressed against the rough bark, ears straining.

What he heard sent shards of icy alarm through him. Lee's voice followed by a stern reply from a male voice Tom didn't recognize. And then Jane's soft entreaty.

He abandoned his hiding spot. Edged around the barrel-like trunk and caught a flash of red hair. *Jane.*

The stranger, Lee's associate, had her. Forcing her in the direction of the cabin, his weapon was trained on the couple walking ahead of them. Tom registered several things at once. Lee's busted-up face. Jessica's very real distress. And Jane...her eyes had a hunted look about them...and her neck...

The wretch had cut her. Badly. Red-hazed rage distorted his vision. Tom very nearly exposed his presence right then and there. Farnsworth would pay and pay dearly.

Calm. He had to calm down. Control his emotions.

Finger on the trigger, he blinked away the sweat dripping in his eyes. He couldn't get a clean shot. From this angle and distance, he couldn't be certain the bullet would find its target. Jane was too close. Too many trees for it to ricochet off and possibly hit Jess.

Caging the fury pushing him to act, he called on all his willpower as he crept silently through the woods, trailing them, waiting for the right opportunity to act.

He couldn't afford any mistakes.

The circuitous ride through the thickest parts of the forest stretched Jane's nerves to the breaking point. She'd stopped trying to figure out their destination and instead alternated begging God for her and Jess's lives and reconciling the very real possibility she wouldn't see Tom again.

More than anything, she hated that their last exchange had been marked with tension and sorrow. Regretted her lost chance to comfort him. Tom would be left with troubling memories of her. She doubted he'd ever have a chance to read her journals. Her mama wouldn't think of giving them to him.

Mama. Her poor heart would crack clean in half. Two daughters lost...

Squeezing her eyes shut, she shoved the morbid

thoughts aside. Now wasn't the time for mourning. There was still a chance for survival.

It's my fault Jess is in this mess. It's my responsibility to get her out.

Turning again to prayer, she asked God to grant her the opportunity to save her sister. She asked Him to make her brave.

The cabin up ahead didn't at first register. Farnsworth had put her on a horse with Lee while he rode with Jessica. Guess he figured the chances of Lee trying to take off were lower that way. She could hardly fathom that Lee had ambushed his own partner. Somewhere inside, the urge to do good existed amid the greed and ambition.

"Why did you bring us home?" Jess demanded.

Home. Jane blinked. She'd been so disoriented, numb with horror, that she hadn't recognized it.

"Those unfortunate O'Malley girls," Farnsworth drawled. "They perished in a barn fire."

His plan finally revealed, Lee stiffened in the saddle, muscles going taut. After the scuffle on the mountain, Farnsworth had given him one more chance, had said he understood his need to protect his girl, but he had to make a choice. The business or her.

Lee hadn't said a word. Did that mean he'd chosen the business?

Poor Jess. What she must be going through right now…

When they came to the barn entrance, Farnsworth was on the ground and barking orders. Gun barrel shoved under Jess's chin, he forced them all inside.

"Lee, douse the floor with kerosene."

Farnsworth gave Jessica a shove that sent her sprawling on the floor. Jane rushed over, crouching close to her face. "We have to stop him," she whispered.

"How?" She spit out bits of straw that had gotten in her mouth. "He confiscated your gun."

The stench of kerosene clogged her nostrils as Lee reluctantly splashed the contents of the container around them. Their chances of escape were narrowing.

Tears brimmed, blurring her vision. "I'm so sorry, Jess. This is my fault. I never should've started this."

Blinking fast, she gave her head a quick shake. "No, it's not. I—I should've listened to you. I was stubborn—"

Sudden movement cut her off. Lee hauled off and swung the canister at the other man's head with all his might. But the swing was too short. He missed.

A loud blast assaulted their ears. Jessica screamed as Lee crumpled to the ground.

"Lee!" She scrambled on her knees to reach him. "No..."

Jane watched in horror as an ever-widening circle of red dampened his chest.

Farnsworth looked unrepentant. "Fool."

"Lee, please." Hovering over him, tears dripped from Jess's cheeks onto his. "Please don't die. I love you. We can work this out. Together."

His face bleached, he lifted a shaky hand to her face. "I love you, too. I'm sorry..."

"No, it's okay..." Jerking up her head, she yelled at Farnsworth. "Help him! You have to—"

"No help for him. You can thank yourself for that." With a smirk, he eyed the dying man with a cold, calculating stare. "Now you can watch your beloved die along with you."

The moment he pointed the gun at her twin, Jane's decision to be brave clicked into place. She acted without hesitation.

She lunged. Leaped between certain death and the sister she loved.

Above the buzzing in her brain, she heard her twin's horrified cry of protest.

Then pain sliced into her, knocking her back. The knowledge of her failure sucked her into darkness, and she hit the ground with a jarring thud.

Jane woke to incredible pressure in her shoulder and searing, tissue-deep pain.

Jessica was very close, sobbing.

She drew in a breath and immediately started coughing. Smoke clogged her lungs.

"Jane! I thought—" Shaking her head, Jess cried, "The barn's on fire! We have to get out."

Blinking, eyes smarting, she started to sit up and realized the pressure was Jess's bound hands on her wound. "Where's Farnsworth?"

"The gun jammed after he shot you," she gasped, cheeks shiny with tears, hair a disheveled mass. "I couldn't believe it...he started the fire and left. I don't know if he's coming back." Glancing over her shoulder, she shuddered violently. "Lee's dead."

They soon would be, too, if they didn't act fast. "Can you untie me? Have to save the animals."

"But your wound—" She dissolved into a fit of coughing.

"I think I can manage."

Unraveling the rope took up more precious seconds than they had to spare. Already Jane was growing light-headed, although from blood loss or the smoke she wasn't sure. With her hands free, she struggled to her feet and lurched to the wall where their tools hung. She used a large knife to cut Jessica's bonds.

Shoulder throbbing, she choked out, "Get the rabbits. I'll get the cow."

With her back to the door, Jessica hesitated. "I can't leave Lee here."

"We'll get him out. I promise." Somehow, she'd find a way.

A hand clamped down on her uninjured shoulder and spun her around. She found herself crushed against a broad chest.

"Jane." Tom groaned her name. "You're okay. When I heard the commotion and the gunshot, I thought the worst." A tremor rippled through his body before he pulled back. "You don't have to worry about Lee's associate."

"What did you do?"

His jaw was like marble. "He won't hurt you again."

"Can you help us with Lee?"

Noticing the still form, his face grew grim. "I'll get him. You two, out."

Ignoring him, Jane rushed past her motionless sister toward the stall housing their dairy cow. "Jess, the rabbits!" she called, gagging at the stench.

It took all her waning strength to lead the frightened animal out. Outside, she dropped to her knees and, bracing her hands in the grass, gulped in fresh air. Tom had dragged Lee's body out, and Jess sank down and took his limp hand between hers. Jane couldn't bear to watch.

Nausea rose up. She sucked in more air.

Over near the horses, the silver-haired man lay unmoving, apparently unconscious. His lip was split, his right eye red and swollen shut.

She was still staring at him when Tom reappeared with the hutch, soot and sweat streaked across his forehead. "He's still alive," he panted, balancing his palms on his knees. "I knocked him out."

When he uttered an exclamation of surprise mixed with horror, Jane jerked her head up. His brilliant gaze was locked on her wound. "You're hurt."

How could he have missed it?

Fear shot anew through him, stronger than when she'd been on the horse with her captor, more devastating than when she'd been inside the barn, out of sight and at the mercy of a killer.

Going on his knees before her, he very carefully lifted the hair tumbling about her shoulders and brushed it out of the way. A hiss slipped between his teeth as he gingerly peeled away the torn, blood-sodden material. The bullet had gouged the flesh where her neck curved into her shoulder. "You need a doctor."

Unlike Jane's, his imagination didn't normally work overtime. All he could think about now, however, was the possibility of infection.

He touched her cheek. She was too pale, her eyes glassy.

"It can wait." Her fingers skimmed his wrist. "Tom, the barn. We can't lose it."

"And I can't lose you," he growled, dipping his head to press a firm, swift kiss on her startled lips. He didn't give her time to react. He could beg forgiveness later, explain it away as heightened emotions.

Avoiding her perusal, he stood.

"Jessica." She looked at him through a shock-induced daze. "Take your sister inside and tend her injury." She hung her head, her grip on Lee unwavering.

Stalking over, he gently tipped her chin up. "You can't help him now. Jane's hurt. She needs you."

Jessica blinked, her focus slowly sharpening. She nodded, lovingly placing Lee's hand on his unmoving stomach. Tom assisted her up, waiting until she and Jane were on the porch before sprinting to the well. Flames were shooting out of the barn door. On his own, he probably wouldn't be able to save it. He could make sure the fire didn't spread to any of the other buildings, though.

Tom wasn't sure how long he worked, lugging pails of water, using blankets to try and pound out the flames, before Caleb, Josh and Sam rode into the yard. Once assured the girls were out of harm's way, they joined him and, together, managed to get the fire out.

Josh slapped him on the back. Like Tom, his clothes stuck to him and sweat dampened his hair. "You look like death. Go get a drink of water."

"Later. I have to fetch the doctor."

"I'll go," Caleb piped up, already striding to his horse.

"Bring back the sheriff," Sam called to his son.

Caleb lifted a hand in acknowledgment, vaulting into the saddle and disappearing down the lane. In the grass nearby, not far from where Lee's blanket-shrouded body lay, the other man stirred. Tom went rigid. The amount of suffering he had caused both twins stirred fury to life once more.

He took a step that direction. Josh blocked his way. "I'll deal with him. You have more important matters to tend to."

Tom stared at him blankly.

Brows lifted, he pointed to the cabin. "Jane?"

"Not sure that's a good idea right now."

"Why not?"

"For one, I'm furious with her." Furious and proud.

She'd squared off against evil in a bid to save her sister. *And was nearly killed in the process.*

He could've lost her forever. The thought of a life without Jane sent rivers of raw grief surging through him.

"You're not the only one." Josh sighed. "But when you love someone, you have to learn to work through it."

"I know." His words sank in, and Tom whipped his head around. "Wait. What did you say?"

"You love my cousin." It was a statement, not a question. He looked smug…and pleased.

Chest tightening painfully, Tom nodded.

Josh smiled. "What are you doing out here with me, then?"

Chapter Twenty-Seven

"I wish you hadn't jumped in front of that gun."

Jane shifted against the pillows propping her up and hid a wince. "I'll be fine, Jess."

Once they'd gotten her ruined blouse off and cleaned up the wound, they discovered that the bullet hadn't lodged inside her body. No surgery for her. She might have to have stitches, and there might be an unsightly scar, but considering the other possible outcomes, she couldn't be anything but grateful for God's protection.

Gazing into her sister's wan, tear-ravaged face, she wished with all her soul that Lee could've been spared.

She laid her hand over Jess's. "I'm sorry about Lee. I regret so many things. Decisions I made. If I'd done things differently, maybe…" She bit her lip, blinking fast to block the moisture filling her eyes. The disturbing sight of his too-still body would be with her for a long, long time. "Maybe he would still be here."

"Don't blame yourself." Jess sucked in a hitched breath. "He made the wrong choices. And I knew—" she pressed a hand over her heart "—I *knew* something wasn't right. I just couldn't accept that he'd put what we had at risk."

Hurt and sorrow clung to Jessica like a shroud. Seeing her twin's despair made her own problems seem paltry in comparison. Jane might not have the man she loved, but at least he was still walking around hale and hearty. She could see him, talk to him, adore him from afar.

Jess didn't have that luxury.

"I love you." Jane gave her cold fingers a light squeeze. "And I'm here for you. Whatever you need, you have it. Space. Privacy. A shoulder to cry on. Someone to yell at."

Looking as if she might shatter any second, Jess abruptly stood. "Love you, too, sis. I—I need to see him again."

"Jess, I'm not sure—"

But she was already gone, her hurried footsteps receding. The main door opened but didn't immediately close. Jane stared out the window at the seemingly innocent sunny day, wishing her view was of the front yard. She wondered if Tom had saved the barn. If he was okay. If he'd ever speak to her again.

Beneath his concern, anger had churned in his beautiful green eyes. Anger at her foolhardy decisions and stubbornness.

He couldn't have been too *angry. He kissed you, didn't he?* a voice prodded.

A throat cleared, and Jane wrenched her head toward the doorway, heart tripping over itself like a too-eager puppy.

Tom stood there, hands in his pockets, his presence solid and reassuring and a tiny bit unnerving. She couldn't decipher the emotions on his soot-streaked face. Shifting uneasily, she gritted her teeth against the pain radiating from her wound.

"If you're here to lecture me, I wish you'd reconsider."

Pulling out his hands, he moved with sure grace to the chair beside her bed and lowered himself into it. The scent of smoke clung to his clothes.

"I won't subject you to what I'm thinking," he said, grimacing. "I'm fairly certain you wouldn't like it."

Grateful for the reprieve, she smoothed the quilt's top edge. "The barn?"

"The structure's intact. The stalls will have to be rebuilt." His gaze drifted to the thick bandage covering her injury, partly visible beneath the white dressing gown Jess had helped her don. "Your cousins and uncle arrived in time to pitch in. I couldn't have saved it, otherwise."

"That's good."

"Sometimes we can't do things on our own. We have to have help." His jaw went taut, and he abruptly shot to his feet. Jabbing a finger at the pitcher and washbowl in the corner, he said, "Do you mind?"

"Uh, sure."

From beneath her lashes, Jane observed his stilted movements as he scrubbed his hands and arms. The corded muscles in his forearms bunched and stretched. Such strength. What she wouldn't give to have him take her in his arms and refuse to let go.

That all-too-brief kiss outside had turned her world upside down. He didn't seem inclined to repeat it, however. Far from it.

Tossing the towel aside, he prowled to the foot of her bed, hands curving around the footboard as he leveled a hard stare at her. "There's something I don't understand."

"What's that?"

"I don't understand why you went off alone." His

knuckles turned white. "Why you didn't turn to me. Or your cousins. Anyone."

"I thought you agreed to wait to lecture me."

Pushing upward, he crossed his arms over his chest, the material straining over his muscles. His boots were planted wide. With his hair in disarray, his skin smudged and eyes burning a hole through her, he looked like an irate mountain man. "I changed my mind."

"There wasn't time!" she said, raising off the pillow and instantly regretting it. "All I knew was that my sister was nowhere to be found and was most likely in danger. I didn't think, Tom. Just acted."

"That's right," he bit out. "You didn't think." Coming around, he sank onto the mattress.

Slowly, he lifted his hand and skimmed the tender skin above her bandage. Prickles of awareness skittered over her nape.

The muscle in his jaw jumped. "You could've died today."

She resisted the pulsing drive to bury her head in his chest. Crumpled the quilt in her fists. "I'm still here," she whispered.

His fingers continued along the top of her bandage, not stopping when he encountered the soft cotton gown, the caress as light as a feather. "I thought we had the kind of relationship where we felt free to share anything with each other. I thought we didn't keep secrets from each other."

Jane's mouth went dry. She'd never seen him in such a strange mood.

"We're friends, Tom." The words hurt to say. "Not husband and wife."

He shrank back as if she'd struck him.

"There are certain things we can't and won't share," she said, insides writhing in protest.

"Right." His lips pressed together in a tight line. "Friends."

A loud rap on the main door echoed through the house. "Jane?"

Tom's lashes lowered to his cheeks. Standing, he crossed to the entrance of her room. "She's back here, Doc." He shot her a quick, unreadable look. "Get some rest, Jane."

When he left, the energy was sucked out of the room. Bruised and battered and empty, she wasn't sure if she'd ever know true contentment again.

Tom didn't visit her.

Jane spotted him at the funeral, standing at the edge of the crowd. Her disappointment had been sharp when he left without speaking to either her or Jessica. That wasn't like him.

She couldn't get their strange conversation out of her head. The intensity of that kiss, the emotion behind it... what did it mean, if anything? And the way he'd reacted when she'd pronounced they were just friends—he'd looked the way she'd felt all those times he'd uttered the same words. Maybe she'd been projecting her own dashed hopes onto him.

After all, she'd been through a major ordeal. Her reasoning couldn't be trusted. Could it?

It took her four agonizing days to work up the nerve to go to him.

A part of her was offended that he hadn't deigned to check on her. A bigger part was terrified she'd pushed him away one too many times.

Clutching the strap of her satchel, she climbed his

cabin's steps and went to knock on the door. It opened before she could do so. Clara barreled into her, small arms going around her legs in a tight grip.

"I've missed you, too, sweetheart." Smiling, she stroked the tight curls, her heart melting. She'd regretted not being around when Tom told her the news about her father. Seeing her made up for the long absence.

Clara peeked from beneath long lashes. "Where have you been? I was sad without you!"

"I wanted to see you, but there were things I had to take care of at home."

Wiping his hands on a towel, Tom didn't appear in a hurry to greet her.

"Hello, Jane." He glanced at her neck, where the high collar of her dress covered the bandage and thin scars where Farnsworth had cut her. Concern flickered. "How are you feeling?"

You'd know the answer to that if you'd bothered to come around, she wanted to retort.

Clara inched backward, waiting for her answer.

"Better."

"That's good."

An awkward silence descended between them. Clara tugged on Tom's trousers. "Can she eat with us?"

His hesitation shook her wavering confidence. *Be brave, Jane.*

"I'm not planning to stay long. I need but a moment of your time," she told him, the leather satchel strap biting into her palm. Senses on high alert, she was shaky and short of breath, as if she'd run a grueling race through the mountains.

"Of course." Lobbing his towel onto the table, he addressed Clara. "Jane and I are going to be out here for a few minutes. I want you to stay inside and play with your dolls. Don't go near the stove."

Her lower lip protruded in a pout. "Yes, sir."

Jane touched her arm. "I'll come and see you before I go, okay?"

"Okay." Dejected, she shuffled inside.

Tom closed the door behind her. Gesturing for her to go first, he said, "We can talk over by the stream."

Neither spoke as they crossed the grassy expanse. Jane wished he'd put his hand low on her back as he used to. Or take her arm. Or smile and say something silly.

At the bank, he slid his hands in his pockets and stared moodily at the water's lazy path.

She soaked in his stern profile. "How's Clara dealing with everything?"

"The days aren't so bad."

"She isn't sleeping well?"

"It's difficult for her to fall asleep. Sometimes she has nightmares."

"I'm sorry to hear that." She took a step closer, aching to hold him. "What about you? How are you coping?"

"Since Charles hasn't been around for a while, it will take time for the reality of his death to sink in." Angling his body toward her, he roamed her features almost hungrily. "Why are you here, Jane?" His tone was soft, sad.

It was now or never.

Lifting the satchel up and over her head, she dug out her journal. Held it out to him with shaking fingers.

Disconcerted, he took it. "Why are you giving me this?"

"You were right. About me keeping secrets." She tapped the cover, anxiety blooming in her chest. Inside that book were her most private, intimate thoughts. And she was giving him permission to read every word. "Contained in this journal is the biggest secret of all."

His brow screwed up, and he pressed the journal into her unwilling hands. Throat working, he said, "I don't want to read about it. Whatever this truth is you want me to know, you can tell me to my face."

This wasn't the plan. Head dipping, she ran her fingers over the worn cover. She'd counted on him going off alone to read about her love for him. She wasn't sure she had the courage to look him in the eye and see his reaction firsthand.

Tom lightly grasped her chin and urged her to look at him. He'd inched closer.

"Don't be afraid, Janie girl. You can tell me anything."

"It will change everything between us," she warned, feeling slightly sick. "Probably not for the better. I'll understand if you don't want to see me anymore."

"That won't happen." He sounded sure of himself.

"You didn't want to see me these last few days," she responded, wincing at the undisguised hurt in her voice.

His hand dropped to his side. "That's because I have a secret of my own." He sighed.

"You do?" Her brain scrambled to latch on to possible explanations. Could he have found her replacement and didn't want to hurt her feelings by telling her? Or worse, could he have decided to court someone? Patricia Vinson, perhaps?

"I do. But you first."

Fumbling to replace the journal, she dropped the satchel and bent to retrieve it. "This was a mistake. Forget I was ever here."

A disbelieving laugh burst out of him. His hands covered hers and, taking the satchel from her and laying it on the bank, he took her elbows and gently pulled her up. His woodsy scent teased her senses.

"I don't think so." Releasing her, he remained very close, a hand's width away. "You like to finish what you start, remember?"

Sucking in a fortifying breath, she fisted her hands and focused on the rapid pulse at the base of his throat. "Ever since I was fourteen, I've had feelings for you. It started out as this childish infatuation, and I thought that, given time, it would pass. That I would stop feeling this way. But I didn't." A dry half laugh, half groan escaped. "Not when you began pursuing my sister. Not when you proposed to her. Not when you left..." Closing her eyes, she recalled the horrid emptiness and desolation his absence had wrought.

Tom's big hands came up to cradle her face. Resting his forehead against hers, he murmured, "I'm sorry I put you through that. I didn't know."

She stared glumly at their boots. "I was prepared to marry a man I didn't love in order to get over you."

"What?" His head lifted, his fingertips urging her jaw up. Meeting his shocked gaze took guts. "*That's* why you were marrying Roy?"

"The day you came back and found me wandering in the woods, I wasn't upset because I didn't get to marry him. I was upset because my plan failed. My chance at rooting you out of my heart failed." Gathering her courage, she placed her hands on either side of his waist. He inhaled sharply, muscles bunching. "These last weeks, my love for you has only gotten stronger. More resilient. There'll be no destroying it now. I know that's not what you expected to hear. Certainly not what you *wanted* to hear—"

His mouth caught hers midspeech, startling her. His

fingers slid into her hair as hers curved into his sides in a bid to anchor herself. Making a low sound deep in his throat, Tom pulled her against him, his kiss fierce and demanding. Wondrous emotion cascaded through Jane. Hope she'd assumed long dead buoyed her. He wouldn't be kissing her this way if he didn't *like* what she'd had to say.

Matching his ardor, she poured the fullness of her love into the embrace, showing him everything she'd felt but hadn't voiced until today.

"Jane." The reverent way he spoke her name made her shiver. When he lifted his head a fraction, she basked in the awed sort of tenderness aglow in his gaze. "I had no idea you felt that way about me. I thought you weren't interested in anything more than friendship. I'll be honest, I came home expecting you to still be the sweet young girl I left behind." His thumb caressed her cheek. "When I saw you in that wedding dress, all grown-up and so beautiful I couldn't think straight, I panicked. We were friends. As an older brother figure, I wasn't supposed to be attracted to you."

His lips turned up in a wry smile that had her heart singing.

"You hid it well." Boldly encircling his neck, she toyed with the ends of his hair, the freedom to touch him a heady thing.

"I can't think how," he said ruefully. "I assumed it was obvious."

"Not to me."

His smile dimmed slightly, and he grew earnest. "I love you, Jane. Only you. Without you, there would be no joy, no purpose in my life. I want you for my bride." Brushing a tender kiss on her lips, he drew back, his hands going to her waist. "But only if you can accept my past."

Her heart stuttered, knocked against her ribs. He looked so serious and somber. "What are you saying?"

"I can't erase what happened with Megan. I have to know you believe me when I say I don't love her anymore. I care for her as a friend, and I wish her every happiness, but I don't want to be with her. I didn't understand what real, abiding love was until I went to Kansas and witnessed what my brother had with Jenny. I didn't experience it for myself until I came home. To you." His fingers flexed on her hips, and his body was as taut as a bow. "I need to know you trust me, Jane. That you trust my love for you is true and loyal."

Any lingering reservations disintegrated in the face of his ardent confession. "I do, Tom. I trust you. Not once have you misled me. Or lied to me." His features relaxed into soft admiration. Jane swallowed against rising emotion. This next part was difficult to get out. "Now I have a question for you. Do you trust that the next time I encounter a problem, I'll come to you instead of trying to handle it on my own in order to prove something?"

"Yes," he said without hesitation. "You don't have anything to prove, my sweet Jane. Like I said before, you're one of the most courageous women I know. You just had to be able to see it for yourself."

She smiled up at him. "I love you." Leaning into him, she feathered kisses along his jaw. "I love you." Continuing her path, she felt his lips curve in a smile beneath hers before she traveled up his other cheek. "I love you, Tom Leighton." Meeting his love-filled gaze, she gushed, "You don't know how wonderful it is to say that out loud instead of in my head. Or on a page."

Laughing huskily, he cupped her cheek. "Oh, I have an idea, because it feels like that when I say it to you. I love *you*, Jane O'Malley. What do you say we put these words into practice? Marry me."

"I thought you'd never ask."

Epilogue

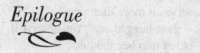

Three weeks later

"You're practically glowing, sister of mine."

Setting her brush on the dresser, Jane took one last look in the mirror, satisfied there were no lingering tangles. She turned to where Jessica sat on the bed, resplendent in a lacy lilac creation that complemented her skin and hair. For once, she'd agreed to have her hair arranged in a becoming, complicated style. A sad sort of smile spoiled the effect. A smile that said she was valiantly trying to mask her grief and be happy for her twin.

Jane ran her hands over her frothy white skirts. "Maybe we should've waited a little longer to get married."

While neither she nor Tom had wanted to postpone their nuptials, compounding Jessica's loss was something they'd intended to avoid. The morning after his proposal, Jane had hesitantly revealed her happy news, prepared to wait until autumn if it would help Jessica.

"You've waited for years to marry your beloved. I wasn't about to be the reason for your delayed happiness."

"Jess—"

"We're not talking about me today." Material rustling as she stood, she came and straightened the wedding gown's swooping neckline. "Today is about you and Tom." Pride and affection turned her eyes a brighter green. "I'm thrilled for you, sis. Truly. You got your fairy-tale ending. There's no one else I know who deserves it more than you."

Jane hugged her. "You deserve it, too, Jess," she whispered into her shoulder.

Surreptitiously wiping a tear from her cheek, Jessica huffed a dry laugh. "No more mushy stuff. I promised myself I wouldn't bawl like a baby."

A commotion outside brought the twins into the main room. Through one of the windows flanking the door, Jane spotted a surprise visitor.

"What is Aunt Althea doing here?"

"She came for your wedding, of course."

The mantel clock showed they had one hour to get to the church. "That's cutting it awful close."

Jessica continued to stare through the glass. "Your wedding isn't the only reason she came." Taking Jane's hand, her expression pleaded for understanding. "I wrote to her the day after the fire. I asked if I could stay with her for a while."

"Why didn't you say anything?"

"You were floating around here with your head in the clouds." Her lips had a rueful twist. "I couldn't bring myself to bring you crashing back to earth. Are you upset?"

"Of course not. If you feel going to Maryville is best for you right now, I support your decision." Lightly touching Jessica's cool cheek, Jane attempted to mask how much she'd miss her. "It's not forever, though, right?"

"No, not forever."

"You'll write often?"

"I'll try."

They shared a smile, both aware Jess wasn't one to put her thoughts on paper.

"I'm sorry about dumping all the baking responsibilities on you," Jess said.

"I don't mind. I've been baking at Tom's all along, so nothing will change except for the fact I won't have to transport all the supplies back and forth."

Her cheeks heated. Starting tonight, she wouldn't be coming here to sleep. She'd get to stay for supper. She'd get to read Clara a bedtime story and tuck her in bed. She'd get to have Tom all to herself.

Shaking herself out of those pleasant ruminations, she said, "When are you leaving?"

"In a couple of days. I'm sure Althea will want a chance to reconnect with Mama first." Once again observing the reunion in the yard, she brought her brows together. "Caroline looks happy. As happy as Caroline can be, that is."

Jane laughed as she studied her friend observing Alice and Althea fuss over each other. It was true. A smile on Caroline was as out of place as a star in the noon sky. Maybe one day that would change. She certainly hoped so.

"She was only being protective. Now that Tom is going to become my husband, there's no further cause for her to worry about me."

Her husband. An impatient thrill radiated outward from her middle. She could hardly wait to see him standing in the church, handsome in his black suit, ready and eager to make her his wife.

"Speaking of your groom, we should probably go. Wouldn't want to make the poor man think you changed your mind."

Her smile stretched from ear to ear. "I'm fairly certain he knows nothing could keep me away."

"Enjoy every moment you have with him." Jess's tone was insistent. "Happy or sad. Good or bad. Each minute, each hour, each day you have together is precious."

Now it was Jane's turn to tear up. "I will, sis. I promise."

"Love you, Jane."

"I love you, too."

Tom stood transfixed as his bride walked the aisle toward him. As he'd requested, Jane's deep red hair cascaded freely to her waist, the glow of candles glinting off the lustrous waves with every step. She was wearing a different wedding gown than the one he'd found her in. This one was softer, flowing and romantic. Not that he paid much attention. He kept being drawn back to her face, peaceful and happy and, perhaps most importantly, confident. In herself. In him. And in their love.

He could hardly believe how much their relationship had transformed in the short weeks since they'd dared to be honest with each other. He was also aware he didn't deserve the blessings that were Jane and Clara, and remembered to thank God on a daily basis.

Their guests watched with obvious delight as Jane paused to give Clara a bouquet of purple orchids and sweet kiss and hug. Only their closest friends and family were in attendance. They'd both wanted this ceremony to be a private, intimate celebration of their commitment to one another.

When she reached him, he held out his hands and she took them, her smile as brilliant as the constellations they'd mapped from his front porch the other night.

"How are you?" he murmured for her ears alone.

And the reverend's, of course, who was opening his Bible and seconds away from beginning the ceremony.

Her eyes sparkled. "Better now that I'm here."

He hadn't seen her since the previous morning, and he'd missed her terribly. The knowledge they'd never have to be apart again flooded his soul with a contentment he hadn't dreamed he'd experience.

Jane was a compassionate, gutsy, *amazing* woman. His friend. His beloved.

And she'd chosen *him*.

She'd loved him from afar all those years. While he regretted the lost time, he understood they hadn't been ready for each other. God, in His infinite wisdom, had brought them together at just the right time.

The ceremony was both poignant and brief, and soon he was taking Jane in his arms, sealing their vows with a kiss. At the whistles and clapping splitting the silence, she broke away and laughed up at him, her cheeks a becoming shade of pink.

"I have a surprise for you, Mrs. Leighton," he murmured, taking her hand and pressing a quick kiss to her knuckles.

She beamed up at him. "I'll follow you anywhere."

Not giving their guests a chance to waylay them, he led her through the church and out into the balmy summer evening, where his horse was waiting. When he'd boosted her up and climbed on behind her, she relaxed into his chest. "Is the surprise at the reception?"

"We're not going to the reception." Guiding the horse out of the yard, he said, "At least not for a while."

"What about Clara?"

"Mary and your ma agreed to keep an eye on her for us. She's spending the night with them, anyway."

Blushing again, a shy smile tipping her lips, she lapsed into silence the rest of the ride. At the sight of his home—their home now—she tossed him a quizzical look.

"Patience, my love." Helping her down, he couldn't resist stealing another kiss. "Close your eyes."

"What are you up to?" Her eyes were alight with excitement.

"Do as I ask, and you'll find out."

She closed them. Guiding her to their spot by the stream, he let go of her arm. "Don't peek."

Working quickly, he dug a match out of the saddlebag he'd left there earlier and lit the dozen or so lamps situated in a circle on the ground and suspended from the branches overhead. He returned to her side, sliding his arm about her waist. "Okay. It's ready."

Her lids fluttered open. Her lips parted as she soaked in the scene. "Oh, Tom."

Several large, colorful quilts covered the grass and in the middle a feast awaited—bowls of fresh berries, platters of ham, cheese and bread, jars of lemonade and a miniature iced cake just for them. The sun had already dipped behind the mountains, coloring the expanse above in shades of pink, orange and blue. In the field on the far side of the stream, lightning bugs flashed in the growing dusk. And the light from the lamps reflected on the water.

Jane took a step, only to whirl around and throw her arms around his neck. "It's wonderful! I can't believe you did this."

Rubbing circles low on her back, he smiled at her enthusiasm. His efforts had paid off. "I admit to having selfish motivations. I wanted you all to myself." He kissed her temple, then her cheek, then the corner of her mouth. Tangling his fingers in her silken hair, he leaned away far enough so that he could gaze into her adoring, shining eyes. "Today you've made me the happiest of men."

Her hold about his neck increased. "Today marks the end of a dream for me. And the start of reality with you, the man I love more than anything else on this earth. Today we begin our future as a family."

Tom was full up with happiness and a deep sense of gratitude. God had brought him through trials and suffering, ultimately blessing him with a family he could love and provide for.

"I love you, Janie girl."

Pulling her as close as he possibly could, he lowered his head and kissed her, showing her without words how much she meant to him.

* * * * *

Dear Reader,

I'm honored you chose to read my book. I hope you enjoyed Tom and Jane's story. Those of you who have read the previous books in this series will have met them before and know that Jane has had a crush on him since her teens. Tom, on the other hand, only had eyes for her big sister, Megan. Quite an obstacle to overcome.

Jane O'Malley isn't the typical spunky heroine, and it took me a while to get her. Introverted and timid, she learns over the course of the story to believe in herself and, ultimately, to be brave. To risk everything for love. Tom's journey was also a joy to write. He's viewed his younger friend Jane almost as the little sister he never had. This mature, beautiful, grown-up version of her comes as quite a shock.

Don't feel too badly for twin sister, Jessica. She'll get her own chance at happy-ever-after in the next book. If you'd like to learn more about the Smoky Mountain Matches series, please visit my website, www.karenkirst.com. You can follow me on Twitter at @KarenKirst or catch up on Facebook. I love hearing from readers. My email is karenkirst@live.com

Blessings,
Karen Kirst

REQUEST YOUR FREE BOOKS!

2 FREE INSPIRATIONAL NOVELS
PLUS 2 *FREE* MYSTERY GIFTS

Love Inspired HISTORICAL

YES! Please send me 2 FREE Love Inspired® Historical novels and my 2 FREE mystery gifts (gifts are worth about $10). After receiving them, if I don't wish to receive any more books, I can return the shipping statement marked "cancel." If I don't cancel, I will receive 4 brand-new novels every month and be billed just $4.99 per book in the U.S. or $5.49 per book in Canada. That's a saving of at least 17% off the cover price. It's quite a bargain! Shipping and handling is just 50¢ per book in the U.S. and 75¢ per book in Canada.* I understand that accepting the 2 free books and gifts places me under no obligation to buy anything. I can always return a shipment and cancel at any time. Even if I never buy another book, the two free books and gifts are mine to keep forever.

102/302 IDN GH6Z

Name	(PLEASE PRINT)	
Address		Apt. #
City	State/Prov.	Zip/Postal Code

Signature (if under 18, a parent or guardian must sign)

Mail to the **Reader Service:**
IN U.S.A.: P.O. Box 1867, Buffalo, NY 14240-1867
IN CANADA: P.O. Box 609, Fort Erie, Ontario L2A 5X3

Want to try two free books from another series?
Call 1-800-873-8635 or visit www.ReaderService.com.

* Terms and prices subject to change without notice. Prices do not include applicable taxes. Sales tax applicable in N.Y. Canadian residents will be charged applicable taxes. Offer not valid in Quebec. This offer is limited to one order per household. Not valid for current subscribers to Love Inspired Historical books. All orders subject to credit approval. Credit or debit balances in a customer's account(s) may be offset by any other outstanding balance owed by or to the customer. Please allow 4 to 6 weeks for delivery. Offer available while quantities last.

Your Privacy—The Reader Service is committed to protecting your privacy. Our Privacy Policy is available online at www.ReaderService.com or upon request from the Reader Service.

We make a portion of our mailing list available to reputable third parties that offer products we believe may interest you. If you prefer that we not exchange your name with third parties, or if you wish to clarify or modify your communication preferences, please visit us at www.ReaderService.com/consumerschoice or write to us at Reader Service Preference Service, P.O. Box 9062, Buffalo, NY 14240-9062. Include your complete name and address.

LIHI5

*Could Hank Chandler's search for a wife lead to
holiday love with schoolteacher Janell Whitman?*

Read on for a sneak preview of
THE HOLIDAY COURTSHIP,
the next book in Winnie Griggs's miniseries
TEXAS GROOMS

"I wonder if you'd mind giving me your opinion on some
potential candidates," Mr. Chandler asked.

"You want my opinion on who would make you a
good wife?" Apparently he saw nothing odd about asking
the woman he'd just proposed to to help him pick a wife.

He frowned. "Not a wife. A mother for the children. I
need your opinion on how the lady under consideration
and the children would get on."

"I see." The man really didn't have an ounce of
romance in him.

He nodded. "You can save me from wasting time
talking to someone who's obviously not right."

"Assuming you find the right woman, may I ask how
you intend to approach her?"

"If you're wondering if I intend to go a'courtin'—"
Hank's tone had a sarcastic bite to it "—the answer is no,
at least not in the usual way. I don't want anyone thinking
this will be more than a marriage of convenience."

"I understand why you wouldn't want to go through a
conventional courtship. But don't you think you and your

prospective bride should get to know each other before you propose?"

He drew himself up. "I consider myself a good judge of character. It won't take me long to figure out if she's a good candidate or not."

"I would recruit a third party to act as a go-between," Janell said. "It should be someone whose judgment you trust."

"And what would this go-between do exactly?"

"Go to the candidate on your behalf. He or she would let the lady know the situation and ascertain the lady's interest in such a match."

"So you agree that a businesslike approach is best, just that I should go about it from a distance."

"It could save a great deal of awkwardness and misunderstanding if you did so."

"In other words, you think I need a matchmaker."

"I suppose. But you *do* want to approach this in a very businesslike manner, don't you?"

Hank nodded. "I have to admit, it sounds like a good idea."

Happy that he'd seen the wisdom of her advice, she said, "Is there someone you could trust to take on this job?"

He rubbed his jaw thoughtfully for a moment. Finally he looked up. "How about you?"

Don't miss
THE HOLIDAY COURTSHIP
by Winnie Griggs, available December 2015 wherever
Love Inspired® Historical books and ebooks are sold.